Man at Arms

The Battle of Poitiers

Book 2 in the Sir John Hawkwood Series

By
Griff Hosker

Contents

Man at Arms

Published by Sword Books Ltd 2020

Copyright ©Griff Hosker First Edition

Dedication

To David Pearson, a loyal and faithful reader.

Real People Used in The Book

King Edward Plantagenet
Prince Edward of Wales and Duke of Cornwall- his son
Lord Henry Plantagenet- Earl of Derby, later Earl of Lancaster
and Duke of Lancaster
Ralph, Earl of Stafford
Earl Ralph Neville
John de Vere, Earl of Oxford
Robert Ufford, Earl of Suffolk
William Montague, Earl of Salisbury
Thomas Beauchamp, Earl of Warwick
Henry de Percy, Earl of Northumberland
Thomas Hatfield, Bishop of Durham
Jean de Grailly, the Captal de Buch, a Gascon lord
King Charles of Navarre
King John II of France
Crown Prince Charles, the Dauphin of France
Philip, Duc d'Orleans
Arnoud d'Audrehem. Marshal of France
John de Clermont, Marshal of France
Gautier de Brienne, Constable of France

Prologue

Southampton 1348

I am John Hawkwood, a warrior and I live for war! I was born to be a warrior and I did not begin to feel as though I was alive until I went to war and learned that I had skills. They were not just the skills of being able to fight and to win. It was not just that I was a good archer, it was more than that. It was as though my mind wanted me to war when there was battle. It did not matter what the size of the conflict was; so long as there was war then I was happy.

That explained why I was not happy for there was no war. With the two men who followed me, Robin and Michael, we had returned to England from Calais rich and well provided for but winter in England meant no war. Worse, we had heard of pestilence or Great Death in Italy and southern France which was spreading north and that meant the constant wars across the Channel had ceased. The Great Mortality as some called the plague was coming to France and the rumours which came from those who fled north was that there was no cure for this curse and whole towns and villages were filled with the dead. There is only so much time a man can spend whoring and drinking. It was when I almost killed a man in a bar brawl in the inn, The Infanta of Castile, that I decided we should leave the city and seek adventure elsewhere. If we stayed there then I might die to a knife in the night or be hanged for murder and, in my bones, I knew I was destined for more than that.

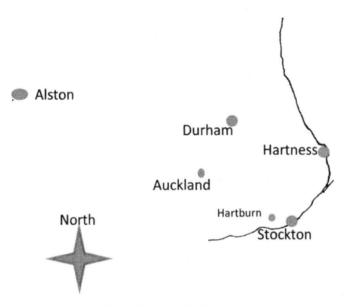

Durham 1348

Chapter 1

When we left Calais after successfully capturing it for the King and his son, we headed for Southampton even though Dover was closer. Basil of Tarsus held money for me and Balin of Bitterne was the weaponsmith we used and each of us wished to have mail and plate. Even Robin wished a short hauberk. We stayed in the Infanta of Castile and there we had parted from the others who been part of my company. All were loyal men, but I could not promise them employment. Ned and Jack returned to the inn in London that they used, and the rest went to their homes. Michael and Robin were the exceptions.

Robin Goodfellow was the one man I might call a close friend although even he did not truly know me. His name was a nickname for he was like Puck and able to vanish from sight and reappear at will. I knew his real name was Robin of Wakefield, but none ever called him that. He was the shortest archer I had employed but one of the best. Michael was the boy we had found, beaten and emaciated. He had attached himself to our company and, whilst not an archer, had skills with weapons and in the time he had been with us he had become a swordsman. He had mail, helmet and shield as well as two good swords.

After the landlord of the Infanta of Castile told us we were no longer welcome we packed our war gear on our horses and left Southampton. The road from Southampton led north and we headed away from the sea to, I knew not where. There was no war and we needed somewhere to winter. We had the whole of England to choose and I wondered where the best place would be to winter. Essex was out of the question for I might meet my father and there would be blood if that happened. London was a cesspit and to be avoided. Where else could we go? I spoke them aloud but both Robin and Michael knew that they were my decisions. When we had left Calais, they had made it quite clear that they were happy to follow me and be my men.

The road was quiet and we rode close together. My words were both for their ears and for myself, "I always wanted land of my own but that means we would be beholden to some lord or other. There are some men I would choose to obey but others…"

Robin nodded, "The King and the Prince, his son, have promised you rewards, perhaps, like Sir John Chandos you will win a knighthood."

"Robin, a King will promise anything when there is war. Then warriors like us have a value. When there is peace, we become an inconvenience. No, we need to find somewhere quiet. I care not for the value of the land I buy for I am no farmer. I just wish a hall where we can gather warriors such as ourselves. I want a company of men that I can lead in war."

This had been an idea which had been fermenting in my head for some time. Increasingly the system of lords bringing men to war had failed. Lords used scutage to avoid risking their own lives and Prince Edward had started to hire men at arms and archers, paying them with the scutage paid to him by his lords. That was why I knew that Robin was wrong. Prince Edward and his father needed us not tied to a land but available to him. I would make my own company, but it would not just be of archers. Archers alone could not win battles; they could decide them but in the end, it was men at arms who would capture the enemy leaders and take the ransoms. At Calais, I had used my sword as much as my bow. I needed men who could fight with swords and pole weapons. I saw myself leading a self-contained company of men who could attack with all the skill of the English archer but, at the same time, defend themselves from the archers' worst enemy, the horseman.

"Hartburn, Captain."

I turned to Michael. Taking him on had been one of the best decisions I had ever made. He was quick thinking and thoughtful. The two were often contradictory. His words seemed unconnected with my musings, "Hartburn?"

"You have chests of gold there and Captain Philip would make us welcome. Hartburn is not subject to the King for it is in the Palatinate and the Bishop of Durham rules. Captain Philip may know of land and it will be cheaper to buy there than closer to London. Do you want a home or just a property, Captain?"

"You are right that we would be welcomed but the Bishop of Durham is subject to the King's command. However, you understand me well. I see this as somewhere to sit out the peace until war comes again." We rode in silence for a mile or more while I mulled over Michael's suggestion. It was a good one and I could find no fault in it. "You have picked the longest journey for us and with the weather like it is then it will not be pleasant."

Robin said cheerfully, "We are warriors, Captain, the hard road is always ours. Let us embrace it while we may. We are young men but one day we will tire of the life and wish a comfortable woman and a family around us."

I shook my head. "Perhaps but that is many years hence!"

The roads of England could be a dangerous place for there were many brigands and robbers but the three of us were so well armed and skilled with weapons that I feared no robber. Of course, we did not court danger. We rode only during daylight and we either used inns and taverns when we could or paid to stay in religious houses. Although quieter places than inns, they offered the best food for that was how most of them remained open. It was at some of these houses that we heard more about the disease which was heading for England and its symptoms. Some of the monks had spoken to those who had travelled from Gascony and further south. That they were worried made me glad that we were heading north away from the disease. The seas around the coast would stop it.

We crossed the River Tees at Piercebridge rather than Stockton. I preferred bridges to ferries. We stayed in a tavern on the north side of the river. It was there we gathered information. We already knew the names of some of the important families: the Nevilles, the de Vescy family and of course, the Percy family who had led the army which had destroyed the Scots at Neville's Cross. What we learned was that all was far from harmonious. The three families would combine to fight the Scots but were not averse to raiding and fighting each other. The most valuable piece of information concerned the Bishop of Durham himself. Thomas Hatfield was a warrior bishop and had fought alongside us at Crécy. He had been in a different division, but we had both been involved in that most important of battles. He had not fought at Neville's Cross, but I hoped he would remember my name. Michael's choice of destination might prove to be fortuitous.

We reached Hartburn in the middle of the afternoon. I saw that Captain Philip had made improvements to his hall. There

6

was now a good stone wall which surrounded it and the gatehouse was substantial with a fighting platform across the top. The gate was open but it was low enough to necessitate us walking through the gate rather than riding. His wife, Mathilde and his young son, John, came out of the door as our horses clattered on the cobbled yard. She recognised me immediately, "John, John Hawkwood!"

"I hope that our arrival is not an inconvenience?"

She laughed, "Philip will be delighted to see you. He and the men are ploughing the east field. Put your horses in the stable and then get in out of this cold wind."

The last time we had been here, more than a year ago, the stable had only been large enough for a couple of horses. Now I saw that there were stalls for eight horses. We did not presume to expect to stay in the hall and we left our gear in the hayloft of the stable. When we knocked on the door it was opened by an older woman.

"I am Gammer Anne, the housekeeper. Wipe your feet and hang your cloaks from the hooks." Her voice told me she would brook no argument.

She had not been here the last time we had visited, and she was a formidable woman. We came to know that she had a heart of gold and was devoted to Captain Philip, his wife, and his son. Her husband had been killed at the Battle of Neville's Cross. In fact, when the Captain told us of him, I remembered seeing him as he was killed. The fire was warming, and Mathilde had arranged the chairs so that all of us could face the fire. John had grown but he was still shy, and he hid behind his mother.

Captain Philip burst into the room, "My men said they had seen riders approaching! It is good to see you again!"

I stood and clasped his arm, "I said to your wife that we did not wish to make life difficult for you. We can sleep in the stable."

Mathilde shook her head, "You will do no such thing! We have plenty of rooms and it is thanks to you that we have them. My husband used the money you left for him wisely and we have spare bed chambers."

I was relieved, "Good."

"And I must hear all about Calais and your life."

I found myself envying the captain of archers. We lived either in camps or in inns. This cosy hall made the three of us feel at ease! I told him of the taking of Calais and my plan to become a leader of a company of men of my own. "I have more money, but I need somewhere to train them."

He cocked an eye at me, "But you are from Essex and this is the north. Would you not have found more men further south?"

I nodded, "I have men already that are trained, Ned, Luke, Alan of the Woods, Walter of Barnsley and Jack but they are archers. Michael here will be the first I train to protect archers. I saw the need for that at Crécy. We protected the nobles but there was no one to protect us. You, of all people, should know that we are not considered in battle. If we lose our lives, there are plenty more to take our place."

"But the King has no need of men at this time."

I nodded, "But there are men in France, Italy, Flanders, Spain, in fact just across the Channel and they would be happy to pay for English warriors. We have a good reputation."

He shook his head, "But you are an Englishman! How can you fight for another king?"

"I will not fight against England but there are many other leaders and I," I spread my arm, "we, fight for gold!"

"I can see that you have thought this through." He smiled, "Did you visit with a fortune teller before you came north this time?"

I shook my head, "I am a Christian and do not believe in fortune-tellers."

He laughed, "There is not a soldier alive who does not believe in luck!" He pointed to the northeast, "There is a farm there, The Ox Bridge House, and old Cedric who was the landowner, died not long before you came here to battle for the Archbishop. It is still without an owner. In truth, it is not a profitable farm. It is on the slopes of the narrow valley. It is the next farm to mine but as different from my manor as a knight to a villein with a billhook. If you were to make an offer, then the Bishop might consider it. If, as you say, you wish just land where you can train men then it would do but I still cannot see why you wish to choose men from here and not further south."

"This is the border and men are used to fighting here. I could have chosen the Welsh borders, but I knew you lived here and besides, we can take a ship to Flanders from one of the ports which are close to here."

"Then ride to Durham and speak with Bishop Hatfield. It would be good to have a neighbour again."

For the rest of the evening, the others all spoke more than I did. I was planning my strategy. I know not where it came from but ever since I had gone to war, I had used my mind to plan how to win. This was peace but I wanted to win. I would pay as little as possible for the farm for when I had no more use for it then I would sell it or, perhaps, make a gift of it to Captain Philip. We rode to Durham the next day. I had plenty of money with me and whatever I spent I had four times as much with Basil of Tarsus.

The city of Durham was like the court of King Edward. There was intrigue as well as plots. Nobles plotted to undermine each other and gain favour from the Bishop. Good land was much sought after and if a knight could take a rich manor from another then he would do so. I had risen early and spoken at great length to Captain Philip. I had discovered as much as I could about the land. It seemed to me that its greatest asset was that it controlled the bridge over the Lustrum Beck. While the waterway could be forded it was the only place for animals and wagons to cross. I intended to use that to my advantage.

I left my two men with the animals and approached the priest who either allowed or denied men permission to speak with the Bishop. I had a plan.

He looked up at me, he was small, and I saw his eyes taking in my status. There were no spurs and therefore I was unworthy of consideration. "Yes? I am Canon Adrian, and I am the one who determines which visitors are allowed to meet with the Bishop," the sneer in the cleric's voice told me what he thought of me.

"I fought alongside Bishop Hatfield at Crécy and I thought to speak with him for I wish to live in the Palatinate."

"Many men wish that, and you need a better reason than that to be granted an audience."

I nodded, "Did I need a better reason when I led the archers of Hartburn at Bear Park and we defeated the Scots? As I recall the only churchmen who fought that day came from York."

He coloured and I realised that I had touched a sensitive subject. "And the Church is grateful for that but..."

I took out my purse and opening it, took out a gold mark, "And my visit will bring profit for both the Church and the Bishop."

The greedy man's eyes widened, "Then I shall see what we can do. Brother Nicholas, take this man to the Bishop.

The young man who had been standing within earshot nodded, and said, "If you would like to follow me, sir."

Canon Adrian held out his hand and I smiled, "When I have spoken to the Bishop, he may well choose to reward you but that will be his decision."

I saw the hint of a smile on the young monk's face. The Canon must have regularly used the ploy to line his own purse. As I was taken into his presence I recognised the Bishop and realised that he looked to be a warrior and not a priest, despite his robes. I still saw him as I had in France wearing a helmet, mail and plate. He was seated at a throne and there was a line of petitioners. I joined the rear of the long line. I did not mind having to wait as it allowed me the opportunity of seeing who else sought favours. The faces that glanced at me dismissed me as soon as they spied me. I was not a knight and so how could I be important. The two overweight merchants also managed to look down their noses at me. I did not mind their contempt. I looked at the weapons of the knights and their livery. They were more important.

The line did not take long to move. Some of those waiting merely had the opportunity to say one sentence and they were answered and left. A clerk made a note of the conversation however brief. More than half of those who were seen did not look happy. When my turn came the Bishop looked up and appraised me from my feet to my face. My archer's dagger was in the top of my buskin. His eyes met mine, "An archer?"

I was not sure how to address a Bishop and I just said, "Yes, my lord. John Hawkwood. I fought at Crécy."

His face broke into a smile, "And while I was away you fought with Neville and the others against the rapacious Scots. You and the men from Hartburn helped to rid Durham of the Scots. It is good to see you. How may I be of service?"

I saw that the two fat merchants who had been in front of me and were on their way out stopped and stared for this contrasted with their reception.

"Captain Philip lives in Hartburn, my lord, and when I visited with him, he told me that the farm at Ox Bridge House is empty and you might be willing to sell it or perhaps lease it to me."

"You wish to be a farmer?"

"No, my lord, I wish a home and I would be a neighbour of the man who made me the archer I am." I was not being entirely truthful, but I knew if I told the truth then I would receive a no.

The Bishop looked at his clerk. "Do you know this property?"

The clerk gave the Bishop a panicked look, "No, I er…"

The Bishop waved a hand, "Then find out all that you can. Hawkwood, I cannot give you an answer now. Come to services on Sunday and after that, we can talk. I am intrigued by your request and I would give it some thought. There is no urgency is there?"

I shook my head, "I would like the land, but I am sure that I can find some lord who would wish me to take a property off his hands."

He smiled, "I am sure they would, but the land is at peace now. Even our Scottish cousins are behaving themselves. I shall see you on Sunday."

As we rode back Robin commented, "I saw men waiting to speak with the Captain of the Guard. They were warriors seeking a paymaster."

I nodded, "It is another reason I am glad that we came north. In the south, there are great lords. Men like the Earl of Warwick pay the best price for the best men. Here, now that the Scots are cowed, knights are cutting their cloth accordingly. Hopefully, the Bishop will see fit to sell me the farm."

Michael said, "You have not even seen it yet, Captain!"

I smiled, "It is down to trust, Michael. There are some men whom I will always trust, and Captain Philip is one. You two are two others but there are few other men."

"The Bishop?"

"No, Robin, for he is not someone that I know, and he will have his own motives. He will see how he can gain from selling me the land. We are not yet desperate. Captain Philip said that there are many small dwellings which lie empty. The lords who own them may well be willing to sell us the tenancy. This is not a permanent move. Giovanni d'Azzo told me that there is an ague coming from Italy. When that has cleared the land of Italy there will be work for hired men like us. I need enough time to train men with swords and spears to protect us and to hire a company of archers."

"That is ambitious, Captain."

"Aye, Robin. Crécy, Calais and the battle here showed me that I have skills and I will take advantage of them."

It was dark by the time we reached the hall and so it was the next day that we went on foot to visit the derelict farm. We walked back and crossed the lane which led to the village and manor house. The Captain pointed up a narrow track which wound through trees. The trees were overgrown and that told me much; no one had been down here for years. The stream to our right did not bubble; it was slow, and I could smell that it needed to be cleared. The animal waste from the Captain's fields had become trapped amongst branches and fallen leaves. When we came to the first field it was full of weeds and overgrown with brambles and elder. It had not been tended for longer than the Captain had said. The house itself stood in an open piece of ground and we stopped a hundred paces from it so that I could assess the worth. It had once been a well-made home. The house, although just single-storied looked substantial. It was attached to the other buildings and I saw the wisdom of that; it afforded strength, protection and defence. It had been well sited at the top of the slope so that it would be dry.

Captain Philip pointed to the overgrown track which led towards Stockton, "We sometimes use this to get to Stockton. The Ox Bridge after which this farm is named is half a mile yonder. There is a better road which leads to the village." He smiled, "It was the road you took last time."

I nodded, "And it is on the land of this farm?"

"The bridge? Aye, it is. Why?"

"Nothing, I am just interested in the strengths and weaknesses of this land. Come, you can show me around the house."

We headed towards it, "It used to be a fine home, but poor Cedric had ill luck. His wife left him, and he raised his three boys himself. One died of the ague and the other two were killed by the Scots in war. He died many years before his body gave up. I barely knew him but the others who farmed around here kept him alive longer than he wished. They are kind people. It was a mercy, they say, when he died."

We had reached the house and I saw that the door barely hung on its leather hinges. The roof had holes and the wattle and daub walls needed work. We pushed open the door and some animal fled from within. The wind had blown in leaves and broken twigs. Captain Philip patted the timber which supported the roof, "This wood is sound. It is like the timber in my hall. The wattle and daub can be repaired."

It was dark and gloomy within, but I saw that, as we entered the main chamber, there was a stone fireplace. Whatever furniture had been part of the family home had long since fallen into disrepair.

The Captain pointed to a doorway which led off the entrance. "His bed is still there and there are three other chambers."

We walked into a kitchen which had another stone fireplace, a more substantial one and there was an open doorway. The wind had taken the door. We left the house to another wilderness of broken tools and equipment. If there had been anything worth taking it had been. The kindness of the locals did not extend beyond death. There was a barn, cow byre and stable but none were large. The bread oven required repair.

I surveyed it. I had grown up on such a farm and I could see how much work was needed. Robin shook his head, "It needs to be demolished and rebuilt."

"That would not suit my purpose. I need it for a short time. It could be repaired. We have endured worse on campaign, but it is not worth expending a great deal of coins upon it. I now know what to say to the Bishop."

I am as religious as the next man, but I do not like churches. I endured the service. The Bishop did not lead it and that confirmed that he was a warrior first and a priest second. Once again there was a gaggle of men seeking his attention, but his guards merely presented a wall of bodies to them. He spied me and spoke to one of the men who ushered me to his side.

I turned to my men, "Robin, Michael. Amuse yourselves!"

Robin grinned, "Aye lord!"

Sunday after the service was when archery practice would take place. Robin had his bow, and I knew that he would take advantage that few, if any, knew him and he would wager with some of the other archers. He would only be able to do it once, but he would profit from it! Every archer worth his salt liked to gamble.

The Bishop took me to his office and when we were alone poured me a goblet of wine. He began without preamble, "I am curious, archer, why you wish this property or, indeed, any property?" He tapped a number of documents on his desk, "As far as I can see the land is worthless and you are no farmer. Why do you want it?"

I smiled, "I am pleased that you think it worthless, Bishop, for I agree, and I was going to offer very little for it."

"You have not answered my question, archer, why do you want a property at all? I am an astute man, and I will not be told a falsehood."

He looked into my eyes and I believed him. I had already decided that if he would not let me buy the land then I would just squat there for Captain Philip had told me that few ever used the track across it and as there was no lord of the manor then who would know?

I nodded, "I wish, while there is not a war, to hire and train men to follow me. I need a roof and somewhere my men can loose arrows and hone their skills."

He smiled, "Ah, that makes sense." He sipped his wine and I saw his eyes flicker to a parchment on his desk. "And how much would you be willing to pay?"

"As little as possible."

He nodded, "How would nothing suit you?"

I looked at him for a hint of deception, but his face looked honest, "I do not understand."

"If this is temporary then it should suit you. All that I ask is that you make the hall habitable and manage the land while you live there."

I had often been told that if something was too good to be true it usually was. "That is very generous of you and under those terms, I will accept but is there more involved here?"

He smiled and held out his hand for me, "There is just one thing." He held on to my hand. I had known there was a catch. "I have a small favour I require of you. You will be rewarded financially and your decision to accept my offer will not influence my decision to let you stay on the farm for nothing."

I took my hand from his and smiled, "Then ask away, I can always say no."

He smiled back, "Of course you can."

I was no fool if I said no then I would have to head south. In this part of England, the Bishop of Durham was as powerful as the King.

He tapped the parchment with the red seal of Durham upon it, "A murderer fled our justice and ran to Scotland. He killed a knight, an elderly one, but a knight nonetheless. A knight who was a good friend of mine and did good for his people. This bandit stole silver and mail. I would have him brought back for justice."

I said, wryly, "That is all?"

"We have tried other ways but the local Scottish sheriffs side with this man who is known as a thief."

"What is his name and where is his lair?"

"Alexander of Roxburgh but he lives in Alston."

I frowned, "Did not King Edward reclaim Alston?"

The Bishop frowned, "He did but his son allowed the Scots to return. By law it is England but in reality, it is part of Scotland for the people there apply Scottish law and appeal to Scottish courts."

This began to make sense. "The knight who was murdered?" We would not be invading another country but acting as guardians of the law.

"Sir Anian Wetherby. He was an old friend of mine and, like you, he fought with us in France. He lived in a cottage on my estate at Auckland." He picked up the parchment, "This is the

15

warrant for Roxburgh's arrest. You would be acting for the Palatinate.

"The two men I have with me are not enough for me to manage this and I would need to find more of them."

He nodded, "I have ten men I have chosen, and they will if you agree, accompany you."

"And why do you not simply send them?"

He poured more wine, "They are good men and skilled with weapons, but they would merely charge in and either get themselves killed or fail. I had thought to lead them, but I was persuaded that such an act might be considered inadvisable for lots of reasons. I remember you and your name. All men say that despite your relative youth you are a talented leader and a thinker."

"And my reward?"

"Fifty marks and I would send to you any men who might be worth training." He shrugged, "I sometimes have fathers and lords who seek employment for a son too many!".

"In theory then I am your man, but I wish to know all that I can about Alston and where I might find this Roxburgh!"

"Then I shall tell you all that I know." By the time we headed back to Stockton, I had realised what was the problem. The Scot, Roxburgh, was nothing more than a robber baron, a brigand. I had met the type before. He probably terrified the locals and seemed unbeatable but as he had only engaged in cross border raids and, by all accounts, had not fought when King David invaded England then it told me all that I needed to know. When we had fetched our war gear we would return to Durham where the Bishop would provide us with horses, and we would meet our men. Alston was not in the Palatinate and that was where the problem began. Although it was a mere forty miles away it had been debatable for so long that there was no law there and every brigand and bandit who wished to hide outside of the law headed there.

I told my men of the task as we headed south and Robin was sceptical, "It seems to me that you need not have accepted the quest, Captain, for is the fifty marks worth it?"

I smiled, "Fifty marks would buy us three warhorses. We could buy good plate and besides it allows me to assess these ten

16

men who come with us. From what the Bishop implied they are swords and bows for hire." I shrugged, "The Bishop of Durham is a powerful man and any friends that I can make in high places will be more than welcome."

Michael's objections were more practical, "Captain, from what you have told us this Alexander of Roxburgh will have surrounded himself with other bandits and brigands. It will be hard to take him."

"The man we seek has a house which is not in the village. It lies more than a mile away across the narrow River Nent. The house is isolated, and we have Robin Goodfellow here. If I did not have such a skilled scout, then I might have refused the offer, but he will find us a way to get close to the house, unseen."

Robin shook his head and smiled, "Do not honey your words, Captain. I follow your commands for I am your man but we both know this is a hard task. If we had the men who fought with us at Calais, then I would be confident, but we go to war with ten unknown men."

We were nearing the Lustrum Beck and the Ox Bridge. I reined in, "Robin, when next I serve the King I intend to have a company of men so that I will be a commander and when the King or the Prince wins we shall be rewarded."

I dug my heels in and my horse walked across the wooden bridge which lay close to a farm on a boggy piece of earth. I could hear and smell pigs snuffling.

"You would win your spurs?"

I shouted over my shoulder, "It would gain me the respect of other lords and mean that we would be less likely to be used."

We rode to Captain Philip's hall and I told him all. He nodded but I could see that he was not happy and he said so, "It is a hard ride and the men there are wild and savage. You need not have accepted the quest."

Robin grinned, "And that, Captain, is what I told him."

Giving Robin a hard stare I said, "Nonetheless, Captain, I will fulfil the commission and I have coins to pay your men to make the house habitable and secure. Could your men do that?"

"Aye, and you need not pay them."

"I will pay for their work for that is my way."

Chapter 2

We rode for war when we returned to Durham. We now had a sumpter which carried our arrows, but Michael, Robin and I wore mail. I had begun to experiment with drawing a bow whilst wearing mail and although I was not as comfortable, I felt safer. I carried on my saddle a helmet as did the other two. We each had a good sword as well as two daggers, one in a boot and one in a belt. Robin and I carried our bows in cases. We had left early so that we reached Durham before noon. We were taken by one of the Bishop's guards to the castle's inner bailey where we saw the ten men we would be riding with. I saw that they each had a horse or large pony of varying quality and that there were four spare sumpters. I guessed that they were for us to use but we would just use them as spares. I did not approach the men but inspected them while I dismounted.

I examined the four archers first and was immediately disappointed. None had their bow in a case. Only one had an arrow bag and the others had a dozen arrows stuffed in their belts. I saw that they had daggers but only the one with the arrow bag had a short sword. It is hard to judge an archer until you have seen them draw a bow, but I was not confident that they were good archers.

The spear and swordsmen were also a disappointment. None wore mail and only two had a helmet. Four of the six had swords; one had two across his back. Four of them wore brigandines but none of them was studded. They each had a shield but only the two spearmen had one which was larger than a buckler. I was pleased to see that all bore at least two daggers and one of the spearmen had a hand axe in his belt.

The Bishop came out and his Captain of the guard had his men clear away bystanders and onlookers, any who might overhear us. There was no one within one hundred paces of us. He came to me and handed me the parchment with his seal upon it. He turned to the ten men, "This is Captain Hawkwood, and he is my man. You obey him as you would me. As I promised all of you there is employment with me for those of you whom Captain Hawkwood recommends. In addition, as I also told you all when

18

I hired you, you will be paid sixpence a day while you are with the Captain. That is twice the rate you would be offered anywhere else and you will earn it. Do you understand?

"Aye, Bishop!" They chorused as though rehearsed.

He nodded to his clerk who handed me a map. "Captain, here is a map and I will let the men introduce themselves." He looked into my eyes, "I want Alexander of Roxburgh alive but if not then I require his body. One way or another the man will be hanged, and his head displayed on Durham's gates. If it is a corpse you bring back, then so be it. I want men to know the price they pay for murder." He turned to me and, taking me to one side, said, quietly, "A messenger has just come to me from the King. There is a disease which has begun to kill people in their hundreds. The messenger says it is a plague sent by God! At the moment it is many hundreds of leagues from here but the less contact you have with others the better. I am asking you to be invisible! That will be better for all! God Speed!" He turned and headed back inside.

I mounted my horse and said to the ten men, "We have forty miles for us to get to know each other and we are wasting daylight. This is Robin and he is my archer. He will scout and lead us. Michael is my man at arms." I saw the sword and spearmen look in surprise at the young man, but they said nothing. "I will speak to each of you as we ride. Mount!" They swung their legs over the horses' backs, and I saw that the archers were unused to riding. "Robin!"

"Right, you are now Hawkwood's men so ride as though you are warriors and not bandits dressed up for the Bishop!"

The looks on a couple of faces told me that Robin was not far from the truth. We headed out through the gate into the town and I waited until we were clear of the noise and hubbub of Durham. I rode next to the archer who had an arrow bag and a sword. "You look as though you have more about you than the rest. What is your name?"

"Martin the Fletcher, Captain and I remember you from the battle here. I was with Lord Henry's men."

I was blunt, "And why are you no longer with him?"

"A woman, Captain. The man who led the archers had a young wife and she took a fancy to me. I did nothing to encourage it, but you know how it is, you cannot have division amongst warriors. I was paid off. That was a year since and I am keen to gain employment again."

"Where is your bow case?"

"I served, briefly, on the border and we were surprised by some Scottish raiders. I lost it."

"And can you fletch?"

He grinned, "My dad was a fletcher, Captain, and I make the best arrows! I can also make a bow. I made my own two."

"Good!"

I had hopes of the fletcher, squat with a barrel chest I could see that he would be powerful. What I did not understand was why a woman would risk the wrath of her husband, for Martin had not a hair on his head and I would not have thought a woman would find him a good catch! I spoke next to the other archers, John of Wark, Wilson the Archer and Peter Longbow. They all struck me as competent archers, but their lack of arrows did not bode well. An archer would sell other gear to pay for arrows or, like Martin, they would make them. Perhaps they had fallen on hard times. We had plenty of arrows and we would be well paid by the Bishop.

It was the others I was most interested in. I already had six archers I could count upon, but I just had Michael to guard us. I was hoping for at least two from these six. Speaking to them did not fill me with confidence. Jack Two Swords looked the best prospect. With two swords strapped across his back, he was the best equipped. He had a brigandine but when he spoke, he was boastful and I did not like that. He spoke of the men he had defeated but as there was no one to corroborate his story then it could have been pure fancy. A good soldier did not boast for such aggrandisements could come back to haunt a man. You let your deeds and the words of others do the talking.

Roger of Norham seemed the best of them for although he only had a spear that was because his sword had been buckled fighting the Scots at Norham. He was keen to impress me, but I wondered why he had not found the means to acquire another sword.

The other four, Much, Ben's son, William of Stanhope, Gareth of Chester and Digby son of Richard did not strike me as men I would care to fight with. They were all vague about their experience and did not seem to know much about battle.

We stopped to water our horses and to rest a little at St John's Chapel. No people were living there any longer. Nobles used it as a stop for hunting and it did no harm to pray. I noticed Michael doing so. While we ate the food which the Bishop's clerk had provided I took Robin to one side. "I have little confidence in most of these men. I fear it will be down to us. They are just bodies to take blows intended for us."

"None are suitable for your company then?"

"Two, possibly, one archer and one spearman. We shall see for I might be wrong and let us see them in battle before we make judgements."

"And do you have a plan?"

"We cannot reach Alston and the brigands' lair before night has fallen and so we shall camp as close to it as we can manage. If nothing else, it will tell us the mettle of these men. Then we scout out the hall in daylight. From the map the clerk gave us there looks to be high ground to the east and a burn between the hall and the high ground. You and I will scout."

"We leave the others alone?"

I shrugged, "I do not think that they will run. Like us, they have not been paid and I do not think that any of them can manage without the Bishop's silver."

We left and headed west. The high ground was to the north and after passing the tiny hamlet of Nenthead we left the road and began to head to the higher ground. There was plenty of cover for this was not a well-farmed area. The odd patch of cleared ground was used for sheep and wary shepherds watched us as we passed. The sun was setting in the west and it illuminated the hall we sought. It was some way away but silhouetted against the sky it gave me an idea of what to expect. We did not have long to look but I saw no tower and that had been my fear. We headed down to the burn and I found a derelict dwelling. There was no roof and some of the stones had been robbed out, but it meant we had walls we could use for shelter and we would be able to use fire. The breeze, slight though it was, came from the west and would not alarm those within the hall. I sent Robin off to do a preliminary scout while we tended to our horses and prepared a fire.

I chose to start as I meant to go on. "John and Jack, you two will have the first watch. Climb up to the top of the half-wrecked wall and be the lookouts. I will have you relieved in an hour or so. The rest of you clear the inside so that we are comfortable. Michael, take charge. I will head up to the high ground yonder and get the lay of the land."

The sun was still slowly setting and sometimes the shadows helped. Robin would already be close to the walls and what he saw would help to determine our plan of attack. We would have most of the next day to sort out the details. I found a piece of rock on which I could perch. I was more than a hundred paces higher than the derelict cottage. I saw the glow from the door of the hall as it was opened and closed. I looked further left and saw tendrils of smoke rising in the light of the setting sun as well as the shadow of a tower. That would be Alston. It looked very close to the hall and posed a problem. The men who lived there might not take kindly to one of their neighbours being abducted, however legally we managed it. I would have to devise a plan to deal with that possibility. I descended when the light went and returned to the camp.

"Gareth and Peter, relieve the other two."

I saw that Michael had organised food. I frowned when I saw that he had allowed the others just to lie down. We all had to work.

"Michael, come here. The rest of you, get the food organised. We have no passengers in my company."

"Yes, Captain?"

I smiled and took him to one side, "You do not have to fetch and carry for everyone. They are being paid. You tell them what to do."

"But they are older!"

"That means nothing. I will wager that you are their superior in every regard!"

We had begun to eat the rough stew we had prepared by the time Robin appeared. It was Martin and Much on duty and he appeared behind them both. He had done so deliberately for he wished them to know he had skills. They both looked shamefaced.

"Well?"

"Numbers were hard to estimate but there were at least eight men that I saw."

"Sentries?"

He shook his head, "I waited an hour, and all were indoors. They were drinking and made the noise drunken men make. I circled the building. There is a low wall all around. I clambered over the rear wall for they lock the gate, and I spied a rear door to the hall. I waited there, hidden by a pile of horse waste for, perhaps, half an hour and I saw that men came out and made water in a pot by the door. While I waited, I saw that they had a barn and a stable. I did not approach the stable for I saw that they had dogs chained close to the door. I think the smell of the horse dung afforded me protection. I returned here."

"You have done well. So, you think that they release the dogs when they sleep?"

"It would make sense. The wall goes from the two sides of the house around to the back. The front is open."

"The man does not bother with wind holes then?"

"They have shutters, but they were closed. Until it is summer, they will not need the through draught."

"Then eat, I need to think." We would have two points of attack. The front door would be barred but the rear one, while open, had dogs for protection. They would have to be silenced. I would leave two archers to watch the front door with orders to send arrows into whoever came out. If we climbed the rear wall, then when the dogs came to investigate, we would slay them. My archers could guard the back door and I would enter with Michael and the four men at arms. Then I remembered that two of the men I had with me only had spears for protection. They would be of little use inside a darkened house. I would leave Digby outside and Roger of Norham would have his hand axe until we could find another sword.

They all looked expectantly at me when I poured some ale into my wooden beaker.

"Tomorrow you will all rest while Robin and I get closer to the house and work out their exact numbers. We need to identify

Alexander of Roxburgh. When we attack them, Martin and John, you will watch the front door. If Alexander of Roxburgh tries to flee apprehend him. If there are others, then stop them!" They both nodded. If I had known their skill level, I might have asked them to try to incapacitate the criminal. I could not risk that. "The rest of us will climb the wall and use our arrows to slay the dogs. I will enter with Michael, Jack, William, Much, Gareth and Roger. The rest will secure the rear door. I am guessing that it will be the kitchen and will be large. Robin will be in charge."

Robin nodded and Jack asked, somewhat truculently, "But how can seven of us guarantee that we can take all the men who are in the house? Robin said that there were at least eight. We all know that there will be more."

I looked at the man who, in theory, should have been the best man I had, "All of you seek regular employment. So far I have seen better buskins on corpses. You have all fallen, for one reason or another, on hard times. Regard this as a test. If you impress me then there might be regular employment with me. If you can show me that you have worth, then I will tell the Bishop so and he will give you a position. For the rest either death or the road awaits you. So, Jack Two Swords, we use our wits. By the time we enter I will be able to recognise Alexander of Roxburgh. Any other man I see who threatens me will be a dead man walking. These are murderers we seek, and we have the blessing of the Church, the Bishop and the law!" I had not been aware of it, but Robin told me later that my voice became more like steel as I spoke and by the end, all of them, even Jack Two Swords, nodded and accepted my command.

I stretched, "Michael, Robin and I will sleep. Assign sentries to watch during the night. I want two men watching at all times." I smiled, not at Michael but the others. "You can all rest during the day tomorrow!"

I wrapped myself in my cloak, rolled over and began to sleep. I was unworried about the sentries. I doubted that any from the house would venture forth, but this was a test for Michael and the others. I would speak to Michael and discover the reaction of the men.

I woke before dawn but that was not because of danger, it was the need to make water. I saw that Roger and Gareth were on watch. They nodded as I unfastened my breeks and relieved myself on the outside wall of the derelict house. I wandered down to the burn to wash my face and to smell the air. I detected no human smell coming from the west. I saw smoke rising from the house of Alexander of Roxburgh. I went back to the camp and after I had nudged Robin awake, grabbed some of the stale bread that was left and cut two slices from it. The fire was almost out but I stuck them on the end of my sword and propped them above the glowing embers to toast. I drank some ale and then went to fetch my bow.

The noise of Robin moving, and my movements woke some of the others. I saw the archers watching me as I strung my bow. That done I fastened a war bag with a dozen arrows onto my belt and then returned to take the toasted bread from my sword. I cut a piece of cheese and placed it on the toast. The heat from the bread began to melt the cheese. By the time the others decided to do the same, there would not be enough heat left in the fire and we would not relight the fire. The walls might have hidden the firelight at night but a tendril of smoke this close to their home would alert them. At night they might be drunk but not during the day. As the sun rose in the east, I nodded to Robin who had eaten and then turned to Michael, "Keep everyone close to the camp. We will return by early afternoon. Stay hidden! We are off the road here and none should visit."

I turned and headed down to the burn. Robin trotted until he was just ahead of me. He was the scout, and I was as noisy as a bull in comparison. He led me along the burn where we used the trees for cover. I tried to be as silent as he was, but I failed. It did not matter for at this hour there would not be any who were about. He stopped and we headed north along a line of hawthorns which must have been planted to give some shelter from the wind. In the winter they would give protection to the sheep. I saw that there were a few animals dotted about the fells. Alexander of Roxburgh was no farmer. There were fields which had been cleared but they were filled with weeds. That helped us for they were tall enough to hide us. I realised that there had been a track of sorts and Robin was following it. He stopped suddenly and held up his hand. I took an arrow and held it in my right hand with my bow. Robin shook his head. He moved towards the hedgerow which was overgrown and needed to be tamed but it suited us that it had not. He lay down and we peered through the stems at the bottom. While the top was an impenetrable mass of growth the bottom was not, and we had a good view of the front of the house just one hundred and twenty paces from us. I lay down too and we waited.

I saw the road which came from the north and turned around the house. I assumed it headed west to Alston. There was a water trough outside the house and even as we watched I saw a man leading a pony and small wagon down the road towards the town. When he hurried past the entrance and the water trough it was a measure of Alexander of Roxburgh. This man was a local farmer and yet he feared the men in the hall. When another three groups of people headed along the road then I knew that it must be the time of the local market. The people travelling down the road had reduced to a trickle by the time that the front door opened and the men from inside emerged. They did not come from the main gate but a small gate in the wall next to the house. Four of them led horses and ponies. As soon as the four animals were mounted, I knew which of them was Alexander of Roxburgh. He rode a courser and had a good sword. The other three riders wore mail shirts. They headed down the road to Alston and were followed by another ten men who walked. They walked in groups which suggested they chose their friends.

When they had gone, I looked at Robin and he shook his head. We waited. Sure enough, the front door opened, and an older woman came out. There were not just men inside. A young girl came with her with a broom. The two cleaned the front of the hall and refilled the water trough. They went inside and we waited. By noon we had seen another six people travel to Alston and when we saw others returning up the road, we knew that it was time to leave. We headed down to the river and back to the camp.

I gathered my men around me. "There are fourteen men, at least, in the house and four wear mail shirts. There are also two women, at the very least. Alexander of Roxburgh is of an age with me and is taller than the others. He is the one who is clean-shaven. The rest can be slain or wounded but leave him for me. There is also a gate in the wall close to the house; Martin, that will need watching. The women will not be harmed. I do not think that the men will wear mail inside the hall. Robin and I will now sleep. Wake us at dusk, Michael."

We led our horses down the riverbank and up to the hedgerow. The trunks were thick enough for us to tether our horses. We had a spare rope upon which to tie, if necessary, our prisoner. We had no spare men to watch the horses, but the only light and noise was coming from the hall. Martin had shown that he could lead, and he silently led John off. I was confident that they would be able to do that which I asked. The others would be with me and I would have to live with any failure on their part.

Robin led us. I left my bow with my horse. We had enough archers and although I was not certain about their ability, I was sure that my sword skills would prove to be more important. Robin, Wilson, and Peter Longbow would have to use their bows to silence any dogs and guards that we found. To that end, the three were boosted up onto the back wall by the gate. The three straddled the wall and I heard growling from within. The three bowstrings thrummed and all that I heard was a slight yelp. The bowstrings told me that the archers had each loosed a second arrow. A moment later the three disappeared and then the gate was opened. I saw the four dead hounds. They were huge beasts and two of them looked to be the Irish Wolf Hound which could bring down a man. Even as I stepped into the yard a movement caught my eye. Robin's hands were fast and the bull mastiff which raced towards me was killed instantly. It was close to me and when I examined the carcass, I saw signs that it had been used for dogfighting. That explained why it had not attacked first. It had fresh wounds and must have fought that day. We were lucky. Had it barked then they would have been alerted.

Robin tapped the other two archers on the shoulder and led them to the stables where they could cover the back door and the gate which was on the wall attached to the hall. I drew my sword and headed towards the back door. This would be the most dangerous part of our task for if we were seen before we gained entry then the door could be barred, and our quest would be ended. I did not look behind. The men had to be following me. I reached the door and put my ear to it. Inside I could hear squeals which suggested women. The old woman I had seen that morning was not the kind to be bothered by men. There could be a problem with innocent people. It could not be helped. Robin had said that the door opened outwards and I lifted the latch and gently pushed open the door. I knew that Michael would be behind me. There was no light burning to illuminate it but the glow from the kitchen range allowed me to see that it was a large kitchen worthy of a great noble. Many meals could be cooked here. I saw the door which led from the kitchen and it was closed.

I risked looking behind me and saw my men; I waved them forward and headed for the door. As I reached for the handle it moved towards me and I quickly stepped back and held my sword across my body. One of the men I had seen wearing mail stepped inside. He had been coming from the light and my men froze. He took one step for I was in the dark and I doubted that he had seen me clearly. Using my body to close the door I put my left hand across his mouth and my sword across his neck.

"One word and you die!"

I saw the anger in his eyes, and he opened his mouth and bit down hard upon my fingers. He was quick and his teeth bit through to the bone. I slashed my sword across his throat and blood spurted. I pulled my hand away and he began to fall. It was Michael who showed he was quick thinking, and he caught the body before it hit the ground. He dragged it towards the range with Roger of Norham helping him. Michael hurried to my side while Roger drew the dead man's weapon. He now had a sword and he looked happier. I wrapped a cloth around my bloodied fingers. This was not the time for hesitation; this was the time for action and, throwing open the door, I entered the corridor which led to the main house. I did not know the house, but I had been in similar houses. There was usually a good passageway from the kitchen to the dining room, or in the case of this house, dining hall. The light from the doorway and the noise told me where that was. As I hurried the eight paces to the door a drunk staggered out and turned to see me. I was running and the pommel of my sword smashed into his face rendering him unconscious. He fell silently but even had he made a noise the din from inside would have drowned it out. I stepped into the well-lit room. There were at least four women, and none were the ones I had seen that morning. Faces turned in shock at the bloody apparition with the sword in his hand and I spied, straightway, Alexander of Roxburgh, he had two of the four women on his lap.

A warrior ran at me with a chair and Michael, standing next to me, hacked him across the middle. I went directly for the murderer, drawing my dagger as I did so. The bite mark hurt and I would only use the dagger if I was in dire straits. I could not count numbers, but I knew that we had surprise and none of the men had weapons in their hands. Having disposed of two the odds had to be more in our favour. A large warrior picked up a jug to run at me. I saw his intent. He would smash it over my head. I thrust my sword up through his neck and into his skull. A sword smashed down on a figure to my right and when a Scot fell at my feet, I knew that one of those following me had saved me.

Alexander of Roxburgh rose, throwing the two women to the ground. He reached up for the two-handed sword above the fireplace. I could not allow him a weapon as I did not know how skilful he was. I stabbed his right hand with my dagger and pinned it to the wood. I tore it out sideways to ensure that his tendons were ripped, and he would not be able to use it. He screamed in pain and I brought the flat of my sword to smash into the back of his skull. He fell into his chair.

"You women, flee while you can!"

Screaming they obeyed me, and I picked up the Scotsman and threw him over my left shoulder. Turning I saw the bloody and chaotic scene behind me. Michael was finishing off one of the men at arms. Of Jack Two Swords there was no sign. Roger was fighting two men, but he was using his axe and sword to great effect. Three dead men lay close to him. Close by the door I saw the bodies of Much and Digby, both had been slain. William of Stanhope was also fighting two men but was not doing as well as Roger. I needed all the men I could get and so I ran at the nearest man fighting William and skewered him. As my sword came out of his front the man next to him turned and William slew him. I saw that the Scots in the room were all dead, dying or wounded. One of the women was weeping and holding the head of a dying man in her arms.

"Michael, William, help Roger and follow me."

I stepped into the corridor and saw Robin. There was still no sign of Jack Two Swords, but three more Scots had been hit by arrows.

"I have him. Cover me and get out of here!" The front door was open, and I ran out shouting. "It is Hawkwood!"

"Come, Captain! We have you covered!" I saw another dead Scot by the door. He had two arrows in him.

Michael overtook me and shouted, "I will ensure that there is no danger, Captain!" Since he had first come to us Michael had become a confident warrior. I was lucky to have him.

I headed down towards the hedgerow and the waiting horses although by my count there were no enemies left or, at least, not enough to bother us. My other men came out and I said to Robin, when he ran next to me, "Wilson and Peter Longbow?"

"They took the horses and will be waiting for us."

Robin looked around and counted the men, "I saw Much and Digby both were dead, where is Two Swords?"

As I ran, I shook my head, "I did not see him."

I wondered if he had taken it upon himself to search the rest of the house, perhaps seeking treasure. When we neared the horses, they neighed, and I held my sword before me. Michael shouted, "Two Swords is with them!"

I turned as William and Roger ran up. Robin would have the archers covering the houses until we called to them. "Tie this man to his horse. Bind his hand I do not want him bleeding to death." Michael mounted and moved behind the mounted horseman. I said to Jack Two Swords, "Why are you here?"

"I thought to secure the horses."

"Michael, take his swords!"

In one practised motion Michael whipped out the swords and examined them. "There is not a mark on them, Captain."

"You did not draw your weapons?"

"There was no need, Captain. You and the others had them in hand."

"Much and Digby died. Dismount!"

He grinned, "Captain, I..."

Michael reached up and dragged him to the ground.

"The rest of you mount. This horse is the Bishop's, and I will not have it ridden by a coward. Start walking, Jack, for you will not be returning with us."

"You cannot leave me here! They will kill me!"

"Luckily for you, we slew most of them now start walking."

He did not move and Robin said, from behind me, "I am loath to waste an arrow but if you do not move then I will pin your foot to the earth so that they will find you all the easier."

He turned and ran for the venom in Robin's voice left him in no doubt that he would carry out his action.

It was dark and the first few miles until we reached a good road were slow but when we did find a surface with cobbles then we galloped. We had spare horses now and could swap. That way we could make the journey to Durham in one ride. Alexander of Roxburgh was tied like a sack of cereal over the horse and he woke as dawn broke.

"Let me off this horse, give me a sword and fight me!"

I laughed, "I fought you once and beat you, besides we are servants of the court and we take you for trial, in Durham!"

His silence told me that he had not realised that was our purpose.

We journeyed for another mile and as the sun rose ahead of us, he asked, "Can I not sit upon a saddle?"

I noticed that he did not have a broad Scottish accent, in fact, it sounded almost Northumbrian. "Robin, cover him, Martin and John, put him on the saddle."

"And my hands?"

I shook my head, "Your hands will be tied. I take no chances with you." My left hand was throbbing. I had washed it and applied some vinegar, but I knew it would take some time to heal for it was a deep wound. When he was securely fastened, I said, "Change horses! I doubt that this man has any friends left but we will put as much distance as we can." Robin kept his bow aimed at the Scot's back until the other three archers had changed and when they aimed their bows, he swapped his own horse.

With daylight, we made faster progress and I let Michael lead. I rode behind Alexander of Roxburgh with Robin and we spoke. Behind us came the archers. All of my men led a spare horse or pony and we cantered. It would take determined men riding hard to catch us and as the nearest help was in Alston, a mile from where we had taken him, I hoped that any pursuit would end before we reached the Palatinate.

"Well, Captain, Jack Two Swords will not be one of your men, what of the others?"

"They did better than I might have expected when first I met them. We shall see what they say when we reach Durham. This sword has two edges, Robin. They may not choose to follow me."

He smiled, "I think that most will."

William of Stanhope rode next to me when noon approached, "Captain, I was born just a mile or two from here. We can take a short cut and save some miles."

I nodded, "And pass your home at the same time?"

He smiled and nodded, "It is a short cut, Captain."

"Then ride to the fore and lead on."

When we changed direction Robin asked, "Is this wise?"

"He fought well enough and if we were passing your home then..."

"When I left home, Captain, it was made quite clear to me that I was not welcome. You and I are alike in that. Come to think of it so is Michael. The three of us have no home to return to."

William's parents had a small farm just outside the village. I saw that they farmed sheep but there was a patch which grew vegetables. That William had a loving family was clear when his parents and the two brothers who lived at home ran to welcome him as we approached. I did not impose on the family for food. I saw that they had little enough, but we drank some of their ale and watered our horses. We ate our own food.

I saw the looks that they gave the Scot. When William told his father why we had hunted the Scot his father suddenly became angry, "Let me know, Captain, when they hang this man, and I will walk to Durham to witness it! Sir Anian was a kind man. I followed his banner when we warred against the Scots. This bandit and his men raped and pillaged this border for too long."

We had allowed Alexander of Roxburgh to dismount so that he could relieve himself. It was not out of kindness; we just did not want to smell soiled breeks. The Scot seemed almost proud of his reputation. He sneered, "I will not hang! I have men in Durham who will support me in court. When I am free, Captain Hawkwood, then I will have my revenge on you!"

Robin's right hand was so fast that it was a blur, but he put the power of his arm and chest into the blow and striking the Scot beneath the chin he rendered him unconscious. He rubbed his knuckles. "Gareth and Peter, tie him to his horse. He does not deserve to be treated well!"

When he was tied on to the horse we mounted and left. Alexander's words worried me a little. I was not afraid of his vengeance for I had the measure of the man, but I wondered about his support. He had taken silver from Sir Anian and, having spoken to William's father I had learned that while Sir Anian had been the only noble who had been murdered and robbed, others had suffered at the man's hands. He was rich and yet we had seen little treasure in the house. Did he have confederates in Durham itself? The Bishop had chosen me to fetch him back and why was that? Did he not trust those from Durham? I thought back and realised that when he had sent us off there had been few men close by.

Chapter 3

It was after dark when we reached Durham. The gates to the castle were barred but when I spoke to the Captain of the Guard we were admitted. The Bishop himself came to supervise the securing of the prisoner. I heard the anger in the Bishop's voice as he ordered him taken to a cell. Robin's punch had broken the jaw of the Scot and he found it difficult to respond but I knew he would offer no more curses for fear of Robin.

When he had gone just the Bishop and his clerk remained. "There are quarters for you in the castle, Captain and there will be food in the refectory. You and your men have done well but you need rest and I shall pay you on the morrow.

I nodded, "Robin, Michael, take the horses to the stable and then go to the refectory I wish to speak to the Bishop, alone."

The clerk nodded and said, "Come with me, good sirs."

The Bishop frowned, "Is there a problem, Captain? I see that three of the men I sent did not return."

I told him of the fight and Jack Two Sword's actions. "But that is not my worry; we can handle the likes of Jack Two Swords. This Alexander of Roxburgh suggested that he would not hang because he had support. Is that true?"

The Bishop nodded, "He has friends and that is why I told no one of your quest. I apologise that I was less than honest with you. You had to be sent in secret for if he got wind of what you were doing he would have been prepared. The trial will smoke out his allies, but he will hang. I have evidence enough and his death warrant is already signed." He smiled, "In this part of the world I am the law and if he thinks that a jury of his peers will save him then he is wrong. You have my word as a warrior who fought alongside you that he will die!" He put his arm around me and led me towards the keep. "And I confess that you did even better than I might have hoped. I wondered how many would return."

"And those you sent with me were expendable?"

"Captain, you have a reputation which is well deserved, and my hands were tied. I could send no one with you who was associated with me for obvious reasons. If any of those who went with you wish to serve me, they have a place here. They were not expendable, but I confess that I did not know their true worth."

I was satisfied. In truth, I was too exhausted to argue.

I slept badly but that was because of the pain in my hand. I woke in the early hours and it had swollen. The Bishop had healers and a hospital. I went to see the monk there and he tut-tutted. He was rougher than I would have liked but he knew his business and after cleaning the wound and applying a salve he wrapped it in a bandage.

"Keep it clean and at the end of a week remove the bandage. The wound should smell clean but if there is any badness…"

"Then apply maggots, I know but I hope that your magic will work."

He sniffed, "It is not magic, it is medicine."

The Bishop was up early because he intended to try Alexander of Roxburgh as soon as possible. We gathered the men together and the Bishop had his scrivener on hand to keep a record of what was said and his moneyer waited with the coins.

"Firstly, I should like to thank you all for your efforts. The coins I would have paid to the three who did not return I will spread amongst you all. I am here to offer any of you who wish employment a paid position in the castle. Threepence a day for archers and two pence a day for the others. I will provide your food, accommodation, and clothes. However, before you either accept or reject my offer then you should know that Captain Hawkwood may also offer a position. Hear his proposal and then let me know."

I had my arm in a sling and I did not realise how much I used my arms to speak until I tried. "I will hire the best of you and until we have finished training, we will live in Stockton. After that, we could go anywhere. It might be England but equally, it could be France, Gascony, Italy, or Spain. If I offer you a position, then you will be my men until you choose to leave. I will house and feed you and, until we are hired then you will be paid two pence a day. You will be Hawkwood's Men."

William of Stanhope smiled, "Captain, as much as I would dearly love to follow you, I cannot leave the north. You saw my family and I wish to be close to them. I will accept the Bishop's offer." He walked over to take his payment. It was as though he had begun an avalanche. John of Wark also wished to stay in the north as did Wilson the Archer. That left four and, in all honesty, I could not reject any of them.

"All four of you wish to serve with me?"

Roger of Norham said, "I think we would serve anywhere, Captain. I can see why the others want to stay in Durham, but I believe we will be richer men if we follow you."

I nodded and Robin added, "Or dead ones!" He said it with a grin and all of them laughed.

We were paid and I spoke to clear the air and remove any misunderstandings, "Bishop we did not try to find treasure in Alston, but we took weapons and animals. They are ours by right, are they not?"

"Of course."

"Then we shall leave now and head back to my home."

"You will not stay for the trial?"

"I am tempted to see him hang, but I have seen hangings before. Just make sure that he suffers, my lord, for he is an evil man!"

It was market day in Durham and while Stockton did have a market it was not as extensive as the one in Durham and we bought items we thought we might need in Stockton. Word had got out about the trial and lords were arriving as we left the city. I wondered if the Bishop's plan would work and he would discover the identity of his enemies. I knew that there were Scottish sympathisers. Many were unhappy that King David had lost his power after the battle. His army had outnumbered ours but his men were simply not good enough.

Relieved of having to watch a prisoner there was a happy atmosphere as we rode home down the Stockton Road. By my reckoning, we had a year before I would need to eke into the chests of coins we had. The farm and the woods would provide food and thanks to Jack Two Swords and Alexander of Roxburgh and his men we had plenty of weapons.

Martin asked me about the trees on my land. I was pleased he did because it told me that he was truly a fletcher. I told him and he was satisfied. "Poplar, ash, chestnut, elm and yew, all good in their own ways. It is important to have a variety. And you have geese?"

I shook my head, "But my neighbour who is an archer has and I can buy some from him!"

Martin nodded, "They make good watchdogs!" He smiled, "And they are tastier when they become annoying or old!"

We reached Stockton in the early afternoon. There was still no lord of the manor in Hartburn, but the Bishop had instructed me to drop off a copy of the deed which granted the farm to me and the right to hunt in Hartburn woods to the Lord of Stockton. The steward of Stockton Castle took the deed and promised that Sir William of Stockton would look at it. It was in the afternoon when we reached the lane to the Captain's manor. I left Robin in charge of the men. Captain Philip's men were still repairing the farm and so I walked across to his hall.

When I was met at the door by Mathilde, she saw my sling and said, "What happened, John?"

I gave her a wry smile, "Would you believe I had my hand bitten… by a man?"

She put her hand to her mouth as she laughed, "I am sorry. I cannot help smiling but it is not a nice thing is it?"

"No, where is Philip?"

"He and some of his men were collecting rabbits from the traps. They have decimated the vegetables. Sit, I pray you."

I had just had half of the beaker of ale when my old Captain of archers walked in. He joined me by the fire, and I told him all. I gave him the whole story, including the threat from Roxburgh. Mathilde was in the kitchen and he shook his head, for he could speak openly, "You should have killed this Jack Two Swords. You have made an enemy!"

"I know but we served the Bishop, and I was not sure how such a murder might look. I can deal with him if he seeks me out but he struck me as a backstabber who would not risk Robin's wrath again."

"Your instincts are good. We will keep an eye open for him. Luckily, there are few people these days who cross the river here at Stockton. Hartness is now the Bishop's port and more traffic goes there. It takes less time to haul goods by wagon than for the ships to take two tides to come up the river!" He smiled and emptied his beaker, "But it suits me for I like the peace and I do not like strangers."

They insisted that I eat with them and it was late when I returned to my new hall. It was still far from finished but my new men were happy there and they had already made it homely. I had the start of my company and the next day we would begin to train. So began six months of hard work that was, in all honesty, joyful! We ate, drank the ale which Mathilde and her women made for us and we honed our skills. I ensured that Roger and Gareth were taught to use a bow. While they would never be as good with one as my archers, they would be able to use one and that could only help. Robin, Martin, and Peter were trained by me to use a sword. Even though Gareth and Roger had been spearmen and could use a sword, they did not have my natural ability. I practised with the swordsmen for my left hand hurt me for months. It was during that time that I began to change from a pure archer to something new, an archer who was skilled with a sword. We practised from dawn until dusk and ate well for tired men always have a good appetite. We took advantage of the licence to hunt and went with Captain Philip and his men to cull the deer. There were no wild boar which was a shame, but it was a good opportunity to practise using a bow with a live target and not just a butt. My hand healed but I suspected that come the winter it would ache with the cold. Wounds close to the bone often did. I was pleased that I had taken on the new men. My initial judgements had been wrong and this was a lesson well learned. If I had not asked them to be in my company then my life would not have been as rich as it became.

When August came the land burgeoned with growth. The fields were full and the animals were healthy. It was then that we heard a rumour of the self-same dreadful disease which had arrived months earlier in the south of England and driven us north. The Captain and most of the locals were sceptical but I told them what my friend Giovanni d'Azzo had told me of this Great Mortality which had killed thousands of his countrymen. So far it was a rumour in the north, but I was worried, and we were wary.

It was late September when it struck and Hartness felt its effect first. A Genoese ship docked and landed its cargo. When it sailed, they left a man who was sick in the hospital of the convent there. A week later we heard that the man had died and some of the nuns and the men who tended the abbey's animals had growths under their arms as well as black spots on their skin. They suffered headaches and vomited. None could keep food down. It is easy to look back and say what should have been done and had we known the true nature of the disease then we would have done so. We would have barred the nuns in their hospital and let the disease die but the folk of Hartness did not. The nuns were popular for they helped all in the town and the disease spread so quickly that the fishermen of the town were convinced that it was brought on the wind and so they hung their nets on the town gates to catch it before it reached them.

I went to visit with the Captain to confide in him of my fears. "Captain, this is a plague which is hitting our lands. When I was in Calais, I heard of this in far off Italy. That it has taken a year or more to travel here suggests that men bring it and the fact that it has spread so quickly is worrying. It is in Hartness now; what if someone who does not know they have the disease flees and comes south? What if they take it to Stockton?"

He nodded, "And then to Hartburn. What can we do?"

"The road from Stockton to Hartburn crosses the beck at the Ox Bridge which is on my land. I could use my men to stop any from crossing. If you could stop any coming along the road from Elton and the west, then we would be safe." I saw him hesitating. "There is no Lord of the Manor and you command the levy. This is a war, Captain. We fight a disease."

"But what if it is not a pestilence, as you say? We would be harming the livelihood of this valley."

"Would we? We have our crops almost gathered in. If we do not sell them in the market at Stockton, then we consume them ourselves. The folk of Stockton have the river they can use, and most travellers cross the Tees at Piercebridge, as we did."

"How would you stop those wishing to cross the bridge?"

I paused, "This is war, Captain, we will stop them."

"Then I will make it legal. We will hold a meeting on the green by the manor. Come, we will go now."

Wrapping our cloaks around us we strode along the lane to the deserted manor house which stood by the green. Captain Philip had taken his hunting horn and when we reached the pond and the green, he sounded it three times. Its strident notes might be heard in Stockton where they might think we were hunting. The men of the village left their homes and made their way to the green. It took those who lived to the east some time to reach us. There were just forty farmers and landowners but their sons and some of their workers came so that there were nearer to seventy who gathered. I recognised some of the archers who had fought alongside us against the Scots.

Edward, Ned's son spoke, "What is this, Captain? Have the Scots come again?"

"No, Edward, but an even more deadly enemy; one we cannot see and against whom there is no defence. You have heard of this disease which has struck Hartness?"

He shook his head, but Harry the Carter nodded, "I heard that it is killing whole families and cares not if they are rich or they are poor." Harry's occupation took him to Stockton and Hartness. He was our main source of information and, indeed, it was he had told us of the first deaths.

"I propose that until the disease ends, we allow no one into the manor who is not here already."

He let that sink in. Matty the Blacksmith said, "What about my iron? If I have no iron, then I cannot work. How will I feed my family?"

There were murmurs and nods of agreement.

"And how will you feed your family if you or they are dead?"

Harry nodded, "The captain is right. I am the one who brought this news, and I can tell you that those who are able to are fleeing Hartness. Some may already be in Billingham or Stockton. I too will suffer but I want to live." Harry's words convinced some of those with doubts.

"This is war, Matty. None will starve. We cannot take our food to market and so we share. I have the largest farm and now that we have the harvest in my granary is full. Those who are short of food come to me. Those who also have a surplus could do the same. The choice we have is a stark one. We share and work together or we die. John?"

He gestured to me and I spoke, "This disease was in Italy two years ago and in France a year since. From what we have heard it has made charnel houses of some places. I will guard the Ox

Bridge and prevent any from entering the village from that direction. The Bishop gave me permission to hunt and my men will do so. All of you will eat meat this winter." I saw some of those who had not met me wondering who I was. I was young and I knew that I must have sounded arrogant to some of the greybeards. "I am only recently come to this land and when this pestilence is gone and my men are trained, then I shall leave but for now I am one of you and I wish to live. I will stop any from crossing the bridge on my land and if I have to use force of arms to do so then I will."

There was silence and Captain Philip said, quietly, "Captain Hawkwood is a friend of the Bishop and fought with us in Durham. More, he served the King and the Prince in the war in France. I have heeded his advice. A show of hands!"

The majority raised their hands.

Captain Philip nodded, "Any who wish to leave may do so but they cannot return until this pestilence is gone!"

In the end, just two families headed to Stockton. They believed that the walls of that town would keep out the disease. Captain Philip gave a parchment to them. It was intended for the steward in the castle and explained what we intended. I had six men with me at the bridge when they left. The Captain was there too. He pinned a copy of what we had decided on the signpost which directed folk to Hartburn. It was on the Stockton side of the bridge.

Oswald was a pig farmer who farmed just across from the bridge and he came over to the bridge. He stared at the parchment and then at our bows, "Captain, I cannot read. What does this say?"

"It says, Oswald of the Beck, that none may enter Hartburn until the plague which afflicts this land is gone."

He laughed, "It is just the winter illness which strikes every year, Captain. Some years it kills more than others. That is all that this is! What if I want to travel to Hartburn?"

"Why?"

"Why?"

"What would make you visit Hartburn?"

I learned later that Oswald was an argumentative type who would argue that black was white if the mood took him. He questioned everything. Captain Philip said, "You have not crossed this bridge since I came to Hartburn, Oswald and I can think of no reason why you should now!"

"But I might want to! You have no right to do so! Who is to stop me? "

I spoke and there was anger in my voice for this annoying little man irritated me, "I will! This is now my land and if any try to cross then my archers will stop them."

He saw me for the first time, "From your voice, you are a southerner and you do not tell me what to do!"

I nodded, "Friend, I am here now, and you will do what I say! Robin, show him!"

There was a wooden post at the entrance to Oswald's farm. It was two hundred paces away. Robin drew an arrow, nocked it and sent it to slam into the middle of the post. It hit so hard that it split the wood. Oswald turned and looked at the arrow whose flights still wobbled from the force of the strike.

"All of my archers have that skill and if any try to cross then they had better learn to use a crutch or eat with one hand."

"This is not right, Captain!" He appealed to Captain Philips for he saw that I would not give him any sympathy.

"Nor is this disease and my duty is to the folk of Hartburn."

The pig farmer stared then turning on his heel stumped up the road towards Stockton. He would complain there. Captain Philip left and I waited with Robin and the others. Michael and the rest of my men were at the farm and practising. It was even more important that we become more skilled. It was late in the afternoon when the ten men strode down the road towards us. I knew that there would be trouble.

"I want none of them killed but if I give the word then frighten them." Drawing my sword, I walked to the end of the bridge. I saw Oswald but I noticed that there were none from the castle and no one wearing the livery of the lord of the manor. The weaponsmith from the castle, Walter of Wulfstun, led them. He had his leather apron and carried his hammer over his shoulder.

Stopping just ten paces from me he said, "What gives you the right, foreigner, to come here and tell us, freemen of Stockton, where we can and cannot go?"

I patted the parapet of the wooden bridge, "The right of ownership of this land and before you threaten me know that I will happily burn this bridge and then all arguments will cease!"

"You cannot do that!" Oswald's whining voice came from behind the huge weaponsmith.

I laughed, "Of course I can!"

Walter's eyes narrowed, "We shall see. I not only make weapons, I know how to use them!"

"And I, my friend, am a warrior and not an overweight bully. Do not try anything or it will be worse for you!"

I knew what he intended for he pulled back his hammer and ran at me, swinging and screaming as he did so. He thought his size and the threat of the hammer would work. The sword in my hand deterred the others; they were followers. When he hit me then they would rush my archers but until then they would watch. I calmly allowed him to swing and, as he did so I spun around on my left leg. His hammer hit nothing but the air on the bridge, and he began to overbalance. Had I wished him harm then I could have hacked across the back of his thighs. He would still have been able to work albeit with a limp. Instead, I swung the flat of my sword into his back which accelerated his fall and he tumbled into the Lustrum Beck. He rose coughing and spluttering and then realised he had lost his hammer. His head disappeared and he searched for it. While he did so I shouted, "The rest of you have the count of ten to return to your homes. If not, then you will need a healer to bind your wounds!" Behind me I heard bows being drawn, "One…" They all ran except for the son of Walter who went to the bank to pull up his bedraggled father. As he came up, I said, "Stick to making weapons, Walter. The next time I will hurt you!"

He nodded, "The sooner you leave this land the better!"

I laughed, "And that is my intention. Let us both hope that this disease does not last long eh?"

We had no trouble for a month and then, while I was practising with Michael on an incredibly chilly day Martin came for me. "Captain. William of Stanhope and a priest are at the bridge."

I was intrigued for we had left William at Durham. I saw as I neared the burning brazier at the bridge that it was Canon Aiden with him. I raised my hand in greeting, "Welcome, William, Canon. What brings you here on this cold November day?" I knew the reason. Someone had travelled to Durham to petition the Bishop.

The Canon gave me a wry smile, "Would that we felt welcomed Captain. The Bishop is concerned for he hears that you have barred the road to the burghers of Stockton."

"Not true, Canon, with the support of all those that live in the village we have barred the road for all and that includes you."

"The Bishop is intrigued, why?"

"We are isolated here and know not these things. How many have died of the plague in Stockton?"

"The last numbers we had was that forty have died."

"And in Durham?"

"Fifty."

"Hartness?"

"More than a hundred and the convent has but two nuns left alive."

"We have had none here in this lordless manor. There has not been a single case and that will remain so until the disease has finished its work. Perhaps the icy air of the north may kill it."

The Canon shook his head, "I doubt it. Perhaps your precautions are wise. I cannot say. I will return to the Bishop and speak with him. He may command you to open the road."

"And I may refuse!"

The Canon laughed, "You are an unpredictable sort of man. May God watch over you." He made the sign of the cross.

I nodded, "How fares your family, William?"

"They survive thus far but I have seen the bodies of the dead from this curse and those who die are in great pain. They say that it comes from the Jews. Many were attacked and killed in York."

The Canon had mounted his horse and, shaking his head, said, "That is nonsense. It was a ship which brought it here, but you are right, it is a curse. Perhaps God is punishing us for our sins."

"If so Canon then it is a harsh punishment!"

No second messenger came. I wondered if that was because too many had died in Durham or, more likely, the Bishop was giving me his approval. Time passed and it was I who was on

duty when Oswald crawled from his house to the bridge. I
nocked an arrow, "Oswald do not try to cross the bridge!"

In answer, he began to cough up blood. His eyes were closed,
and I thought he was dead already, but he made a monumental
effort, raised himself on to his elbows. "My family are all dead! I
beg you to burn our bodies lest they infect others I..." He fell
forward and I knew he was dead.

Peter Longbow shook his head, "The man was a fool! You
were right, Captain, and he has paid the price."

"Yet he is right. We have to burn the bodies and the house. If
we do not, then rats might feast on the dead and they could infect
us or our animals."

"But we will catch the plague!"

I shook my head, "I will do this. I will cover my mouth with a
cloth soaked in vinegar and wear gauntlets upon my hands."
When I have burned the bodies, I will sleep on the other side of
the river and live there for a week. If I have no growths under my
armpits or groin and no headaches, then I will be well."

Peter looked appalled, "You will freeze!"

"I will have a brazier and you can fetch me wood. I will go
back to the farm and prepare."

I did not want to do this but there was no other way, and a
leader did not ask a man to do anything that he would not do so
himself. As I expected I had arguments from all my men except
for Robin who simply said, "Let me do this Captain."

"No, this task is appointed to me and I will do it. If God
spares me then it shows me that I am destined for higher things."
He nodded. "It might be as well for all of the guards on the
bridge to wear vinegar-soaked cloths. The pestilence might travel
by air for all that we know."

Before I touched the body my men and I made a camp just
down from the bridge. We were adept at building hovels, and
they piled the firewood there for me. I had my bow and a war
bag of arrows as well as my sword and daggers. They each
clasped my arm as they returned across the bridge. Robin was
the last.

"You have nobility in your bones, John Hawkwood, and I am
happy that I chose to follow you. Leaders like you are rare. I will
speak with the Captain and tell him what it is that you do." I

nodded. "And do not worry, while you are here I will work them even harder."

I nodded and after donning the thick gauntlets which I would burn when I had done with them, I took a brand from the fire and walked down to the house. There was no sound from the pigs and I guessed that they must have either escaped or been killed. All of that fine food would be gone for who knew if the plague could infect an animal? I confess that I was terrified. Oswald had been a fool, but he had been a brave man. What had kept him alive when he had crawled down to speak with us? It took every ounce of courage to step inside the house. The fire had long gone out and even through the cloth there was the stink of death. I rammed the brand into the ground and went back to fetch Oswald. I grabbed his boots and pulled him back down the track. I saw that his breeks were bloody, and his front was also covered in a bloody flux. It looked as though he had been gutted by a butcher, yet this was a disease. Perhaps there was no cure and one day all of us would die. I put that unhealthy thought from my mind and pulled. I had to step inside the door and then jump over his body to get back out. I went around the back of the house and fetched all of the kindling and firewood the family had kept for the winter. I built a fire as carefully as I had ever done and when I was happy, I lit the kindling. The wind was from behind me. It was not a strong one, but it would fan the flames and fire the interior. I would continue to pile wood on the fire until it had crumbled to black dust.

I had made a good fire, but it took all of my will power to stand there once the plague-infested flesh began to burn for the stink of burning flesh was almost unbearable. To help myself I said a prayer. Perhaps if I spoke to God, he would help me, "Oh lord, take the souls of Oswald and his family. I know not if they confessed before they died but I pray that you show them mercy."

It was almost as though I was answered for a sudden gust of wind made the flames flare and the roof caught fire. Within moments the whole house was ablaze, and a black column of smoke rose. I took off the gloves and threw them and the vinegar-soaked cloth into the inferno. My men could leave me a new pair and a fresh cloth at the bridge. I stood and watched the fire eat the farm. I hoped it would kill the disease. I was still standing there an hour later when a figure rode down from Stockton. I saw him descending from the low ridge and I hurried back to my camp. By the time they had reined in, I had an arrow nocked, "Friend come no closer. I have just burned the bodies and farm of Oswald as he asked me to do. We have no plague in Hartburn and I intend to keep it that way."

I saw that the cloak covered man was a priest. "I am Father Paul, and I came to see what the cause of the fire was. You are lucky that you have no deaths. In Stockton, there are whole families who have died, and they all realise that you were right. We have now barred the river and the road from the north. None come to Stockton. The numbers of those dying have lessened since then." He made the sign of the cross, "May God be with you!"

And then he went. My men had watched from the other side of the beck with nocked bows and now they unstrung them.

"I need another vinegar covered cloth. Leave it with my food."

It was later in the afternoon when they brought me the bread platter covered in food and the skin of ale. I had my own beaker. Michael said as he left the skin hanging from the parapet of the bridge, "There is two days ale in there, Captain. We have another four skins we will bring."

"Thank you."

I went to my hovel and sat there. My men were forty paces from me, but it felt further. It was as though I was on an island in the middle of the sea. I felt like a hermit priest in a tower and all that I could do was think. I had been a man of action and the time on the bridge was good for my soul. I reflected on what I had done and what I might do in the future. If nothing else the plague gave me clarity of thought and a vision of the man I would be.

I ate each meal slowly for I had little else to occupy me. When it was dark, I slept. That was my routine for a week. Each morning I stripped to the waist and searched my body for the tell-tale signs. When there was none I would wash in the river and then dress. It passed the time. It was while I washed that I saw the rats. That gave me occupation. When I was not asleep, I hunted rats along the river with my bow and war arrows. At first, I missed more than I hit but I developed the skills necessary and when my isolation was over I had killed thirty rats.

I felt no ill effects and I carried my bow case back to the bridge. I smiled at Robin who was there to greet me. "God has other plans, it seems!"

Chapter 4

As a precaution, we kept apart from the rest of Hartburn until January. I shouted to the Captain what had happened and included the news from the priest, but I did not risk getting closer than fifty paces. The snow was so bad at the end of December that we had little choice about our isolation; God made sure we stayed apart. It was a cheerless Christmas, but we were alive, and it seemed that many others were not. The plan was working but we dared not relent. The visit from the priest had proved us right. It was February before the snows began to disappear and the Captain insisted that I join his family for food. I found it quite hard to do. I had lived for almost five months under the same roof as my small band of men. That we were all closer was an understatement and it was difficult to walk the few hundred paces to the Captain's farm. I just had to cross a grassy greenway and over steppingstones and I was there yet it felt like a journey across a mountain. Mathilde was the first woman I had seen since I had spied the bloated corpses in Oswald's home. What if I carried the deadly disease within me? I knew not how the disease moved. Perhaps my men and I would not be affected but Mathilde and the Captain's children might. Even as I knocked on the door I contemplated turning and running. I would make my excuses and leave without any contact at all. It was not fair on the family.

The door was opened not by the Captain, but Mathilde and she threw her arms around me, "You are truly Christian! My husband told me what you did for Oswald and his family. You are a saint."

"Mistress, I do not wish to bring even a hint of harm to your home."

She smiled, "God will protect us for we are all good people; you most of all!"

I felt almost shy in the company of the family and I washed more than I would have in my hall. I had my own knife, spoon and beaker and I tried to avoid touching anything. As the two of them chatted about John and what he had done lately I wondered if life would ever get back to something like normal and I was so distracted that I almost missed Mathilde telling her news, "I am to have another baby in August, John. What do you think of that? At my age!"

"What?"

"A baby, John, my wife is expecting another child!"

I could not help grinning, "Good! We need more children!"

For some reason, the news that there would be another child made me happy. The Captain and his wife were good, and they would not mistreat their children as I had been mistreated by my father. One day I would father children, but the plague meant that would not be any time soon!

Life went on in our isolated village. No one had tried to enter the village since our confrontation with Walter the weaponsmith and that, perhaps, showed me the effect of the pestilence. We continued to train and as we had nothing else to do it meant that all of my men, Martin and my archers included were more than competent swordsmen. We used wooden swords which were heavier than real ones and harder to use. I knew it could only make us better warriors. We also made shields for each of us. We had the time to make them better than any we had seen on other warriors. We had plenty of timber and we used alternating layers of wood which were bent so that the shield was curved. They were glued and nailed before being covered in leather. On the back we fitted three brases which were carrying straps as well as a guige strap which was a longer piece of leather that allowed the shield to hang down our side; that enabled us to use two weapons and still have protection. We had no livery and so I left the leather blank. We used a sort of varnish to help protect the shield and they made it look white. As far as armour and helmets went only those who fought with a sword had a helmet and Michael and I had a mail hauberk. Mine was the best as it had been made by Balin of Bitterne. My next purchase would be metal coifs for my men, all of them. Our shoulders and our heads were the most vulnerable. I became as skilled as any with a sword and shield. Robin said I was the best but I was not sure about that. I certainly felt comfortable and found that wearing the mail hauberk was not as constricting as I had thought. When the time came for us to go to war we would be the best-trained men outside of a rich noble's retinue.

We had geese and Martin made good arrows. He was right about their employment and it was the geese who saved us. As April drew to an end I was thinking we should risk one of us riding to Stockton to discover if the plague persisted. To that end, we had begun to exercise our horses. With two men on the bridge, the rest of us were grooming our mounts after a day of riding around the paddock. It was the geese who alerted us to danger. Martin had said that they made the best watchdogs and, hitherto, we had doubted him but that late afternoon he was proved right for the geese began to make such a racket that all of us turned. They had squawked and hissed at us for the first two months that they had been with us. When Martin collected their feathers, they still hissed but this was different and Martin turned when they began their squawking, "Captain, they are warning us!"

"Get your weapons! Michael, go to the greenway, summon the Captain. Peter and Gareth guard the house. Martin, come with me."

It did not take any of us long to string our bows. Even as we ran for the bridge, I heard the cries. Robin and Roger were having to defend the bridge. Running confidently along the familiar track I was weighing up the problems of fighting an enemy with the plague. We could not allow them to get close to us for they might have the pestilence. As we neared the bridge I shouted, "Martin, take the right. I will take the left!"

Robin and Roger would be in cover and both would have bows. We knew the land and the enemy, whoever it was, did not. They could cross the beck almost anywhere, but would they have the confidence to do so?

I saw, close to the entrance to Oswald's farm, a body with an arrow in it. It was an armed man, and he wore a leather brigandine. I could not see any others. I used the cover of the undergrowth to approach the bank unseen. I saw a crossbowman rise and before he could release his bolt Robin's arrow smacked into his head. Three men rose from the bushes and ran towards the riverbank. I took in that Roger of Norham sent an arrow at one, but the man blocked it with his shield. At that distance, a real archer would have aimed for the head. We still had work to do. The range was long, but I was hidden by the scrubby undergrowth and I nocked an arrow and waited. Sure enough, another two men rose from the same place as the other three. I was ready and my arrow hit one in the shoulder while Robin's snap shot still managed to strike a second in the leg. The three men who had made the bank of the beck leapt into the water, but Martin was ready, and one was hit in the chest. Even Roger could not miss and a second fell with an arrow in his neck. The last man turned, realising he was alone, but it was too late, and Robin's arrow hit him in the back.

I whistled and Martin turned. I signalled for him to cross the beck. It was a risk, but we had to ensure that all of our enemies were dead. I slipped into the water and with an arrow nocked I slowly waded across. Robin whistled and when I looked, I saw that he and Roger had moved to the end of the bridge. We were covered in case any of these attackers were left alive. I headed to the bodies and kicking each one saw that they were dead. I knew none of them. Were they opportunists looking for a safe place or was there something more sinister?

A voice from behind the hedgerow close to Oswald's farm made me pull back on my bow. "Captain, they made me come here."

I knew the whining voice, "Jack Two Swords?"

"Aye, Captain. They held me prisoner and Alexander of Roxburgh's brother led this raid to have vengeance on you for they hanged his brother."

"Come into the light!"

He moved from the shadows of the hedge and I saw that his fingers were blackened. He saw my look and nodded, "I have the plague. God has punished me. I should have fought for you but...."

"And you have been with them ever since?"

"Aye, Captain. We were all infected and they were dead men walking. I beg you, end my suffering. I have confessed all of my sins to God and I would not suffer the bloody flux I have seen take other men."

I nodded, "Go with God!" The arrow I sent was the truest I ever sent, and it struck him dead in the centre of his head.

I shouted, "We will need to burn these bodies. It will be us four which take the risk. Roger fetch cloths and gauntlets. Tell the others to stay apart. We will sleep in the stable for seven days and the other three will have to guard the bridge."

"Aye, Captain!"

I knew that I was less fearful as we began the grim work of dragging the bodies to the pyre we had built. I had done this once and I believed that God protected me. However, it was worse than with just Oswald for some of the bodies had been in the beck. It took some time for the fire to take and even longer for the flesh to begin to burn. We stood, cloth masks in place and watched as the flames from the kindling ignited the logs and then the dried cloth. Steam rose with the smoke and the fire spattered and spat as the clothes and bodies dried out. It was an even grimmer duty to stand there when the fire really took hold, and the flesh began to melt. It was dark by the time the fire went out, but we could see the metal in the ashes. Their coins, swords and daggers remained intact. "If they are still there a year from this time, I may touch them."

Martin said, "They are the Devil's now, Captain, and I will not touch them." We did not and they were buried a month later. I do not know but they may be there to this day, buried by the side of the Ox Bridge. Whoever digs them up will never know their story nor the danger they present.

The Captain and his men arrived when they saw the smoke. I told them what had occurred, and he left us to our grim duty. "I will have my men watch this bridge for a week. This is Hartburn and our land. It is not right that you have had to endure this duty."

That made it easier for the ones who had not fought or touched the dead were able to cook for us and leave the food outside the stable and they enjoyed more rest than they might have done. A week later none of us showed any sign of having contracted the disease and I conjectured that perhaps it was the vinegar-soaked cloth and the gauntlets we had burned which saved us. While we had waited in the stable, tending to the horses, we made new gauntlets. Who knew when we might need them again?

I had promised the Bishop that I would care for the land so long as I lived there and as summer began to approach, I had my men tend the fields and the hedgerows. We should have used the bill hooks on the hedges in autumn, but the plague had distracted us. We tended to them now and the work helped us for it worked different muscles. We knew that for even though we worked hard each day, when we rested for the night there were aches and pains we had not suffered before. It was as I rubbed my aching shoulder that I realised my plan to build up a company in the north had not worked out as it should. I had counted on hiring men I met here in the hard north of the land but the pestilence had ended that dream. However, I knew that wintering in Hartburn had saved our lives. Here we had protection from those who brought the diseases. That was clear now for none in the village had contracted the plague. The Captain was now the leader of those in this land. That was confirmed in August when, a week before Mathilde gave birth to a daughter, Eleanor, the Canon, this time escorted by those men I had left in Durham, arrived at the bridge.

"You are still alive Canon, as are you others, I give thanks to God for that. We still bar the bridge for none has died of the disease and we intend to keep it that way."

The Canon nodded, "It has been a hard winter, and many have died." He shook his head, "It has been like one of the plagues visited upon the Egyptians, but we have had no more deaths in Durham for a month and Stockton for two months. We came to tell you that." I nodded. "I also come with this." He took from his saddlebag a parchment, "The Bishop has conferred a knighthood on Captain Philip and named him as Lord of Hartburn. The family which held the title and the deed all died. There are no heirs left and Bishop Hatfield feels that Sir Philip deserves it. When he is happy to travel then the Bishop will dub him. In any case, he needs to visit with the Bishop to discover his duties. The time will be of his choosing, but he will have to leave the village at some point and the disease is on the wane."

"How do you know, Canon?"

"Because some suffered the headaches and the sweats but not the growths in the armpits. They did not develop the black skin and fingers. They were unwell but they recovered. I believe it is because priests prayed with them but, in any case, they survived. The disease still spreads. It now sweeps through Scotland. Only those who do as you do or are in such a remote place that there are no visitors can hope to escape the fingers of this black death."

"Thank you. I will take the parchment to the Captain as his wife is in the last month of her pregnancy, I am not sure that he will read it but I will tell him and he can decide."

The Canon made the sign of the cross.

"And if any of you warriors wish to serve me you know that there is always a place here."

William nodded, "There would have been a time for such a decision, but the world has changed. We have grown closer to each other and the Bishop and you, Captain, and your men have become closer than brothers. This was meant to be but I hope that you fare well. You are a good leader and while your words are harsh you are fair and that is all that any warrior can ask of his leader."

I delivered the parchment to the Captain who pointed to the wooden seat outside his hall. "Leave it there, John and when my wife is safely delivered, I will read it. From what you say we have defeated this disease and we should give thanks to God in a church. That means either Durham or St John's in Stockton. We will enjoy a better Christmas this year."

I nodded, "And we will stay here until next Spring and then journey south to seek work. We are warriors and we have skills. The two skirmishes with the Scots did little other than to whet our appetite for war."

We left before Christmas. In fact, we stayed just until late September for after the birth of their daughter, the Captain and his family went into Stockton to pray in the church. It was a symbol that he believed the disease was gone. He came back with a sad face for more than a third of the families had perished. There were derelict farms and, as he told me, there would be an even harder winter to follow. "This will be the same all across the country, John. Who will plough the fields and raise the animals? The lords who survived in their castles cannot plough. This plague has changed the land forever. You and your men will be even more valuable from now on. Lords who called upon a levy to fight their wars for them have fewer men to do so. If a lord wishes to war, he will have to hire you."

I had not thought of that, but it made sense. Hartburn had survived, prospered even but we had been an island in a sea of death. If the country had suffered the same and one in three had died, then England had changed forever.

When the bridge was opened and we had visitors passing through once more we questioned them for we were hungry for news of the outside world. We had conjectured and speculated but speaking with visitors gave us real news. The first thing we discovered was that travel by sea was less popular for that was how the disease had entered England and at the Cinque Ports unknown ships were often refused the right to dock and any visitor from France, Italy or Spain had to endure the indignity of baring flesh so that they could be examined for growths. It was, however, a Scot returning the long way back to his home in the borders who gave us the reason to leave. He had walked from York having returned from Gascony. We put him up in the stable and fed him and, in return, he told us of wars. That was what we craved. Not a war against a disease but the clash of steel!

"The war in Gascony ended when both sides lost men not to war but this pestilence. Ten of us left Gascony with our lord, Sir Henry of Whorlton and half perished before we reached London. That great cesspit suffered as badly as anywhere. It is said the royal family barred themselves in Windsor and that probably saved them. The lord I served lived close to York and there I was paid off and left to walk home."

Robin had looked at me and I nodded. He said, "We have a pony you can have." He grinned, "We took it from a Scottish bandit so…"

"I thank you for your kindness and I shall say a prayer for you all when I reach my church. I confess I was offered work. When we passed through Lincoln, we heard that the young Baron Mortimer of Wigmore Castle in Herefordshire was seeking warriors for a campaign against his Welsh neighbours. The Welsh, it seems, suffered less than the English and sought to take advantage of the plague."

"Herefordshire?"

He nodded, "Aye, the Baron is young but he has an old head upon his shoulders. His father, Sir Edmund, was a descendant of

King Llewellyn of Gwynedd and Joan, the daughter of King John. He has royal blood."

"We thank you for that information and our gift of the pony is now payment."

After he had gone, we debated our course of action. I knew what I wished but, in those days, I wished to have the agreement of my men. They decided, thankfully, that they wished to go to war. We told Sir Philip, who was all ready to travel to Durham and receive his spurs, of our decision and whilst sad to see us go understood our reason.

"I will tell the Bishop. Now that the farm has been improved and I am moving into the manor, there are two farms which will have new owners. Know that the folk of Hartburn will say prayers for you. It is thanks to you that they all survived."

"If we had not done so then we would have died too. I am pleased that you prosper, Captain. I am not sure that we shall meet again but we are warriors, are we not?" We clasped hands. Mathilde and his son John were tearful as we mounted our horses and headed south and west. We were leaving the north, never to return, but it had saved our lives and we were grateful.

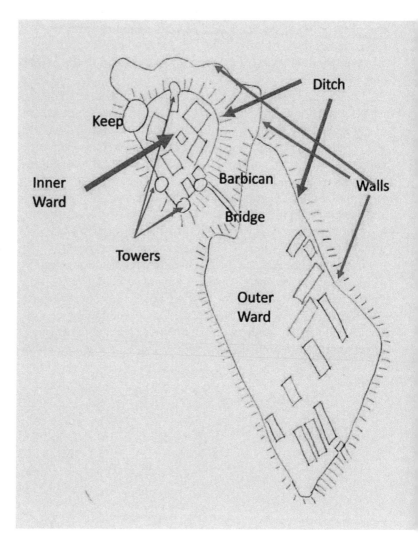

Wigmore Castle

Chapter 5

One unexpected result of the plague was that not only were we welcomed at the inns and taverns, not to mention the holy houses, but the prices were lower as they were desperate for business. I was eking into my coins but when we, eventually, reached Southampton I could always acquire more from Basil of Tarsus. Wales would be a stopover on our journey back to France and profit! It was when we were at Sheffield that we came across an old comrade. Walter of Barnsley had been one of my best archers, but he had chosen to head to his home. It was Robin who spied him when we emerged from the inn close to the mighty castle to visit the local weaponsmith. We did this in each town through which we passed in the hope that they might have coifs. We had managed to buy just one thus far but we were ever hopeful.

Robin spied Walter although how he recognised him, I did not know. It looked like a bundle of rags which someone had discarded in an alley between a bakery and a smithy. Robin hurried over, "Walter! Is that you?"

When the head appeared from beneath the rags, I recognised him. My voice conveyed the shock I felt, "Walter of Barnsley, what happened to you?" I saw that even though he had sunk far he still had his gardyvyan. The bow and the arrow might have gone but he had kept the bag which kept the equipment to maintain his weapon. I knew that beneath his hat he would still have bowstrings for the day he could acquire a bow once more.

Robin put out a hand to help him to his feet and when Walter spoke, his voice conveyed the weakness in his body. "The pestilence, Captain; I left you to be with my family and the plague struck our home. That was almost a year since." To be fair to Robin he did not withdraw his hand. "All of my family died, and I buried them." He shook his head, "I did not suffer at all. Why is that, Captain? When I had buried them then I was thrown out of the village and I have wandered ever since. Doors were shut and for a while, I lived in the forest of Sherwood until the local lord scoured it. I was lucky, I escaped. The rest lost their fingers! A shame for they were good archers."

I nodded, "And you are a good archer. Come we will get you cleaned up and then get you fed."

"But Captain, I have nothing!"

"And you are of our company! Do not worry, Martin the Fletcher can make you a bow and I will furnish you with new boots and clothes."

He did not move, "Captain there is another archer. This is where I live for the bakery and the smithy provide warmth. I share it with another archer, Richard of Loidis. He is seeking food. I cannot abandon him for he is my friend."

I hesitated and Robin said, "Captain, we need archers. We know not this Richard but if Walter speaks well of him ..."

"Then wait here, Robin, and fetch them both. I will return to the inn and arrange a chamber." This was more expense for me but if I could help Walter to recover and if the other archer was good then I had increased my company! All I needed then was Alan of the Woods, Ned and Jack. They would do as a start. They were all that I could afford! Of course, the landlord was not averse to the extra coins. I had planned on leaving the next day but that was out of the question. I worried that Baron Mortimer would not need us over winter, and we would be stuck without employment in the Welsh borders!

When Richard of Loidis arrived, I saw that he was not in such a pitiable condition as Walter. His story was a similar one to Walter's. He had been with Lord Henry in Gascony; indeed, we had fought in the same battles but as we had different commanders we had not met. When we had gone north and ended up in Calais he had stayed in Gascony. The plague there had meant that the war petered out and coming home he found not only no employment but a disease which wiped out his village, albeit before he arrived.

"I do not think that every villager died, Captain. Many must have left but my family died. My parents were old and the Great Mortality seemed to take the old first. I burned our home for the priest was not there to bury them."

The two of them were happy to be employed by me. We had spare bows, they were the ones used by Roger, Michael and Gareth. Martin promised that when we found the right wood, he would make them both a better bow than they had ever used. We headed west for Wales.

By the time we reached Shrewsbury, we had managed to buy four more mail coifs from weaponsmiths who were desperate for an income and we paid less than I expected. Both Richard and Walter had benefitted from the food and beds. It was as we walked around the market, seeking coifs that we found Alan of the Woods. In his case, he had not fallen on hard times. Shrewsbury was the King's castle, and he was one of the garrison. He had been lucky but, like the rest of my men, starvation and old age, compounded by the plague, had taken his aged parents.

"I am glad that I went home, Captain Hawkwood, for I was able to speak with them, but it was hard to watch the two of them die over three days. They did not have the growths nor the blackened fingers and arms but the disease's milder form was too much for them. I confess that for a week I was ill, but I did not have the growths. When they were buried, I headed here for I heard they sought archers."

"And I am pleased that you have employment. We go to Wigmore Castle to seek work with Baron Mortimer."

He grinned, "He is a lively young cockerel, Captain! He is married to a beauty, Lady Philippe de Montagu who seems to be a force of nature. Both are young to be rulers and yet they have put their mark upon the land. The Baron hates the Welsh."

"Would you not relish the chance to serve him?"

He rubbed his beard thoughtfully, "You know I think I might, but I have a contract here. I will speak with the Captain of the Guard and explain what it is that we do. Where are you staying?"

"The White Hart."

"A good inn with fine ale! I will join you later when I have spoken to him."

I knew that, if nothing else, a conversation with Alan of the Woods would give me more information about the activities on this border. I knew that the Welsh could be as dangerous as the Scots and I knew as well as any that they were good archers.

When he came, he had his war bag and cased bow. He was grinning, "It seems that the young Baron has been pestering all and sundry with requests for archers. The Captain was delighted that you were going to offer your services and was happy to let me go. I got on well with him. but I am new and being an old hand I would be more likely to rub against him. I am better with familiar faces like Walter, Robin and Michael here who appears to have spent the last year or so doing nothing but eat! He is a giant!"

Alan of the Woods was good for my company. He had a sense of humour as well as archer's skills. While we ate and drank well, I had to spend a whole florin but it was worth it, Alan told us of warfare in this part of the world. "You will need few bodkins for the Welsh do not use many knights. None of their spearmen or swordsmen wears mail. You need to be aware that even a rustic, a farmer or even a labourer has weapons, and they can all use a bow! If Baron Mortimer wishes to control them then he will need a good castle and be able to hunt them down in their mountains!"

"I have heard it is a poor country, is it?"

"Not so, Captain. The parts close to the mountains are but in Powys, just to the west of Herefordshire, it is rich farmland. The Severn Valley is very fertile!"

"And can we make money?"

Alan laughed, "It is good to see that you have not changed, Captain!"

"A warrior is worth his hire. We have skills and we should be rewarded. I cannot see that a stripling youth will know more about fighting than I!" I suddenly realised how arrogant I sounded. I had been little older than Baron Mortimer when I went to war and began to lead men but I had been a quick learner. Perhaps the young baron would be as quick.

We rode, the next day, down a road which whilst beautiful in its own way belied the description given by Alan of the Woods. We passed over a high piece of wooded ground but once we passed Stokesay I saw what he meant. Cattle and sheep grazed the uplands, and the valley bottom was studded with farms. It was harvest time and the fields were filled with men toiling to bring in nature's bounty. I suspected that this year there would, thanks to the pestilence, be fewer men. Perhaps they would be paid more?

We reached Wigmore Castle and I was taken aback by its size. There was an enormous outer bailey with several large buildings. A good ditch completely encircled it and while there was no huge gatehouse on the outer wall, when we were admitted I saw that the reason was the main castle and the inner bailey. It was built on a massive rock and the barbican not only had a deep ditch but a walled bridge with defences at both ends. Baron Mortimer had inherited a fortress. The men at the gate in the curtain wall merely wanted to know our business. Although we were well-armed, we were English. It was at the main gate to the castle where we had to dismount. A Sergeant at Arms spoke to us to discover our business.

He nodded, "The Baron may well choose to hire you, but you can't come in the main castle until he invites you." He pointed to an open area to the left of the track which led from the outer gate to the main gate. "Camp there for now and I will send a message to his lordship."

As a welcome, it was not as warm as I might have wished but times were strange and it was a new world in which we sought work. We had food we had bought in Shrewsbury and so we did as we were bid and made a camp. I looked at the sky and hoped that the rainy reputation of the west would be a myth. We had no tents and naught with which to build hovels.

As it turned out the Baron was keen to meet me and I was summoned by a page. I felt dirty and travel soiled. I did not have the time to change and I dared not delay.

I knew that the Baron and his wife were young but until I met them I did not know how youthful they really were. To me, they looked like children. It was his wife, however, who drew my eye for she was stunningly beautiful. I could not take my eyes from her. I think she knew that she was alluring but I do not think that she did anything to encourage it except to be what she was.

The Baron was red-haired and had an eager look in his eye. He leaned forward in his seat, "I have heard of you, archer. You fought against the French when we took their treasure and ransom! You fought at Durham. Lord Henry spoke of you in Gascony! For one so young you have a well-deserved reputation. You are a Captain now?"

"I have a small group of men at arms and archers. Until the King or the Prince require us for France and Aquitaine again, we need employment for we are warriors. We heard you needed men such as we."

He nodded and held his wife's hand. They were young and in love; I could see that immediately. "We do for the Welsh sorely try us and since the plague came and took so many of our men we are in danger."

His wife nodded, "I believe that this plague came from the Devil and the Welsh are in league with them. It is why they lost so few men. They are witches and wizards you know? They should all be burned at the stake."

As I came to realise, she was a woman of strong opinions.

"I have ten men, my lord. Three men at arms and the rest of us are archers but all my men can draw a bow, and all can use a sword. We have our own shields, and we are mounted."

He sat back, "Then you are valuable as well, so far as I know, unique. I shall hire you all."

"You know, lord, that when the King needs us for Gascony, we will have to leave your service?"

Lady Phillipe clapped her hands, "I like this man, my husband, for he is honest!

The Baron inclined his head, "You need not fear for when the King calls, I shall go to France with him. By then we will have quelled this Welsh spirit. Now as to pay…" I had the sum of three pence a day in mind but before I could suggest that he said, "I will pay you all fourpence a day and no more. You, as Captain, shall have sixpence a day with a bonus of a florin for each month that you serve. For that, you will be fed and wear my livery. If your horses are hurt whilst serving me then I shall recompense you. You have your own arrows?"

"Aye, my lord. We make our own."

"Then I shall pay you sixpence for every five hundred arrows. I will have my scrivener draw up the contract and you shall sign it on the morrow." He waved over the Sergeant who had brought us in. "Egbert, there is room in the stable for these men's horses and the warrior hall in the outer bailey has space too. House them there and feed them."

"Yes, my lord."

He turned back to me, "It will just be one night for you are to be the new garrison at Knighton. We will leave in the morning."

"Knighton, my lord?"

He nodded, "It is one of my castles and is ten miles west of here. It is on Offa's Dyke and marks the border with Wales. It was recently raided and the men there suffered deaths and wounds. The people had their homes burned. I will not have it. You will be the garrison there, but I wish you to patrol the Welsh side and make them fear my surcoat!" He smiled, "That is for the morrow. I will come with you for we wish to see the suffering that the folk there endured."

"How many are in the garrison, my lord?"

"There are seven who survived but I will bring them back here for their nerve may be broken. I have another six men I have hired. There will be sixteen of you in total." My face must have fallen for he smiled and said, "Fear not, I will send more men as they become available but the archer who helped to break the French and King David will not fear Welsh brigands!"

As the Sergeant took me from the main castle, I shook my head, "He is a whirlwind is he not?"

The Sergeant smiled, "He was well trained by his father. The old lord was a good man who was taken too early, but his son has inherited all of his skill. He may be young, but he has an old head on his shoulders."

My men were relieved to have a roof especially when drizzle began to fall. The Sergeant introduced me to the one armed old soldier who was in charge of the warrior hall. He had lost it in Gascony and when he heard I had been with Lord Henry on the great chevauchée, greeted me like an old friend. He opened a new barrel of ale and food was fetched by the servants. I spoke to him of the other battles and a wistful look came over his face. "But for a French axe, I would still be serving the Baron. He will be as good a lord as his father."

"He said that we were to be the garrison at Knighton?"

Old James nodded, "The Sergeant in charge, Wilfred of Yarpole, is a good enough soldier but he stayed inside the walls. He had no idea what the Welsh were up to. You need to have eyes and ears beyond the border, John Hawkwood. You have to be ready when the Welsh come. You can't sit and wait until they are in the village. You have to have the people inside and defending the walls."

"Are they stone ones?"

"No, it is the same castle erected by Fitz Osbern almost a hundred and fifty years ago. Oh, they have maintained and improved it but it is still the old castle that holds back the Welsh. Even though they hurt the village and the garrison, they didn't take it and had it not been for the pestilence the garrison might have sent them back to their mountains. You will do well, young man. I have heard your name, but I confess I thought you older. Perhaps this was meant to be, the young baron and the young captain!"

I was flattered but I had hoped for an easier first position than being on the Welsh border. We sat around the large table and spoke with the other warriors. I knew from the Baron's words that some of these would be with us and so I was guarded in what I said and, if anything, a little more distant than I might have been. I was used to command but I was aware of the responsibility of this position.

I found time to speak alone with Robin and Michael. Those two had been the ones who had followed me without question, and I trusted them more than any other warriors. I told them all that I had learned.

Robin seemed quite happy, "I care not that it is just a wooden castle. We have walls and ditches, and the old soldier is quite right. You do need to ride amongst the enemy if you are to stop them. We can do that. You have the best equipped and trained men, Captain. The pestilence was a curse, but you made it a blessing. When we need to, we have extra archers and that is always useful and if we have to then we can all use a sword. The Welsh will have seen nothing like us and you have gained us extra pay."

I was not sure when the Baron would wish to leave but I took no chances and, rousing my men early, we prepared our horses while it was still dark. We found food and had breakfasted before those charged with serving food were awake. The time was not wasted for as the sun rose, I wandered around the outer bailey and marvelled at its size. It told me much about the border for this was the sort of castle a King might build close to his capital. The Baron was a minor lord and yet there was enough money to be had to build and maintain a strong castle. As was my wont, as I looked at the defences, I sought a way to overcome them. I came to the conclusion, which stood me in good stead later in life, that if I could avoid trying to take castles then I would have more victories than defeats. The trick would be to bring an enemy to battle on ground of my choosing. As I headed back to the horses, for I saw the main gates opening, I could not help smiling to myself. I was barely a vintenar and yet here I was commanding armies. Such are young men's dreams.

The Baron smiled when he saw that my men were all ready. I viewed the other ten men who would be part of the garrison following from the castle. He was giving me good men to lead. "Good, Hawkwood, you are eager, and I like that. Ride next to me so that I may speak with you as we ride."

The Baron's Sergeant, Edmund of Lucton, shouted, "Open the gates!" I later learned that the old Sergeant had served the former Baron, Sir Edmund, and regarded himself as Baron Roger's guardian! He was very protective of him.

As we passed through the village the villagers who were out and about bowed or doffed their hats as we passed. The Baron greeted them all and when we had passed the last house said, "We lost too many in the pestilence but not as many as in other parts of the land. What was it like in the north?"

"The village where we spent the Great Mortality, lord, lost none but those around, Stockton, Durham, Hartness, lost more than one in three of their people. I do not think that the true numbers will be known for some time. There will be isolated farms which were touched by the disease and none yet know that those within lie dead."

Baron Mortimer nodded, "When the time for taxes draws nigh then the numbers will become clearer and this means that our King cannot reclaim our French lands yet for there will not be the coin the plague has made us poor. When he does, Hawkwood, know that Baron Mortimer of Wigmore will ride behind his banner!"

Once we passed through the village, we entered a huge forest which threatened to engulf the road. The young Baron and his Sergeant did not seem nervous about the ride, but I was. This was ambush country yet the two did not seem concerned. I was a soldier, and I asked the question, "My lord, this forest would seem to be the perfect place for an ambush. If I was alone, I would have an archer on each side and ahead of me in the forest looking for signs of danger."

He smiled and I saw the flaw in his character, arrogance, "I am Baron Mortimer and if I cannot ride through my hunting ground safely then I would be a poor lord of the manor."

Sergeant Edmund, who was behind us said, "It is good that you are cautious, Hawkwood, for that might keep you alive. His lordship employs many gamekeepers. They watch, not only for poachers but also for enemies. They know the trails in these forests as well as they know their family's faces. They have not reported intruders in this part of the land."

The Teme was the border and both that and the Dyke built by the Mercian Offa were striking features. The other was the Norman castle on the mound. The village of Knighton was tiny. Its very name told me that it was not Welsh, and the first Normans had built a castle here and settled the land when William the Bastard had conquered England. The wooden walls were a clear indication that this was England.

The Baron reined in and swept a hand before him, "Well?"

"A good site and I can see why this was chosen. The castle guards the bridge, and the dyke will deter large numbers of men."

The Baron was astute, and he threw me a sharp glance as he said, "There is a 'but' in your voice, Hawkwood!"

"The river is only an obstacle to mailed men, my lord. My men and I could swim it and the same is true of the dyke. From what I have learned the Welsh do not use many mailed men but their archers and those who fight with spears can be dangerous. Is that not how they hurt your village and garrison?"

I heard Edmund chuckle behind me. The Baron nodded, "I can see that I have made a good choice in my castellan. You are right. How would you make it safer?"

I remembered the words of Old James, "I would have my mounted men patrol the other side of the river. If you know where to look then there will always be signs." I was thinking back to Alston. If Alexander of Roxburgh had been a better leader then he would have kept watch and discovered that horsemen had been scouting out his land.

"And what would you do if you found such signs?"

"I take it you wish us to be aggressive, my lord?"

"They killed my people. I want them to fear us. Be as aggressive as you like."

"Then, under your authority, my lord, I would punish them."

He pointed a gloved finger to the west, "My authority ends at the river but one day I will take the land on the other side for it once belonged to my family until a misguided treaty gave it away. You are my first footsteps there."

He spurred his horse and we headed into the castle.

Knighton

Crug

Rhayader

Wigmore Castle

North

2.5 Miles

Chapter 6

This would be my new home and, more importantly, my first command. I took everything in as we crossed the wooden bridge. The ditch needed maintenance. Weeds were growing in it and the sides were not as sharp as they ought to be. The ropes on the bridge over the ditch needed to be replaced. There was a stone gatehouse which was relatively new and well carved, but the mortar was crumbling. That would need to be renewed. The outer bailey seemed tiny after Wigmore, but it was still as large as any other that I had seen. There were dwellings within, and I saw that the bread oven, as well as the smith, were in the outer bailey. The land rose towards the inner wall, ditch and the keep. Although it was wooden in structure, I saw that someone had added stone. The Baron let me inspect the whole edifice without comment. The ditch which surrounded the inner bailey also needed repair, but the gate and the walls were solid enough. We dismounted in the inner bailey and I saw an older warrior walk towards us. He had a studded brigandine and carried a good sword. He wore a mail coif, and I took him to be Wilfred of Yarpole. The Baron spoke to him while I examined the keep. It had a wooden staircase on the outside of the building which gave access to the lower floor but the bottom of the keep now had stone instead of wood. That had been replaced. It meant that fire was less of a problem. I spied a door at the base of the keep which I guessed led to the stable. In winter that would heat the castle. The keep itself had three floors and that was rare in a largely wooden building. I could see that from the ends of the beams which were clearly visible. The first floor would be the Great Hall and above that would be the castellan's chambers. When Fitz Osbern had built the castle he and his family would have stayed there. Above it was a guard room and then the fighting platform. I turned and walked back to the baron and his castellan.

"Well, Wilfred, I have brought men to replace those who served here during the plague. It is time you had a rest at Wigmore Castle."

"We are still happy to serve, Baron Mortimer. I swear we will not be caught out again!"

The Baron showed his ruthless side, "That you were caught out once was unforgivable." He smiled, "It is my fault for you had been here many years and viewed the border with old eyes. You saw what you expected to see. Captain Hawkwood has new eyes. Let us see how he fares! While I show the new castellan his home I would have you and your men quit it." With that, the old soldier was dismissed, and the Baron turned to me, "Well, Hawkwood, what do you think?"

"I think that between now and Christmas we will have two tasks to do. While my archers and I acquaint ourselves with Wales, the rest will improve the defences. Those ditches would barely stop an ancient cripple!" I suddenly felt guilty for Wilfred was still in earshot. I had not meant to offend him but, as he turned sharply, I knew that I had.

The Baron seemed oblivious to my words and he waved over a greybeard who was not dressed in military garb but a simple tunic bearing the livery of the Mortimers. "This is Iago, he is the Steward of the castle and acts as a reeve for me. He is Welsh-born but trustworthy for all of that." Iago was impassive even though he had just been insulted. "He will handle the food and your accommodation. You need not worry about that. He handed me a purse which jingled. "Here is your first month's pay in advance. You will be paid your next instalment at the end of six months. I will pay my own men as and when I see fit." He had just four men left to him and he said, as he mounted, "I think that I shall do what you intend, Hawkwood. I will ride a little way into Wales. Let the locals see that the new Baron Mortimer is like his father and is unafraid."

I contemplated dissuading him or asking if he wished me to accompany him but that would be a mistake and so I just nodded.

He turned to Wilfred, "When you have shown Captain Hawkwood around you and your men can collect your war gear and make your way back to Wigmore. That will be your new home!"

I waited until the Baron and his men had gone and then turned to Iago and Wilfred. "I am sorry that you have lost your

position, Wilfred. You should know that it was not of my doing.
I happened to come seeking work."

His smile was a sad one and I saw that he was prematurely
old. "My son died six months ago of the plague and my wife
followed while I was in here and untouched. I do not think my
heart was in the task and that it cost men their lives will be on
my conscience. I will ask Baron Mortimer to release me from the
oath I swore to his father."

I did not ask what he would do. The man had mail and a good
sword, but he was not a man at arms; he just had the
accoutrements of one. He looked too old to hire out his sword. I
wondered if he had money. Then I put those thoughts from my
head. I did not know him, and I had enough souls to worry about
as it was. Nodding I turned to Iago, "Iago, my men and I have
simple tastes. So long as the food is wholesome and the ale
plentiful, we will not complain but what of the servants? You
trust them all?"

I was looking in his eyes for signs of deceit for the question
included him. "Captain Hawkwood, this has been England for
four generations. We have Welsh names, and we have accents
which mark us as being other than either English or Norman but
we are English. Knighton would not have existed but for Lord
Fitz Osbern. We are loyal and not only soldiers died in the
attack, but some servants and villagers perished for we all fought
the attackers."

"Then I have a question for the two of you, what prompted
the attack and who was behind it?"

Interestingly it was Iago who answered, "There is a Welsh
lord who lives just sixteen miles west of here at Cefnllys. Lord
Rhys ap Bleddyn was given the manor by a descendant of
Dafydd ap Gruffydd. He is supposed to be an English ally
but…Until Lord Rhys is given a bloody nose then this will be a
dangerous place."

I looked at Wilfred, "Do you concur?"

"Yes Captain, Welsh politics are complicated and none of the
local lords is to be trusted."

"You think the Baron needs a knight here?"

They both nodded and Iago said, "I mean no disrespect, but it
is horsemen that the Welsh fear."

"I am not insulted, and I would have you remain as honest in the future, Iago. Even if it upsets me, I will punish no man for honesty." I turned to Robin, "Put the horses in the stable and then take the men and inspect the ditches. They need repair and I want a new rope for the bridge over the ditch."

"Aye, Captain." Turning, he rubbed his hands and addressed the men we had brought, "Right then my lovely lads, let us see what work there is to do." I knew that there would be more than just an inspection of the walls. The two groups of men would be inspecting each other. There might be blows and bloody noses. It would just create a hierarchy. That my men would be at the top was never in doubt. The ones we had brought from Wigmore all had the look of men who had served in a garrison for a long time. They would be soft. Mine were hardened steel!

As the two of them took me around the castle I realised that I had been given a poisoned chalice. I did not have enough men and we were, in effect, the edge of the border despite what the King in Windsor might think. The castle was well made and looked reasonably well furnished, but I could see that there had been no lady living there for some time. That suited me. My men could all live in the keep and the rest could use the warrior hall in the outer bailey. When I climbed to the top of the keep, I saw that we had good views of the surrounding land. It raised a question and I asked it of the two men, "What was the weather like when they attacked?"

"Foggy, Captain!"

I saw that the bridge was about a hundred paces away from the castle, but the houses obscured the bridge. From the top of the keep, there was a clear line of sight. "Wilfred, did you have bowmen or crossbowmen?"

"Two of each, Captain." I had another question to ask but Wilfred answered it without me having to ask it, "They are only adequate bowmen, Captain. They could not hit the bridge from here."

I knew that I could as could any of my archers. I would have one on duty here all the time. I would rotate them for this would be a mind-numbingly boring duty. I was aware that Wilfred had ten miles to walk and so I turned and said, "Wilfred, you and your men have a long walk. I will not detain you. Iago can answer any further questions." He nodded, "I hope that fortune favours you now, Wilfred, for I can see that you have had your fair share of misfortune."

He looked at me with dead eyes, "My life is now over. I shall find a monastery and work as a lay brother. Perhaps working for the lord will ensure a place in heaven for surely my wife and son are with Jesus now."

He sounded like a man who was desperate for answers and tired of life. I hoped that I never became like him.

I stood with Iago and I saw that Robin had already divided the men into four groups. They were a mixture of both sets of warriors. Some were working on the outer ditch while others toiled at the more important ditch, the one around the inner bailey. Iago said, "It is not Wilfred's fault, Captain. Old Sir Edmund did not pay much attention to this border and did not see the rise in the attacks on us. He allowed the Welsh to cross and to steal cattle and sheep. His son is different, but Wilfred had old men serving him. You, I feel, will be different."

"There are no Welsh kings are there? I ask because I come from London and served in France more than England."

He smiled, "The last Welsh King was Llewellyn the Last but there are many who claim to have royal blood in their veins. If you believed them all then the old Welsh kings would have spent more time visiting women rather than fighting. The Welsh are a romantic people, Captain, and no man likes to believe he is ruled by a foreigner."

"Then tell me what we face."

"Lord Rhys is a knight although who knighted him, I do not know. He has a warhorse, and he wears plate and mail. Some say he fought in Gascony. He tends to spend more time at Rhayader these days as it is a better castle and Cefnllys village has fallen on hard times of late due to the plague. There are half a dozen men at arms or men who wear mail. I confess that I would be hard-pressed to know the difference. Then he has a warband. I use that old-fashioned term for when they attacked and stole our cattle and sheep, they appeared to have little discipline. There are sixty or so in the band and none wear mail. A few of the spearmen wear helmets. He has fewer than fifteen real spearmen and the rest are archers. They think they are good but looking at the way your men carry themselves I would say that yours are better."

"Do not try to flatter me, Iago! I need the truth."

"And I speak the truth. Your men have good bows or at least I assume they are good bows for they are in cases but the men of Lord Rhys do not use cases and I saw that all of your arrows were fletched with goose." The man was observant. "Lord Rhys' men use any feathers that they can. They will outnumber you, but you will have more skill."

He was a clever man who used his eyes and mind well. As we talked I discovered that he was married, and his sons were not warriors. Both were employed at Wigmore Castle as scriveners. His eldest, Madog, hoped to become a lawyer. It was high ambition for the son of a steward. "Lord Edmund told me that he would pay for my son to become a lawyer, but he died before he could put that in writing. Baron Mortimer knows what his father promised. It is too soon now but one day I shall ask him if he intends to honour his father's wishes. The Baron is one of the richest men in England!"

"I shall rely on you, Iago."

"And I will not let you down, Captain."

"Tonight, I will dine with all of my men in the warrior hall. I will not leave a guard, but I shall bar the gates. It is important that I get to know my men."

"As you wish but we have some boys, they are the sons of the women who cook. They could watch on the walls. If you give them each a farthing, they will think that they have a king's ransom."

I saw that the steward was as valuable as half a dozen spearmen. By the time we had fetched our gear to the keep and I had allocated beds and sleeping spaces, it was dark. I sent Michael and half of my men to walk the fighting platform of the inner bailey, while I took Robin and the rest of what were, effectively, Hawkwood's men to walk the longer walls of the outer bailey and bar the gate. There were four boys at the gate. None was older than ten, but all held a sling.

"Now you know what you are to do while we eat?"

The eldest nodded, "Aye, Captain Hawkwood, we walk the walls and if we see any danger, we fetch you!"

Iago had briefed them well, "Good lad. What is your name?"

"Dai son of James, Captain." He added, almost as an afterthought. "The Welsh killed my father the last time they attacked and I would have vengeance. One day I shall be a warrior!"

That I could understand. I counted out five farthings, "Then tonight you shall be Captain of the Guard. There is a farthing for each of your sentries and two farthings for you!"

His eyes lit up as he took the coins. I descended the ladder followed by my men. As we walked across to the hall where the others would eat and sleep Robin chuckled, "When I was his age that would have made me think I was the richest boy in Wakefield!"

"And it is little enough to ensure that we can eat for an hour or so and speak with the men. You have met them, what do you make of them?"

He lowered his voice, "They all talk like warriors and I have no doubt that they will be able to use weapons, but they are not yet truly warriors. They have watched the walls of Wigmore. When I spoke of Durham and Gascony and the battles there it was as though I was speaking a foreign language. If the garrison of Knighton was the same, then it is no wonder that they lost men and did not slay any of the Welsh."

My heart sank for that meant I would be reliant upon my men only and from what Iago had told me we had seventy men who were potential enemies.

When we entered the hall Michael and the other half of my men were there already, and the murmur of conversation ceased. I allowed the silence to reign while I walked to the seat which had been left for me at the head of the table. The table filled the centre of the hall while at each end was a stone fireplace with a roaring fire. Along the sides were sleeping platforms. Simply made they were a box filled with straw. The straw would be changed once a week and burned on the fires to kill the wildlife within. Each man would make his bed and area his own. I looked at the faces of the men I would lead. I had been busy speaking with the Baron when I had journeyed here and now, I looked at them. The youngest was twenty-five or so but he was unusual. The rest were all thirty or more. I reached the seat and said, "Sit!

Fetch food and I will speak as I eat for I have much to say!" I saw my men sitting, not with their friends, but interspersing themselves on the benches with the new men. They had been so instructed by me.

The four serving women must have been briefed by Iago for they wasted no time, and a stew was ladled into the wooden bowls before us. I took out my spoon and tasted it. It was not unpleasant and had been seasoned. I saw beans, cabbage and meat which looked like rabbit. There was also a taste of ham. We could live on such fare. I took out my beaker and held it up. A young girl of ten or so poured the ale from the jug which looked almost as big as she. It was good ale and I nodded.

"We have been sent here by Baron Mortimer to protect the bridge, the village and his castle. It is not the fault of any in this hall, but the castle has been allowed to become vulnerable. Tomorrow we continue to clean the ditches, sharpen the edges and bury stakes. That work could take us past All Saints Day. At the same time, I will lead ten men every day to ride the country and let the Welsh know that there is a castellan who will not be threatened by Welshmen. We will ride armed and be ready to fight."

My men continued to eat but I saw that the ten men from Wigmore, in my mind they were Wigmore men, paused and look at each other.

I dipped some of the rustic bread in the juices left in the bottom of the bowl. I wanted to enjoy the last of the food and I wished to let my words and their implication sink in. I wiped my hand on the cloth over my left shoulder and drank some ale. I nodded to the girl who scurried over to refill it.

"I know that some of you have not fought as often as my men and so only two of you will have to ride with us. Over five days each of you will begin to learn to become Hawkwood's men and by the end of the month you should all be better warriors."

One spoke. He was an older man whose hair was thinning and had flecks of grey in his beard, "But Sunday we rest?"

I put down the beaker, put my fingers together and leaned forward, "We are the guardians of the castle. We do not have a day off. You can go to Church…?"

"Maelwyn, Captain."

"Maelwyn, on Sunday, men will watch my walls, others will ride on patrol with me for I shall ride every day and my archers will train those in the village to use a bow. We do God's work by fighting the evil Welsh!" I waited for more questions but there were none. "Now get to know your shield brothers."

I was at the head of the table and was the only one who did not get to speak. That was my choice for I used my ears and eyes. I learned much. I discovered that the plague had been less virulent here. They had suffered deaths and losses but not as much as in England. It gave me another reason why the Welsh had become so belligerent. They saw the chance to take back part of their land. I also learned a little of the politics of this part of the world. Prince Edward was, in theory, the ruler of Wales for his title was Prince of Wales. King Edward the First had made that decision and built castles to control the Welsh but he had left the nobility in place. While Rhuddlan, Beaumaris, Caernarfon and Conwy might be new towns filled with English settlers and protected by a fortress, the heart of Wales, the villages and towns were still Welsh. They did not like English law and that their courts spoke English, resentment burned and Lord Rhys was just a symptom of this disease!

I had finished and so I rose, "You may all continue but this will be a rare occurrence. Perhaps at Christmas, God willing then we shall do so again. You, Maelwyn, will ride with the patrol tomorrow, as shall you." I pointed to the youngest of them. "Robin here will command in my absence. I shall go and relieve the boys. Michael will allocate the sentries of the night watch. Each of us will enjoy that duty and that includes me. You may come to hate me but know that I will get the job done for Baron Mortimer and when that job is done then Hawkwood's men will move on!"

The boys were still where they had been placed and I said, "Thank you, boys, you have done your duty now find your beds for Captain Hawkwood is here."

They looked disappointed and Dai said, "Any time you need us, Captain we will do this, and you need not pay us."

I nodded, "You said that you wish to be a warrior, Dai?"

"Aye, Captain, for the Welsh slew my father who was one of the garrison."

Here was a tale! "Then know that a warrior is worth his hire. The Lords who pay us have the coins to do so and it is not right for the poor to pay for their castles with their lives. Duty is to God and then men should look to themselves and their families. I will take you up on your offer, but you shall be paid."

They had not been gone long and I looked out on a darkened village with the sparkle of the river below it. It was a cold night and there might be a slight frost, but it did not bode fog. I heard the feet on the ladder, but I did not turn for it had to be one of my men, "Captain, I asked for the first duty for I wished to speak with you."

I turned and saw the youngest warrior, the one who would be riding on patrol the next day, "What is your name?"

"Stephen of Shrewsbury."

"And what did you wish to say?"

"I cannot ride, Captain, I am willing to learn but could another not go in my place tomorrow?"

I smiled, "You are afraid you will fall off?" He nodded. "That may well happen and if it does will be a good lesson for the next time you will ensure that you do not." He still did not look convinced. "I tell you what, the horses and ponies all belong to my company. I will choose a small one so you have not far to fall and she shall be a quiet one. You will ride next to me and I can teach you as we ride." I saw the resignation on his face. I wondered if the question about the horse was just an excuse not to ride. "What made you become a soldier?"

"My father is a sergeant at arms at Shrewsbury Castle. He fought at Crécy and has scars to prove it."

I nodded, "I fought there too and, as your father will tell you, the odds were against us. Why did you not join the garrison there?"

He hung his head, "I knew how to use weapons but when the Captain of the guard tested me he said I did not have the skills yet and as they guarded the King's castle I should gain experience elsewhere. Old Baron Mortimer took me on."

"But you have not had an opportunity to improve." He shook his head. "Well now is your chance. You are young and any man can wield a sword and use a shield. It just needs practice."

Alan of the Woods arrived with another of the Wigmore men, "I am Captain of the night watch, Captain Hawkwood, I will help Robin in the morning." That made sense for Alan, although much recovered was still not the man who had fought at Calais.

"I will see you in the morning, Stephen."

It was not just the new men who would be learning; their leader had many lessons ahead of him!

Chapter 7

I slept as well as I might have expected but my mind was too busy with all the things I had to do for a truly restful night. The night before Michael had brought food and ale for our breakfast as there was a hall for the lord and lady to use. It was perfect for us ten and I sat and ate while I worked out my strategy. Michael rose soon after I did and joined me, "I have arranged with one of the women to fetch food each day for us to eat for breakfast and to clean the hall. Iago suggested the woman."

I nodded and drank some ale to wash down the semi-stale bread and cheese, "When you ride with me feel free to help make the new men better warriors. I fear that they will not last long in combat. There are up to seventy men at Cefnllys. True, most of them are untrained but it seems to me that half of our men are barely trained."

"We need Ned and Jack!"

"If you are wishing for the unattainable then make it twenty men at arms! We work with what we have!"

"And you have a plan?"

"I do. We use our greatest skill, archers. After today it will be the three of you who remain here with the garrison. I need to be able to hurt the Welsh. Today I will visit Lord Rhys and warn him of my intentions."

"Is that not dangerous? Better to surprise him."

"This will give me the measure of the man. I will use the fact that I fought for Prince Edward. It will do one of two things. It will either make him acquiesce…"

"Which you doubt!"

I nodded, "Or it will prod him to anger and he may become aggressive. Thanks to Baron Mortimer the castle and the village are well supplied. If he tries a siege, then it suits us and if he just raids then we can ambush him. He does not know of our skill."

As we rode to Cefnllys I discovered more from Maelwyn. I still saw him as the weak link, but he knew the land. "The problem, Captain, is that this castle has always been a bone of contention. Eighty years or so ago the first Baron Mortimer tried to build a castle at Cefnllys. Llewellyn the Last tore it down. In the peace, the first King Edward gave the land to the grandfather of Lord Rhys who had been a supporter of the King. As Baron Mortimer had partly rebuilt the castle he was not pleased. Now Lord Rhys has forgotten that and seeks to enlarge his fiefdom. He sees himself as a prince!"

Now I understood.

The land was farmed but I saw to the north a line of wooded hills and low ridges. They could be used. We passed through the tiny hamlet of Crug where we saw scowls. They were far from friendly. The place was too small for defences, but they would favour the Welsh and news of our movements would be passed on. I would have to find another route the next time I came. I saw the castle on top of the ridge above the River Ithon. The tiny village lay at the bottom of the slope. There were fewer people than I had expected. We watered our horses at the river. I was not worried by the villagers. We had ten armed and in some cases, mailed men. Leaving my horse with Stephen I walked over to a blacksmith who was making horseshoes.

"I seek Lord Rhys." I tried several times, but he feigned ignorance of our language. I waved over Maelwyn "Ask him where I can find Lord Rhys." The man's face adopted a scowl before Maelwyn could even begin and I knew that he had understood. "Tell him if he does not answer we shall see if he can shoe horses with one hand!"

The smith spat in the fire and pointed west, "He is at his castle of Rhayader." He grinned, "There he is eating Mortimer sheep!"

I drew my sword and pricked his neck with the end, "Friend, you do not know me so I will let that pass. I am Captain Hawkwood and I have slain Bretons, Frenchmen, Normans and Scots. I have yet to kill a Welshman, but I am happy to make you the first. My men and I will now be riding this valley which is English! If I see any eating Mortimer sheep or cattle then they will lose a hand. I am not Wilfred and I fear no Welshman!"

We mounted and Maelwyn said, "Did you mean what you said, Captain?"

"I never threaten idly. I will do as I said. How far to Rhayader?"

"Another twenty miles."

Then we will ride to this castle and tomorrow I will see Lord
Rhys in Rhayader."

"That is a stronger castle, Captain."

I smiled, "Then he will not mind losing this one will he?"

After riding beyond bowshot and examining the defences we
returned to our own castle in the middle of the afternoon. Our
presence had made the garrison of Cefnllys slam the gates, but
we did not allow them the chance to send an arrow at us. I
realised that I did not need to take the castle. I could destroy the
village if I had to. Then the whole purpose of the castle would be
gone!

I dismounted and let Stephen take my horse to the stable. He
had not fallen off and found, after a mile or two that riding was
not as hard as he had expected. In five days, when next he rode
with me, I would give him a bigger horse. Robin and Alan came
over. "From now on I take archers and just one of my
swordsmen. Michael and Roger can command the workers
tomorrow. We ride before dawn for we have thirty miles to go.
We will be heading back in the dark. I wish to show Lord Rhys
that his main castle is not out of reach!"

We chose our best horses and left a good three hours before
dawn. We passed through Crug before the villagers were awake
and reached Cefnllys in the mid-morning. We stopped to eat and
rest the horses at Nantmel which was almost deserted and had
more empty houses than ones which were occupied. We had no
Welsh speaker with us and could not ask but the signs on the
doors told us that this village had been struck by the plague. We
had barely left when Robin's keen senses heard and smelled
something.

"Captain, there are horsemen in the distance. I can smell their
riders and hear the jingle of mail!"

I looked around and saw that we had just passed some
hawthorns. "Turn and follow me!" We rode back the two
hundred paces to where hawthorns, blackthorns and brambles
sprouted from the remains of what looked like an ancient and
long-abandoned farm. "Robin, hide the archers there. You know
what to do!"

"Aye." He needed to give no command for the others were
my archers. "Gareth, next to me. Rafe and Edward flank us." I

sensed that they were nervous. "Do not worry. If I give the command, then dig your heels into your horses' flanks and charge them." They nodded, "Do not forget to draw your swords."

I wondered what the riders would make of us. Edward and Rafe had the livery of Baron Mortimer upon their shields and jupons. The yellow and blue colours were well known. Gareth and I had our plain white shields. I wondered then if we should use a white surcoat and cloak as well. They would be easier to keep clean as we could just use the piss pots to bleach them. I liked that idea. I always had a mind which liked occupation.

The riders were a column of horsemen. The livery was colourful. It was bright yellow and on it was some sort of red symbol. They were too far away for me to make out. I could see my archers, but I doubted that these horsemen would be able to for there was still enough foliage left to hide them. When the horsemen stopped my archers would have a good and close view of them. I wondered if they would simply charge us.

I saw them halt when they spied us, and the two leaders turned to speak. I saw then the symbol on the shields and tunics was a red claw! The horsemen drew their swords and rode towards us.

"Do not draw your weapons yet but keep your hands on the hilt. If we strike, we do so like lightning."

The three murmured, "Aye, captain!"

I could see that one of the two who rode towards us was a knight and that there were just two with mail while the other twenty were just mounted spearmen and swordsmen. They had shields with the red and yellow livery, but none had jupons. They rode ponies and sumpters. Hawkwood's men rode palfreys!

The knight spoke to me but in English and that told me much, "Who are you that you bar the road to the rightful lord of this land?"

"I am Captain Hawkwood who now commands the garrison of Knighton to which you laid waste and did great mischief, for I assume you are Lord Rhys."

I am Lord Rhys ap Bleddyn and I am descended from the prince who ruled this land before the English came,

Gwenwynwyn ab Owain. Begone before I have my men ride you down!"

I smiled, "I was about to offer you the same courtesy. If you turn and ride back to Rhayader when I have given you my ultimatum, then you and your men shall live, but if not then we shall gain some horses fit only for eating and swords which can be melted down for pots. Baron Mortimer will have reparation for the damage that you do and I am here to tell you that we will guard his land better than the other men you slew!"

He laughed but the man at arms next to him looked around nervously, "There are but four of you!"

Just then the man at arms must have spotted a movement, "Lord, it is an ambush!"

Shouting, "Now!" I drew my sword and rode at the two leading men. Six arrows flew through the hedges and six men were hit; while not all were mortally wounded it would attract the attention of the rest. I could leave the others to Robin. I pulled my shield around and had my sword out before the knight. Now would be the test of the training during the plague. I heard arrows again and the screams and shouts as men were struck. I won the race to strike the first blow for the knight was still trying to swing his sword around. He wore plate above his mail but my blow was well struck and I hit his shoulder. His face showed the pain of the strike. To my left, I heard a cry but did not turn. Another flight of arrows struck the spearmen who were trying to get at Robin and his archers. I swung my shield horizontally and hit the knight so hard that he almost tumbled from his horse, but knights are usually good riders and although he retained his seat he was forced to turn.

He saw that he had lost many men and he shouted, "Fall back! Fall back!"

I risked turning and saw Rafe dead in a pool of blood next to his horse and Edward was struggling to fight the man at arms. I was not a knight and honour meant nothing. I let the knight flee and I turned. Swinging my sword, I hacked across the back of the man at arms. I am an archer and the blade hacked through the mail but it was the weight of iron which broke his back and he fell from the horse.

"Get the horses!"

I had no intention of pursuing the Welsh. We were too far from home and besides, we had a victory. I was annoyed that it had cost me one man but that could not be helped.

"Edward, put Rafe's body on his horse. Gareth, recover the man at arms. Robin, collect the horses and any weapons we can use."

I heard him shout out the orders and add, "Martin, collect the arrows!" We wasted nothing!

We had four poor horses as well as the good one ridden by the man at arms. He had lamellar armour and would serve one of the Wigmore men. Five of the Welsh were dead although Robin was convinced that another six were so badly wounded that they would either not recover or be crippled. We took their swords and the few coins that they possessed and headed back to Knighton. Walter of Barnsley and Richard of Loidis rode fifty paces behind us to protect our rear.

Robin and Gareth flanked me, "What happened to Rafe?"

Gareth shook his head, "He could not control his horse and when it lurched forward, he was unable to slow it and had no weapon raised. He was an easy kill for the Welshman. Rafe's horse got in the way of mine and the Welshman had the first strike. I owe you, Captain."

"We are all one company, and it is my fault. I thought after Stephen did so well yesterday that the others would find it as easy. We do not need to rise as early tomorrow, and we can give them rudimentary lessons."

"You have a plan for tomorrow?"

"Aye, Robin, we ride to Crug and let the villagers there know that we are now the landowners and not Lord Rhys."

"The old Baron has allowed this situation to develop. He should have nipped the incursion in the bud. Baron Mortimer needs to make war and reclaim his land through force of arms."

"And he may do. When Christmas comes, I will return to Wigmore. By then we will know how determined this Welshman really is. I think we gave him a shock today. I want to give him time to worry. When word reaches him from Crug he will wonder where we will strike next. We keep him guessing until we have our defences stronger."

Robin nodded, "And when we do not raid again, he will come and attack us."

"Aye, and if he does not then that shows that we have won."

"You think he will return."

"I do but we have weakened him, he had seventy men and he now has almost ten fewer. One is a man at arms, and they are expensive to hire. He will use his archers. We saw none today for they do not ride. I am guessing he will have ambushes set out for us. We will patrol but closer to home and we will make life hard for Welsh warriors to travel the road."

It was dark as we rode through the gates. The Wigmore men looked apprehensive but my two men just grinned when they saw the captured horses and the dead body. I think it was the body of Rafe which upset the Wigmore men. I saw Maelwyn look at Stephen. They were the old and the young. As the gate was slammed shut and the bar dropped, I said, "Before we eat tonight, we will bury our dead comrade. I hope it makes you all realise that one mistake can be fatal. If I strive for perfection with you then there is a good reason."

Maelwyn said, "Mistake, Captain?"

Edward nodded and lifted his friend's body from the horse, "Rafe could not control his horse and he had no sword ready. His death was quick but," he glanced at me, "it could have been avoided."

"And that is why, Ben and Dafydd, you will be given a lesson before we leave tomorrow." I turned on Edward, "If however, any is at fault then it is your Sergeant at Arms from Wigmore, Edmund. If he had done his job, then I would not have to waste time training you to be that for which you are paid!" His head dropped as he realised the truth in my words. "Michael, have the animals and their cargo taken to the stables."

After we had buried him in the small cemetery inside the outer bailey, I said a few words over him. I did not know him but felt obliged to do so. I noticed the freshly turned mounds which showed those others who had died at the hands of the Welsh. I think that was the moment when the nine remaining Wigmore men realised the reality of their situation. That evening as we ate it was not a sombre atmosphere but the Wigmore men were certainly serious about becoming better warriors. This time when they talked to my men the questions had a purpose. I chose not to sit at the head of the table but as one seat was vacant, I sat there and chatted to Stephen and Long Rob. I spoke of the wars in which I had fought and also my journey to reach where I was.

When we had finished, I said, "And now there is a treasure to share." I saw the surprise on their faces. "Let us go to the stables."

Abel Abelson said, "But Captain, we were not part of the patrol; why should we be given anything?"

"Because you are now part of my company and in my company, once I have taken that which is due to me, we share the rest. You worked on the ditch today and one day that might save us."

That moment changed them all. They would always be Wigmore men but they also became part of Hawkwood!

The next day I took two different men to Crug, but we spent an hour first mastering the horses. I had chosen a quiet horse for Stephen but not for Rafe and that was a mistake which had cost me a man and I could ill afford such losses. When we rode out, I was able to see the progress which had been made on the ditch. Our first line of defence, the ditch around the outer bailey, was almost completely cleaned and now just required the stakes embedding in the bottom. We soon reached Crug, after the last day's journey it seemed to take no time at all. I dismounted in the centre and, cupping my hands, shouted, "All men in the village, I wish to speak with you! Come here to the green."

There was no movement. I had my bow with me, and I nocked an arrow. My injured hand hardly ached at all these days. The smith who had spat in his fire put his head from the smithy and then pointedly went back inside. He had his tools hanging from a metal rail and I sent an arrow to split the sledgehammer's shaft in two. The arrow carried on and I heard it clatter against some metal, it sounded like church bells. The smith and his boy raced out.

"I will not ask again! I will have my men string their bows and begin to kill every man and boy in this cesspit of rebels!"

They came out and their women followed them fearfully. I hung my bow from my saddle horn and walked towards them. My men fanned out behind me. I waited until I was level with the smith. He must have thought he was the toughest man in the village, and he knew he was the biggest. I was as big but there was no fat on me. I put my hands on my hips and balanced on the balls of my feet in case he became violent.

"Yesterday I met Lord Rhys and he ran from me. One of my men now wears the mail of the man at arms we slew. The other men we slew we left for carrion. I told Lord Rhys what I will tell you. This land is Mortimer land, and you will all pay taxes to him as you once did. You will show him fealty and you will shun any attempt to subvert your loyalties." I looked at the smith and held his gaze. He looked away. "If you feel that you cannot do so then leave for any who stay here and show disloyalty will be punished as traitors by me!" Men looked at each other and I saw some of the women clutch their children closer. "You have one week to make your decision. Cefnllys and Rhayader are the lands of Baron Mortimer and over the next year, they will be returning to his control. If you leave then you have a long journey! In the next days, we will repeat this message to all the settlements within range of Knighton. Law has returned to this part of King Edward's lands!"

As we rode back Richard of Loidis asked, "Will the Welsh not seek to plead their case to a Sherriff or a court?"

I nodded, "I hope they do. The Sherriff and the Court are both Baron Mortimer's men or men appointed by him. They will get short shrift there. No, Richard, I had been so unpleasant and aggressive to force the hand of Lord Rhys. I do not wish to have to spend the winter riding across this land ensuring that the Welsh keep the peace. I want them angry enough to attack us at Knighton so that when we defeat them they will not be in any position to cause more trouble."

"But we have just nineteen men."

I nodded, "And the village. This time we will be vigilant. I have kept an archer on the top of the keep when they could have been toiling on the ditch and there was a reason. By the end of the week, my men will have an eye for this country. Unlike Wilfred, we will know when the Welsh are coming and every villager and animal will be within the walls of Knighton. We have arrows and food aplenty. They will bleed on our walls and when the time is ripe, I will lead my men, my mounted men and we will take Lord Rhys in chains to Wigmore where he will face Baron Mortimer's justice!"

As I said it, I knew it sounded plausible, but I also knew how many things could go wrong. I was an arrogant young man in those days. I suppose I always was.

Chapter 8

After three days there was not a Welshman within fifteen miles who did not know my intentions. We had almost finished the ditch around the inner bailey, and I knew that Lord Rhys would be gathering his forces to come and punish the arrogant English archer. I had sent Michael to Wigmore to tell Baron Mortimer what I had done. When Michael returned, he said that the Baron approved completely of all my actions. Had he not done so then I would have left his service.

My patrol spotted the men moving along the road to Crug. It was a week after Michael had returned from Wigmore. I only used four men on my patrols now for the new warriors had learned to ride and I needed more men to make the castle more defensible. The ropes on the bridge had been renewed but I wanted hoardings on the outer bailey gatehouse. Four cloaked men were harder to see than the knight flanked by mailed men at arms and marching Welshmen with spearpoints gleaming in the autumn sun. We spied them and I do not think they saw us.

I had Gareth with me as well as Stephen and Maelwyn. The oldest and youngest of the Wigmore men appeared to have formed a bond and I knew the value of such things. I said to them, "So it begins, and we no longer need to ride out each day."

Stephen was a curious man and he asked, "Do we not need to know when they will reach Knighton, Captain?"

Maelwyn answered for me, "Most of their men are afoot and they will be picking up men at the villages as they come. We do this journey quickly, but they will not reach Knighton until tomorrow or the day after."

"Maelwyn is right and that gives us the chance to finish our defences and warn the families in Knighton of the danger." As we turned to ride back, I waved a hand at the thin sun above us, "The weather at this time of year is predictable. The slightly warmer days are followed by cold nights and that makes for a mist. From what I was told by Iago and Wilfred the last time they attacked there was fog. There may not be fog around but morning mist will aid our foes. Lord Rhys will wait for a mist. I would."

Maelwyn asked, "How would you take the castle, Captain?"

"I would attack at night. I would make crude bridges to cross the ditch and with archers picking off sentries, climb the wall. Unless you have the walls fully manned it is difficult to fight such an attack. Of course, I do not think Lord Rhys knows that we have improved our ditches for we have seen no trace of scouts. He will have a rude shock if he tries to attack them the same way as when he did so the last time."

"How do you know there have been no scouts, Captain?"

"I have had the bridge watched from the keep by one of my archers and they have watched for strangers. They saw none and you may not have noticed, Stephen, but we often come back along the river. That is not just for a change. That is because my men and I have been looking for the signs of men fording the river. It is what we would have done had we been the ones seeking to take the castle. Lord Rhys, from what I can see, has ambitions which are far greater than his ability to achieve them."

Maelwyn said, to no one in particular, "And that shows that Wilfred should not have been the man to command."

"I do not blame him, Maelwyn. The old Baron Mortimer should have realised that events in Wilfred's life had to take effect and change him. That is the past. The only point in looking back is not to repeat the mistakes you made. All else is waste."

While the horses were taken to the stable, I waved over Michael and Robin. Both were stripped to the waist and toiling on the walls. "We need to see Iago."

Robin nodded, "Lord Rhys comes?"

I nodded, "Tomorrow or the day after is my expectation. How goes the work?"

"The hoardings on the first gatehouse are almost done but we have not yet begun to work on the gatehouse to the inner bailey. We have placed all the stones we recovered from the ditches on the fighting platform."

"Good and I have had Dai and the boys who watched for us collecting river-washed stones for their slings. Had we had time I would have had more darts made."

Iago had seen us approach and he left his house to come towards us.

"I did not see numbers, Robin, but if he has much more than a hundred men I will be surprised. While the pestilence appears to have taken fewer families in his land, enough have died to make a large army unlikely."

"Captain?"

"The Welsh are coming, Iago. I wish you to tell the villagers of the danger. I believe the attack will be in the next few days. If any wish to come within our walls now, then they may do so but when I sound my horn then I want everyone and their animals inside immediately. Is that clear?"

He smiled, "Aye, Captain. I think only old Siôr and his family will stay outside until they hear the horn. He is an obstinate old fool who will argue with all. He has the large farm half a mile down the Wigmore Road. He will come when the horn sounds but not before. When the Welsh came the last time, he led his family away from the castle, but he lost some animals."

"Just so long as he knows that I will brook no arguments. If he is not here when I sound a second blast, I will have men drag him and his family hither!"

Michael asked, "Why, Captain? Surely if he and his family are of that mind then we leave them to their own fate."

"Hostages, Michael! They could be used as a shield of bodies. I would slay them but that would take the heart from the others. No, my will shall prevail! Go tell them, Iago!"

That evening I told my men my orders. "From now on we have two shifts. There will be four hours on watch and four off. There will always be nine of you on duty. My horn will be in the keep. Robin and Alan of the Woods will command the two watches and one of those will watch from the top of the keep. The Welsh will come over the bridge and my guess is that they will wait until a misty morning to do so. We sound the horn for any who are without and all the walls will be manned. There will be three of my archers in the keep and the others on the gatehouse. The rest of you will spread yourselves out on the walls of the outer bailey. As soon as the walls are manned sound the horn a second time. I will lead men out to drag to safety any villager who is tardy."

My Hawkwood men looked happy but I saw the doubt on some of the faces of the Wigmore contingent. I decided to explain my thinking.

"It is hard to attack walls which are well defended. The villagers of Knighton will not wish to suffer again, and their menfolk will use their bows to great effect. This time we have archers who can use bodkin arrows. The seven of us will give their men in mail a shock. I intend for this to be the last battle. When we win then their archers will lose two fingers from their right hands. Their men at arms will be hanged. Lord Rhys will be taken to Wigmore and the farmers will have their weapons and boots taken."

Siôn looked puzzled, "Boots, captain?"

I smiled, "The men who are not archers will have walked more than twenty miles to get here. If they have no boots then that twenty miles walk home over autumn roads will hurt them and make them less likely to wish to repeat their mistake and men who have no footwear are more likely to spend their time making boots rather than weapons."

My time at Hartburn had been productive. Those days watching Oswald's farm and when we had been isolated, all I had to do was practise. I exercised my mind and worked out ways of winning wars other than simply killing an enemy. My mind was as potent a weapon as my bow or my sword.

It was Richard of Loidis who woke me. I was awake in an instant and I followed him to the fighting platform of the keep. It was still some hours before dawn. He pointed and I saw the mist along the river. It covered the bridge. "Is there a sign of the Welsh?" He shook his head. "Then you stay on watch and at the first hint of a Welshman sound the horn."

"And if they do not come?"

"It will be a test of our reactions. I will wake the others."

Almost all of the village had spent the last day and a half in the inner bailey. Old Siôr had not been the only one to stay outside. The rest, however, were within hailing distance of the walls. I shook the others awake, "Robin, get to the bridge and sniff out the Welsh. Michael, go and bring in the other villagers. Alan of the Woods, fetch old Siôr and his family. The rest of you rouse the villagers in the bailey and have the walls manned. There is a mist, and it is perfect conditions for an attack!"

I returned to my chamber and donned my padded gambeson and studded brigandine. I slipped my coif over my head and strapped on not only my sword but also my hand axe and daggers. Finally, I took my bow from its case, strung it and fitted my bracer. As I left, I picked up a warbag of arrows. The others had all left by the time I descended the stairs to the inner bailey. There were now three archers on the top of the keep while the others were rushing to obey my orders. It was all eerily silent and there was some mist gathered close to the village gate. I heard the bar as it was removed and by the time I ascended the fighting platform some of the Wigmore men were rushing to their positions. That there appeared to be little panic pleased me, but I knew that, in all likelihood that was because they thought this was a false alarm. I knew, in my bones, that it was not. I seemed to have a sixth sense about such things.

It was Maelwyn who had captained the night guard and he said, quietly, "We heard nothing."

"That was because there was nothing to hear. There is a chance that they will not come but Lord Rhys would be a fool not to take advantage of this. You cannot even see the ditch the mist is so thick." He looked over and saw what I had already discerned, it was an autumn river bottom mist. It would last barely an hour once the sun came out. I could see the clear skies above me which had helped to create the fog. The villagers with noisy sheep and cattle began to move across the wooden bridge and I knew that it would alert the Welsh. However, once they were on the bridge they would be seen by my men on the keep's fighting platform.

Suddenly there was a cry from the bridge and a shout. The horn sounded and I shouted, "Nock an arrow!" I saw Robin running back towards the gate. The bridge was more than two hundred paces from the gate, but it was uphill. "Prepare to close the gate! Richard, sound the horn again!" Alan would have to use his sword to persuade old Siôr if he would not come peacefully. I saw Michael wave as he crossed the bridge and stood below me with Gareth. They would be the ones to raise the bridge. Robin stood on the bridge and nocked an arrow. He had the best eyes of any of my men. I aimed towards the bridge and as Robin loosed I saw what looked like a spear above the mist. I adjusted my aim and sent an arrow into it. I heard a Welsh voice shout something and even as I prepared to give the order to raise the bridge saw old Siôr with a bloody nose. He and his family were less than thirty paces from the gate. "Release arrows into the mist. Aim at the bridge." The bridge was narrow, and the Welsh would be more congested there. The villagers' arrows might be lucky. I saw Dai and the boys with their slings. They were at the far end of the wall and could obviously see more than we. Their stones flew.

Alan and Robin rushed in and I heard Robin shout, "Raise the bridge!"

I saw a man at arms hiding behind a shield emerge from the mist. I had a war arrow, and he had a shield but I aimed it where I thought his leg would be and when he dropped I knew that I had hit something. A horn sounded three times and I knew by the tone that it was not ours.

Pulling my coif above my head I shouted, "Stand to! They come. Every man and boy to the walls!"

Arrows descended from the sky and although they were sent blindly some struck. One hit me square on the top of the head. My coif and archer's hat afforded some protection, but it still hurt. The ones in the newly finished and roofed gatehouse were safe. Within the next hour, it would be daylight and the mist would begin to dissipate. For the moment, the three archers on the keep had no targets but it would be foolish to move them. I knew that the Welsh, once they crossed the bridge, could make their way along the curtain wall and they had to be stopped.

Shadows could be seen and we loosed at shadows. Cries from the Welsh and the walls told me that the blindly loosed arrows were hitting. The odds on a fatality were slim. Welsh arrows were sent in reply but the Wigmore men all wore helmets and some of the villagers, old soldiers, had helmets made of leather or hide. Along with the recently built hoardings we were less likely to suffer deaths. The Welsh horn had an effect and a sea of Welshmen surged forward. Their lower halves were hidden by the mist but their upper bodies and heads were not. Those on my walls with spears and swords began to hurl stones as the Welsh protected by shields ran eagerly towards the ditch. This was a different prospect from the one they had crossed so easily. There were screams as the first men landed on the stakes. A couple landed on the top of wounded comrades and they found that the ditch was too steep to ascend. Rocks dropped from above ended their suffering. That would have been the time to withdraw and wait for daylight to see the size of the problem, but Lord Rhys just remembered Wilfred and his weak defence.

I realised that I could see mail and I drew a bodkin. The man at arms had a hauberk down to the knees, a good helmet as well as a metal coif. In his hand, he held an axe. Behind him were six men with shields and helmets. He thought we could not hurt him, but the trouble was that he was just forty feet from me as he was standing at the edge of the ditch. I could see that he planned on using the bodies of the wounded and dead as a bridge. They were piling up because, for some reason, they had tried to attack close to the gate. Had I been leading then I would have spread the attackers out around the whole of the curtain wall. They had the weight of numbers but were not using them. I pulled back and aimed at the head of the man at arms. He was peering over the top of the shield and I guessed that he thought the metal rim would protect him. At such close range, it would not. One of the villagers sent a hunting arrow at him a heartbeat before I released. His arrow made the man at arms turn slightly and lift his shield. The arrow bounced off the well-made shield. It meant my arrow missed his head but sank deep into his right shoulder. The combination of the two arrows made him pitch forward and he fell into the ditch. Fortune did not favour the man at arms for he managed to fall face down on one of the sharpened spikes which drove into his head. He died. Their metal protection gone, the six men behind him became easy targets for the villagers. Three were hit and the others ran back into the mist. The sun was beginning to rise behind us and soon the protection of fog would be no more. It was at that point that Lord Rhys realised that his attack had failed. The horn made one long mournful sound and was, clearly, the signal to withdraw.

I turned, "Michael, I want my swordsmen mounted. We will attack."

Iago had been on the wall with us and he turned with a fearful expression on his face, "Is that wise, Captain?"

I smiled, "Iago, if you were the Welsh and falling back across the bridge would you expect to be charged by horsemen?"

"No, Captain."

"And they will not. Robin, you command. Bring down the archers from the keep. They are no longer needed there."

"Aye, Captain!" He shouted to the defenders, "Keep the arrows falling into the fog!"

The Welsh archers were now able to send their own arrows once more and I saw a villager, I did not know his name, pitch backwards into the bailey. I dropped my bow and arrows onto the fighting platform and ran towards the gate of the inner bailey. It took time to saddle the horses, grab our shields and then mount them. The three archers from the keep had just reached the gatehouse as I led my men towards the main gate. The mist had cleared from our gatehouse, but I knew it would still hover close to the bridge. The morning light had done little to lighten the gloom.

I raised my sword and two of my archers lowered the bridge. Then they lifted the bar. As we galloped through, I saw that some over-eager Welshmen, hearing the bridge, had raced back to enter the castle. Michael, Gareth and I came as a complete shock to them and even Stephen and Maelwyn, who had yet to fight from the back of a horse, managed to swing their swords and split skulls. The slowly thinning mist hid our horses, and the Welsh must have been terrified to see the disembodied warriors slashing their swords down on them. We had an effect far beyond the numbers who attacked. At the bridge, the fleeing Welsh warriors who had heard the hooves thundering were packed closely together. The horses made some throw themselves into the river and others were easily slain. We were briefly stopped, in the centre of the wooden bridge, until we managed to kill four men and carve a path through them. For the Wigmore men, it was a new experience and part of their training I could not have envisaged.

I knew that Lord Rhys and his mounted men at arms would not have their horses close to the bridge and so it proved. They had a distance to run before they could mount them. The Welsh foot soldiers took to the fields in an attempt to escape us. The horsemen would have to use the road. We had the twin advantages of fresh horses and no mail. We would be able to ride them down so long as there were not too many of them. We also knew the road as well as any. I had ridden down it almost every day since I had arrived, and I heard the hooves ahead of us just as the first rays of the thin autumnal sun shone from the east. As the road rose anyway the six horse riders were soon clearly visible. More than six men were riding away but only six of those men rode horses. The rest had ponies and old sumpters.

I shouted, over my shoulder, "Michael and Gareth, flank me. The rest be ready to support us but remember Rafe! No heroics!"

I saw now that there were just a few riders ahead of us. This would be a long race for they had more than a two hundred paces start, and they were desperate to escape. We must have killed more men than I had thought. Perhaps the stakes in the ditch had hurt them. I had seen at least twelve men impaled on the walls close to me. All the work we had put in had been worthwhile.

I saw that there were four mailed men ahead of us and as one had to be Lord Rhys the others would be men at arms. One might be the knight's squire. My shield hung from its guige strap and that allowed me to use my left arm to hold the reins. I had my sword in my right hand. I wanted to be able to strike as soon as I came within range. I knew that it was almost impossible to fight an enemy who was behind you. We began to draw closer to the rearmost riders as they spread out in a long line. Lord Rhys had the best horse. The last man looked around in panic and seeing an open field to the right jerked his horse around. He hoped to escape us.

"Ben and Dafydd get after him."

There were still ten men with me and that would be enough. I had learned to ride through necessity but Captain Philip had given me the odd lesson and one was that when you looked around while riding you looked under your arm and only when the road was straight and flat. I had remembered that lesson. The new last man had not had that lesson or perhaps his horse was lame. Whatever the reason he turned to look behind when the road began to dip and he did not look down. The result was that as the horse swung right around the slight curve and the road fell away the rider lost his balance and was thrown from his horse. Fate placed a large rock where he landed and as we passed him, I saw that his head was like a squashed plum. His horse, now riderless, had stopped and was happily eating grass less than twenty feet from its dead rider. That left seven of them and ten of us. Just as important was the fact that each time the last men fell or disappeared it made the others more nervous. When they turned to look, they saw us with drawn swords closing with them. Thus far it had been men in brigandines who had fallen. I saw now that the last such rider had begun to overtake the mailed men whose horses looked lathered and exhausted. We had the six mailed men in sight and two of them flanked the knight.

Michael and Gareth were lighter men than I was and they closed with me so that the three of us filled the road and when the mailed man at the rear of the line began to slow I knew that his horse had pulled up lame. He was a brave man, and he turned his horse to face us. He had a sword and a small round shield but there were three of us and we were not knights. We cared not for honour. I took his sword blow on my shield while Michael rammed his sword into his skull and allowed his hand to fall back so that his blade sliced open the lower half of his face. I knew that Michael would be pleased with the strike.

The Welsh must have known that they could go no further. The five of them stopped and turned their weary horses. They did not rate our skill and hoped that they could defeat us and allow Lord Rhys to escape. I did not slow and like the point of an arrow, I barrelled into the first man at arms. He had expected that I would slow, and he was slow to strike. My arm held my sword out before me, and it hit his chest above his shield. He had on mail, but the sword tore through the mail links and then slid up under the man's throat. My men hit the others and then, as I slipped the sword from the dead man, I was face to face with Lord Rhys. I was quite happy to fight him for nothing about the man made me fear him, but I wanted him taken to Baron Mortimer for trial.

"Surrender!"

"To a low born commoner? Never!"

He stood and raised his sword to strike down. I slipped my hand into the brases on my shield and blocked his strike easily.

He was not as strong a man as me. I heard shouts and the clash of steel on steel behind me, but I ignored it. My men would either succeed or I would ride home with a body or two draped over saddles. I now had the shield secure and I looked for the knight's next move. He told me with his eyes. He saw that I had no helmet and he stood again to swing at my head. To negate his strike, I stood and held my shield before me whilst swinging my sword horizontally. It was the end of his sword which hit my shield and whilst it cut the leather it did no harm while my blow smashed into the centre of his shield and rocked him in his saddle. He had a knight's saddle with two high cantles but that made little difference when my fast hands struck again, and he tumbled to the ground. I leapt from my horse and had my sword at his throat while he was still trying to catch his breath.

"Yield!" His hand dropped the sword and, unable to speak, he gave a tiny nod.

I turned to see the last man at arms who was still fighting killed by Stephen. The other two had surrendered. We had won.

We took them back to Knighton and reached there before noon. I sent Robin to Wigmore Castle to tell the Baron of our victory. Already the villagers were piling up the dead, now stripped naked, and placing them on a pyre they had made. The three survivors looked on in horror as those who had lost family in the two battles despoiled the dead.

Siôr came over to me. He had fought on my walls and he held out his hand. His accent was so thick that I could barely make out his words, but I managed to understand him, "Than you, archer, you were proved right and we owe you and your man our lives. Now that you have this killer, perhaps we can live in peace."

I nodded, "That was why I took this course of action. Winter will be upon us before we know it. Come Spring it may be a different story but for now, we have won and we have control of the land." Michael was leading the three men at arms, who were tethered to each other. "You and Gareth take them to the stable. Remove their boots and mail. They will be less likely to run that way but as they would have to run through the villagers it may well be that they see captivity as the safer choice."

"Aye, Captain!"

"Roger of Norham, take Lord Rhys to the Great Hall. Help him to remove his armour. I will follow shortly." As Michael led the men at arms past me, I saw that one had a dagger in his boot. I bent to retrieve it, "And make sure you search them for hidden weapons." I tossed the dagger to a watching Dai, "Here slinger, one day you will be a warrior. This will be your first weapon!"

"Thank you, Captain!"

I looked for Iago. He had a bandage around his head, and I walked over to him, "A noble war wound!"

"At least we fought them off this time and it feels better."

"How many did we lose?"

"Two men died and five have serious wounds but when I see what we inflicted then I know we got off lightly."

"The villagers can go back to their homes but until our prisoners are delivered to the Baron then my men cannot relax. Put the extra horses in the outer bailey. Will there be food?"

He beamed. "Of course, Captain, and the women have been working since the savages fled. It will be a feast!"

As I walked up to the inner bailey and the keep, I saw Stephen. He was carrying the mail he had taken from the dead man at arms he had slain. He looked jubilant. "You did well today and came of age. Few men who are not knights get to slay a man on horseback. You have skill and yet a month ago you could not ride."

He shook his head, "It is you, Captain, you are a good teacher, and you give a man confidence. I would stay with you when you leave."

We had reached the main gate and I paused, "Leave?"

"It is no secret amongst your men that this is just a way for you to earn money and then you will be away to Gascony."

I continued to walk, "I had not decided where I would go but Baron Mortimer hired me to do a job. We have, I believe, done that job. If you stayed here, you would have an easy life."

He grinned, "I enjoy winning and with Lord Rhys taken there would be no one left to defeat!"

For some reason, I was happy that the least experienced of the Wigmore men had chosen to follow me.

We shackled the men at arms and two of the Wigmore men agreed to be their gaolers. I took responsibility for the Baron but as he had yielded, he would not need to be watched. Robin arrived after dark with the news that the Baron wanted the four prisoners taking to Wigmore the next day where they would be tried for their crimes.

As we ate that night Lord Rhys, who had lost all his arrogance, asked, "What will happen to me, do you think?"

I shrugged, "Ransom? I know not." That did rankle a little. I had taken him, and he had surrendered to me but I was not a knight and the ransom would go to my lord. I would not grumble about it nor let it sour me, but it was another incentive for me to rise through the ranks and become a noble. It had happened to John Chandos and I wanted it to happen to me!

Chapter 9

I took just three men at arms with me: Michael, Gareth and Roger. There was work to be done on the ditches and the castles. We took the four worst horses with us just in case the Baron tried to claim them, and we kept the mail and weapons in the Keep. Wigmore village was little bigger than Knighton but the castle was enormous and being built of stone seemed much more imposing. The sight of it affected Lord Rhys who visibly shrank in his saddle. He had dreamed of a fiefdom which was enormous and now he saw the castle which was merely one of Baron Mortimer's he realised that he could not have fulfilled his dream. Once more we stopped in the outer bailey and walked our prisoners up to the walled bridge over the ditch. We were expected and the responsibility of keeping weapons in the backs of the men at arms was handed over to the Baron's men.

I turned to my men at arms, "Go to the warrior hall where there will be food and ale." I leaned in and spoke to Michael, "Keep your ears open!"

"Aye, Captain."

I followed the prisoners, and we were taken into the Great Hall. I could see that the hall was set out as a court already. Baron Mortimer had much faith in me! I also saw a knight I recognised from the campaign in Gascony. It was Sir Walter Pavely, and he was one of Prince Edward's retinue. He stood just behind Baron Mortimer. The Baron nodded to me and then to the Bishop of Hereford who was seated next to him.

The Bishop stood and began to read. The first part was in Latin which I did not understand and then he spoke in a language which I could understand, French. "Lord Rhys ap Bleddyn, you have been apprehended by Baron Wigmore's men after attempting for a second time to cause mischief at the Baron's castle at Knighton. Captain Hawkwood, tell us of the Battle of Knighton and your pursuit of Lord Rhys. Place your hand on the Bible when you do so and speak the truth."

I stepped forward and, after placing my hand on the Bible, went through the whole of the battle from the attack in the mist to the ride towards Crug.

When I had finished the Bishop said, "Do you dispute any of Captain Hawkwood's testimony?"

Lord Rhys glanced briefly at me and then his hand went to the cross he wore about his neck and which he had fingered since the Bishop first spoke, "No, my lord."

The Bishop nodded and said, solemnly, "You have murdered the innocent of Herefordshire and slain Baron Mortimer's officers. What have you to say to these charges?"

Every eye was on the Welsh knight. I had expected defiance at the very least, perhaps some legal justification, but all the fight seemed to have been sucked out of him. "I throw myself on the mercy of the Baron."

The look on the Baron's face told me that it would not be forthcoming or at least not in the manner the Welshman expected.

The Bishop looked at the Baron and said, "It is for the jury to decide his guilt, my lord."

It was then I saw that there were eight other knights apart from Sir Walter and they were seated close by the Baron who turned and said, "Verdict?"

One by one they all gave the same one, guilty. This was the first trial I had witnessed. I had missed Alexander of Roxburgh's, but I had assumed there would be arguments and counter-arguments. I suppose the fact that I had taken him after the attempt to take Knighton was irrefutable proof of his guilt.

The Baron had grown since I had seen him last. His beard was fuller, and he had filled out a little more but to me, he still looked like a youth. He stood and spoke, "Lord Rhys ap Bleddyn for your crimes you could be dragged around the town of Wigmore before being hanged alive and then disembowelled and quartered but we have heard your plea for mercy and as Christmas does approach we commute the sentence to beheading. You will be taken from here to a chamber where we will provide a priest so that you may meet your God prepared. You will be executed on the morrow. Now as to the three men taken by Captain Hawkwood." They all looked up. "You will be taken from here now and hanged!"

One dropped to his knees and cried, "Mercy, Baron, mercy!"

The young Baron smiled, "But this is mercy for you will not be tortured first. You deserve such torture for it was not just warriors whom you slew, there were farmers and their families."

It was at that moment that I saw one of the men who had served at Knighton. Of Wilfred, there was no sign, but Baron Mortimer had other witnesses ready in case there was a counter-argument.

"Take them away and have their heads removed after the execution. Captain Hawkwood can place them on spikes at Knighton when he returns tomorrow morning."

The three were unceremoniously dragged away while a pair of men at arms led Lord Rhys out. It was then that eyes turned to me. The Baron said something to the Bishop and then said, "Hawkwood, come and join us."

I walked to the table behind which the Baron and the jury were seated. Sir Walter also sat down and gestured for me to sit between him and the Baron.

"Sir Walter remembers you from Gascony and the chevauchée which the Duke of Lancaster led. You were modest when you came to seek employment, archer, but I can see that you did not boast for this victory with just twenty men against a much larger force is impressive."

Sir Walter said, "Twenty men?"

I nodded, "We were behind walls and ditches we had improved, my lord, and the Welsh were poorly led."

"Yet from what I heard yesterday when your archer reported to the Baron, you and some of your men rode on horses and fought and defeated men at arms and a knight. You, indeed, unhorsed and defeated Lord Rhys!"

I smiled, "He was not a very good knight, my lords. He rode too far and exhausted his horse and while I have limited skills, I saw little evidence of much training in his strokes!"

The Baron beamed, "You have secured the border for me and in the Spring, I can retake Cefnllys and Rhayader."

It looked like I would have employment for another year. I was wondering if it would be impolite to have increased pay when he continued, "I shall need you to winter at Knighton but in February Sir Walter wishes men to serve with him, Prince

Edward and the King in an action against the French and the Castilians."

I turned to Sir Walter, "The King asked for me?"

He smiled, "I was sent here to ask the Baron for men at arms and archers to serve on ships. I had not even thought of you until your man came yesterday and I remembered that you had fought at Sluys with Sir Walter Manny. The Baron was more than happy to release you."

"Then I would be honoured. Baron, would it be rude of me to ask for a couple of the men who fought with me at Knighton? I know that it would weaken your garrison, but some have shown skill."

I thought he might be angry, but it was the opposite. He seemed delighted. "Of course! I have hired more men who will come in January to relieve you. I would have the change of garrison effected smoothly. Sir Walter will speak with you now and then we shall see you at the execution tomorrow. I will have decent food sent down to the warrior hall."

Sir Walter smiled, "Come with me, Hawkwood, and we will take a turn around the battlements."

He led me up to the top of the walls where we could walk and talk without the risk of being overheard. "This is fate, you know. I came here without much hope for I knew that the Baron was young. When I heard your name yesterday then I saw an answer to our dilemma. The Castilian pirate, although he calls himself a lord, Charles de la Cerda, has attacked and murdered the crews of many English and Gascon ships. Trade between Gascony and England has been interrupted and a fleet of over forty ships now lurks in Flanders threatening our trade. The wine ships cannot sail from Gascony!" I hid my smile. Lords could not be deprived of their wine. "This is not the season for sailing, and we are safe for the moment. The King is using a papal envoy to attempt to end this piracy, but we are not hopeful. The King and the Prince are gathering a fleet at Wynchchelse and the Cinque Ports. We need men like you to man them. When the talks fail and fail they will, then we will sail and end this pirate's reign."

"The King would hire us?"

"Aye, until the Castilian fleet is destroyed you and your men will be King's men."

"And how many men do you expect?"

He smiled, "If they are Hawkwood's men then as many as you can manage. You are to be at Wynchchelse by the first day of April. You will need to equip your company for battle. The King hires warriors and does not provide weapons."

I nodded and we agreed on a rate. We stopped at the top of the huge donjon and I said, "My lord, may I ask a question? It is not about the battle ahead but the trial." He nodded. "Why did the knight not defend himself in court? He must have known that there could be but one outcome."

Sir Walter smiled sadly, "That was down to you and your presence in the court. He was not defeated by a knight, nor even a man at arms but an archer. He was ashamed. You are right that he was a poor knight, but he was a knight, and all honour went the moment you unhorsed him."

"Ah."

"You know, Hawkwood, from what I have heard you could be a man at arms. Consider it, for there would be more advancement. Had you been a gentleman at arms then you might have dined with us in the Great Hall rather than with the garrison in the warrior hall."

"My lord, I am content. I lead my men and it is their respect which means more to me." I smiled, "Besides, regardless of the quality of the food, I will be more comfortable eating with the garrison. I will not have to worry about making a mistake!"

He laughed, "Aye, you are right there." We looked down and saw the three men at arms being hanged. Their bodies had been hauled up while we were speaking and now, they wriggled and struggled as they were slowly strangled. It was not the way a warrior should die.

I left the castle and went to the warrior hall. Michael said, "Do we leave now Captain? We can be back at Knighton just after dark."

I shook my head, "We leave on the morrow for we have to take the heads of the men at arms back to Knighton, but I have good news." While I enjoyed the ale provided I told them about our new contract."

Roger and Gareth looked apprehensive, "Fighting at sea, Captain, but we have no experience!"

"Roger, it is like fighting on land for a man with a sword. You do not have to ride but the ship does move. You keep your feet well apart." I shrugged, "And if you fall overboard then you have a swift death for your mail will drag you down. Do not worry. I fought at Sluys with Sir Walter Manny and I have confidence."

That evening two of the garrison who had left Knighton when we arrived sat with us. They wanted to know how we had succeeded when they had failed. We told them of our work on the defences and my strategy.

One of the men, John, nodded, "Wilfred had lost his desire, Captain. He is now a lay monk and he is at peace. We lost men we should not have lost."

"And will you be returning to Knighton?"

They both nodded, "The Baron has already told us that we have an opportunity to redeem ourselves and next time the Welsh will lose!"

"I think the heart has gone from the Welsh," I told them of the pile of bodies we had burned. "The plague and their foolish attack have stripped the land of warriors. You will be redeemed!"

I was keen to return to my castle, but I had to await the punishment. A raised platform had been erected in the centre of the outer bailey and as the chief witness, I was required to attend the execution. I confess that I had never seen one and was intrigued. When I had lived in London and served as an apprentice tailor, I had been unable to attend the many such executions. I stood with the Baron and the nobles as well as the Bishop. The executioner was one of the Baron's bodyguards and he looked as though he knew how to wield the axe. I knew, from others, that it was not as easy to chop off a head as people might think. Bones could get in the way. A drum began to beat and the Welsh knight was led from the donjon. He was not fettered, and he looked resigned. The steps he took were in time to the drumbeat; they were his last steps on this earth, few men had the dubious honour of knowing when death will strike. For most men, death came as a surprise on the battlefield, but Lord Rhys saw the manner of his death and it would be a very public one. I wondered what thoughts would be in his mind, his last thoughts on this earth. Would he be cursing me? The raised dais was not high and he took two steps on to it. He knelt before the Bishop who gave him his blessing. A priest had shriven him. He stood and took his purse from his belt. He took a golden florin from it and then handed the purse to the Bishop. "Would you see that my mother gets this, my lord?"

The Bishop nodded.

Lord Rhys turned and handed the florin to the executioner, "I pray you to make this a swift end."

The man nodded, "I will do my best, my lord, and you shall not suffer."

He placed his head on the block and, after looking at the Baron, who nodded, the executioner raised his axe and in one lightning quick move, took the knight's head. It was as clean a strike as I had seen. It was so swift that there was not as much blood as I had expected. The head would be displayed on the gatehouse. I had done my duty and so the four of us mounted our horses and led the ones we had brought for the four prisoners. If we were travelling to the muster, we would need them. The Baron did not come to see us off, but Sir Walter did. We took the heads of the men at arms with us.

"Captain, the Baron says you have between ten and fourteen men?"

I nodded, "Close enough."

"If you can hire more who match your high standards then the King or the Prince will pay. We can get warriors for hire anywhere but we would prefer warriors of quality."

"I will do my best. I intend to visit my archers who live in London and see if they can be persuaded to leave a life of peace."

He handed me a parchment, "Here is a royal warrant made out to you. It should mean you can stay in the holy houses along the King's Road. You will have to pay but they will not turn you away."

"Thank you, Sir Walter."

As we rode back to Knighton, I spoke to Michael about the archers who had served with us at Calais. My memory was shocking for I named archers who had died there. In the end, we could only name three still living. Ned and Jack could be sought in Southwark, but Luke could be anywhere. "When February comes, and we are paid off then we shall travel to Southwark. It will cost us coins but that cannot be helped. We have not done as well from this contract as I might have hoped."

Michael had a clever mind. "Captain we now have many more horses and once we reach London then we shall not need them all. We could sell them. The poor weapons we took from the Welsh can be melted down. They too can be sold."

"Aye, you are right, and I still have my chests with Basil of Tarsus." I realised, even as I spoke, that I also had the chest of coins I had recovered from Captain Philip. My men were my investment and when I led my own company and we hired out to princes in Italy, Spain and France, I would be a rich man! At least that was my dream.

The first thing I did when we returned, for it was not long before noon, was to gather just the warriors in the hall. I sent all else away, even Iago for this was not his business.

"We have been offered the chance to fight, for the King and the Prince have hired us for an indeterminate period from the start of April. We are paid here until February. Any man who is within this hall can come with me and be a Hawkwood man. You do not have to do so and any who choose can stay here at Knighton and be part of the new garrison." I looked around at the faces. My original men would all come, and I knew that without asking. I guessed, from what he had told me that Stephen would wish to join us, but I did not know the rest well enough. "If you choose to join me then I will be your paymaster and I will issue the orders. The King and the Prince may well appoint another to command me, but I will be the one who issues the orders in battle."

Maelwyn nodded, "You do not want a decision now, Captain?"

"No, you have until the first day of January and if you do not wish to serve there will be no hard feelings. I know that I am a hard taskmaster and that I have ruffled some of your feathers. I will not be changing. I am what I am and make no apologies for that. Do not expect honeyed words for it is not in my nature."

Over the days leading to Christmas, some of the men came to tell me that they wished to follow me. Stephen was no surprise.

Edward, Ben and Siôn surprised me by asking so quickly. The rest pondered. I would see them at night as they sat in the warrior hall debating. The other four tended to sit together.

Christmas was similar to the last one. The plague was not only fresh in people's minds, but there had also been another few outbreaks close to us. Lucton just south of Wigmore was completely wiped out. A soldier returning from the Holy Land brought it and within a week all were dead. There was suspicion once more of all those who came from the south and east. I explained this particularly deadly plague by rationalising that it was not an English plague but one from the far east. I thought back to Oswald's death and my burning of his house. I had not caught it. When we had disposed of the dead Scots who had attacked us, we had not caught it. We had been briefly unwell but there had been no growths nor blackened skin. We would still stake precautions and use vinegar-soaked cloth when we came to a place we did not know but they were just that, precautions.

On the first day of January Maelwyn, Dafydd and Dai came to the keep to speak with me. Maelwyn spoke, "Dafydd here would follow you but I am here to say that I will not."

"Thank you but you need not have done so."

He said, "I am here to give a reason. I am to marry Dai's mother, Myfanwy."

"Congratulations."

"All is well with Dai, her eldest child, and he is happy for us to wed but he would serve you." My eyes bored into him. He shrugged and explained, "I spoke with Myfanwy and he heard. He wishes to be a warrior and although he is not an archer, he can use a bow. You will need a servant and Dai is happy to perform that service. His mother knows she cannot keep him here."

I nodded, "Thank you Maelwyn and, Dafydd, welcome to my company. You may leave. Dai, take a seat and we will talk."

I interrogated the youth, for he had grown over the past months, and I discovered that he had very genuine reasons to become a soldier. I used every argument I could conjure to dissuade him but he was happy to clean up horse muck so long as he could be a Hawkwood man. In the end, it was the memory of me walking up the Great North Road and falling in with four archers as well as the discovery of an emaciated Michael which persuaded me. This was meant to be!

Old James rode with eight men to the castle in the middle of January. He had news for me. The winter had been remarkably mild. Iago thought that was the reason for the return of the plague. The previous winter had been colder, and he was certain that the cold killed the disease. I was not sure for it had been much colder in Hartburn and yet the plague had still killed.

"The Baron sent me for he is sending the new Captain in a week. I am to be part of the garrison."

"We are to be released early?"

"Aye, but he will pay you until the end of February. When he went to Rhayader he claimed the land and made Lord Rhys' widow a ward. He took the treasure from the hall and is much richer now." He added quietly, "He knows he owes this to you."

I was relieved. The snow had yet to come and I wanted to be deeper into England and further south when it did arrive. My Welsh adventure was almost over, and it had not cost me anything. I had more men and thanks to the Baron, more money than I might have expected. God was smiling on me.

Chapter 10

We reached Southwark after a two-week journey. I saw the effect of the plague in the deserted and often burned villages and farms which lay along our route. The monks in the houses we used told us tales of barrowloads of bodies being buried in quicklime or burned to prevent the disease spreading, as they told us it was not yet eradicated and would return. They advised us to wear garlic and pray to God!

The Castle Inn at Southwark was a popular tavern for many pilgrims travelling to Canterbury used it. Since the pestilence had come its business had almost dried up and they were more than happy to accommodate the eighteen of us. It would cost me, but the inn was friendly, and I had the money. It also reunited us with Ned and Jack. I had wondered if they had gone off with some other captain, but they had spent the time since Calais drinking, eating and enjoying the company of women. Ned had even married but his wife had died of the plague.

Robin asked his old friend, "How is it that you did not catch it? You are not a ghost, are you?"

He smiled, "I honestly do not know. I cared for her when she was sick, and I became a little unwell but I developed no other signs. For that reason, Captain Hawkwood, I will follow your banner again. I will become Ned the Wanderer once more."

Jack nodded, "And I cannot let this old fool go alone so I will come, too!"

I patted his belly, "And will that be before or after you have given birth?"

My archers, especially Robin, found that hilarious and Jack nodded. "Once I work at the bow it will go, Captain. If we are not needed until April, then I have time!"

"And I will go with Michael and Dai to Southampton. I need more of my coins and there may be archers who seek employment there. Robin, you can command here and seek any archers who wish to join my company."

Ned shook his head, "Captain, London was hit hard by the pestilence. It is only because we were south of the river that we did not suffer more. You crossed the river by the bridge, but most people use the ferries, and the ferrymen were amongst the first to die. Now the new ones charge five times what the old ones did."

"Our world will be changed by this. Ned and Jack if you change your mind about leaving before we have to leave for Wynchchelse I will understand."

They both shook their heads and Ned said, "We have missed the world of war and our comrades too much. The pestilence has spread across our world and if we can make a profit from it then so be it."

It was a grim three-day ride to Southampton for the pestilence had struck hard in this part of the world. The monks with whom we stayed told us that the disease had landed in Dorset and spread north. The people in the south found that they had the disease before they knew that the pestilence had landed. I realised how fortuitous was our decision to go north for we had more warning of the imminent arrival of the invisible, creeping death. It had been so bad that my misbehaviour in the inn we used was forgotten and we even found news when we asked for rooms.

"An archer came to seek you six months since. His name was..." the innkeeper turned to his wife, "Ada, what was that archer's name? You know the one who asked for Captain Hawkwood?"

She scratched her head, "It was a name from the Bible, one of the gospels I think."

"Luke?"

"Aye, that was him."

"And where did he go?"

The man looked at me dumbly and said, "He had no money. We threw him out."

Suddenly I did not feel so bad about my poor behaviour. I owed this man nothing. "Dai, see to the horses and then arrange our gear in our room. We will just stay one night. You had better guard our belongings."

The innkeeper could hear the anger in my voice and he said, "Captain, there is no need for that!"

"I will be the judge of that. Come Michael, we will search Southampton for an hour and then seek Basil of Tarsus."

We went to all the places where an out of work soldier might seek shelter. There were others there who were in the same position as Luke, but we did not find our friend. As it was getting on towards dusk, I went to find Basil of Tarsus. The Jew had two huge bodyguards, Hob and Tam. They had tried to intimidate me when first I had visited but they had quickly realised that they were no match for me or my men. I was expecting them but when the door opened it was Luke, my archer who opened it. My mouth dropped open and Luke grinned.

From within came the Jew's voice, "Who is it?"

"Captain Hawkwood and one of his men!"

"Then get them in and quickly!"

Questions were dancing around inside my head. They were like angry wasps. I knew I would have to wait for answers. The Jew looked ill and my hand went to my cross. Where were Tam and Hob? Did he have the plague?

He seemed to read my mind for he waved a hand, "It is just the winter coughing sickness. This island is the wettest I have ever endured, and this sickness comes each winter. Sit before the fire. Luke, take the Captain's man and fetch wine and food. I will answer the questions I see in his eyes." They left and he folded his hands, "When the pestilence came I closed my doors for I knew that was the safest thing to do but the mob, when families started to die, blamed the Jews and they broke in. Hob was killed before Tam, although wounded, managed to rid the house of them. We summoned the watch, and we were protected." Luke and Michael returned and served us food and wine. "What we did not know was that Tam's wound was mortal. Perhaps some cloth was on the blade but, whatever the reason, over the next month he deteriorated and then died leaving me helpless. The plague meant that people remained indoors or else they could have come in and taken all of my treasures. Then Luke, looking a lot thinner than he does now, came to my door seeking help. God sent him. He has been my bodyguard since then." He smiled and sipped his wine, "And you have survived too. Let us drink to survival."

"To survival." The wine was good as I knew it would be.

"You have come for some of your money?" I nodded. "Your investments have done well. The pestilence hurt people, but it made goods more expensive. You are almost a rich man although if you take all of your money from me you will be losing future profits."

I put my hand up, "I have no intention of taking out all of my money. I need money to keep my men while we await our next commission."

Basil leaned forward, "You go to war again? Where?"

"Why do you wish to know?"

"There is always a profit in war. If France is attacked or there is war in Gascony, then wine is in short supply. I can buy now while it is cheaper. If there is war when the harvest is being collected, then prices will be higher and I can buy cereal and keep it stored."

"And if I tell you then what is in it for me?"

"I will invest your money and you will be richer!"

That made perfect sense to me and I nodded, "In the summer we fight the French and Castilian ships which cause havoc with our ships!"

He beamed and clapped his hands together, "Then I will wait to buy wine until you have won when the prices will begin to fall and I will now invest in ships for King Edward will need to hire ships. If they are sunk, then he has to recompense the owners. I will buy old ships for a low price and claim back more. You, Captain Hawkwood, are good for business. And how much do you want from your account?"

"Just a hundred florins and I would like Luke to rejoin my company."

Basil shook his head, "Luke has replaced Hob and Tam and he is valuable to me."

"And he saves you money for you only need one man rather than two." I did not look at Luke, but I said, "And we both know that if I asked Luke to rejoin my company he would do so for he is an archer!"

Basil's head slumped, "Aye, you are right. We are a cursed people!"

"I do not need him yet. It will be on April the first when we need to be at Wynchchelse. You have until the end of March to replace him." I finally looked at Luke, "You wish to come?"

"Aye, Captain, but I have neither bow nor arrows. I was forced to sell them."

"Fear not, we have a fletcher who can also make bows. There will be a bow for you. You still have your gardyvyan?"

"Of course."

"Then replace what you need, and I shall see you at Wynchchelse."

Basil gave me my money and the written account I insisted upon. I did not think he would cheat me, but I needed to know what I held. I was pleased that Luke had found a home, but I was still angry with the innkeeper. When we returned, he was beaming, "You completed your business? Good. My wife has a fine meal prepared."

I shook my head, "It would taste like sawdust for you are not a Christian man that you throw out my friend."

"But we did not know and if we had…"

I gave him a thin smile, "Then you would have rooked me. We will find a more wholesome table, and this is the last time we will stay here. More, I will tell all that I meet that this inn is to be avoided." I waved to Dai, "Come Dai, let us go to the harbour where there are good places to eat! I have a mind to eat fish and shellfish!"

Sometimes you make a decision, and it sets you on a path you might not otherwise have chosen. That happened to us as we headed to the harbour and inns which were by the waterfront and rough but also served the best food. Archers all have broad chests, and I was no exception. Michael too had filled out so that when the three of us entered the harbourside tavern, The Siren's End, every eye turned to us. Inside there were mainly sailors or those who went to sea but others in the tavern looked to have interesting tales to tell. Compared with the rest of the customers Michael and I were well dressed and the owner or at least the man I took to be the owner scurried over and led us to a table occupied by a single man.

"Old Tom, join another table for I have three customers here who look like they will do more than nurse a pot of ale until they can cadge another!"

The old man stood and went off to another table with a single occupant. The diversion of our entrance over, the rest went back to their ale and their platters of food.

"What is good to eat, innkeeper?"

"Why everything, my lord."

"I am no lord as well you know so do not try to rook me by inflating your prices. I am Captain Hawkwood and I serve the King."

I had spent enough time in Southampton for my name to be known and his attitude changed, "The fish soup is the best value, Captain." He shrugged, "It is what I would choose."

"Then fetch it and a jug of ale for three thirsty men." I smiled as Dai sat up a little straighter. I had called him a man.

While we waited for our food and ale we chatted. Dai's eyes were wide as he looked at the mix of men in the room. He heard accents he had never heard before and the shades of skin varied too. There were no Moors but there were sailors from Lusitania as well as Norway. The pale Norse contrasted with the olive coloured Lusitanians. Michael said, "Who would have thought that Luke would end up as a bodyguard for a Jew?"

I nodded as the jug came and I poured us three beakers, "Yet he came back to our service quickly enough."

"Do you think that Basil will be able to replace him?"

I shook my head, "Not with just one man. Luke replaced two and it will take two to replace Luke. With the pestilence taking so many, it will be hard but there will be men who lost their paymasters. The trick will be to choose the right ones. He has time."

I saw a man slip into the tavern. It was his almost furtive movements which attracted my attention. I was used to looking for such things. I did not recognise him, but I knew the type. He was what used to be called a hobelar or light horseman. In the time of the first King Edward, they were common. Now there were fewer of them. There had been some at Crécy. His clothes, however, told a tale. I saw that the sole was hanging from one buskin and his scabbard was empty. He had a dagger and a hatchet instead. His brigandine was worn while his breeks needed repair. There were a couple of upturned empty barrels and after he had bought a beaker of ale, he sat on one which was in the shadows of the corner. He needed ale but he did not wish to be seen.

Michael asked, "What is so interesting about the man, Captain?"

"The fact that he does not wish to be seen and that ale is his priority when, from his gaunt features, food is the priority."

Dai said, innocently, "Perhaps he prefers ale to food, Captain."

I smiled, as our food arrived, "And such men have a weakness. I like ale but given the choice of food or ale, I will take food every time. And now let us see if we were advised well." I looked up at the tavern owner.

He smiled, "If you are unhappy with the taste then the bread is free!"

I nodded, "Put an extra loaf on my bill and give it to the hobelar who just entered and sits alone."

He looked over and said, "You mean Henry the Luckless?"

I nodded as Michael asked, "Why such a name?"

"He fought at Crécy and captured a knight as well as slaying four others. Prince Edward himself gave him a reward of fifty florins. He came home and spent most of it on ale. He used to drink in here all the time. Then he found a woman, Mary, and she saved him from himself. He became sober and found employment with Lord Hardacre. The pestilence took his lordship, his family as well as Mary and Henry's daughter. He lost his position and he dived into the bottom of a jug again."

Dai said, "But if he survived and the others died surely that makes him lucky?"

I shook my head, "No, he is well named. Give him another ale with the bread, innkeeper for I see why he wishes to lose himself in ale."

I began to eat, and the fish soup was good. It was more of a stew and cooked in the French style. Many small fish and shellfish had been cooked until the flesh had fallen from the bones. Roughly sieved, winter greens and dried beans had been added along with garlic and the last of the autumn onions. I liked it. I took the small pouch of pepper I carried. I had acquired it in the chevauchée in Gascony. It had been much larger in those days and I did not share my bounty but a few grains in whatever food I ate transformed the food into a feast. I never used it when I dined in monasteries or the halls of the great and the good. They would have considered it an insult.

The hobelar was served the bread and the innkeeper pointed over to us. The man raised his beaker in acknowledgement, and I nodded. As I ate, I watched the way the hobelar ate the bread slowly as though eking it out. When we finished the food, I waved over the innkeeper. "You were right. Bring us the bill and another small jug of ale and then we shall leave."

We had almost finished when I saw three men enter who looked like bandits. They wore hoods and unlike the rest of the men who wore hoods they kept them up covering their features. The knives they had along with their swords were killer's weapons. It was not just me who recognised the type for the other customers viewed them with suspicion in their eyes. When we three had entered it had been curiosity only. Henry the Luckless saw them and I saw his eyes dart nervously to the door. He was working out if he could reach it before they did.

"Drink up, boys."

Dai said, "But I have only just started this one!"

Michael laughed, "Then drink it quickly and if you fall then I shall carry you." He became serious for he saw my gaze, "And besides the Captain spies trouble."

I drank the ale in one and stood, I raised my hand and said, louder than was needed, "Thank you, innkeeper. I shall recommend your ale and food." As I had expected the three hooded men all looked around at me and Henry the Luckless took his opportunity and headed for the door.

He was quick but the three men saw him and began to move. As I stood, I feigned a stagger, and my left foot tripped the second of the three and he brought down the last one. As the customers laughed I put my hand down to help the man I had tripped to his feet, "I am sorry, my friend, it is always the last jug of ale that makes a man forget to know how to stand."

The scar-faced bandit shook my hand free, "Get off me you fool!"

He and the other bandit hurried out of the door. I had given Henry the Luckless less than a few moments' grace, but I hoped he would use it wisely. As we stepped out, I saw that close to the edge of the dock, Henry was fighting with the first bandit. The other two were hurrying to finish the job.

"Dai, find the watch. Michael draw your sword. Let us see if we can scare them off."

I saw that Henry the Luckless had felled the man with whom he had been fighting but the other two had reached him and he had no avenue of escape left except to jump into the harbour. We ran and I held my sword before me. I heard one of them say, "You thought you could hide from us, did you? The Frenchman does not like those who owe him money to leave his service."

"I owed him no money!"

The scar-faced man laughed, "Then tell him that and he might only take your left hand!"

My voice made the three bandits start for we had approached silently. "Friend, step away from this man."

The one who had been felled stood and the three turned. Seeing our swords, they drew their weapons, "You again! We shall have your purse and your weapons, and this man will still pay the price for flight!"

They did not see us as a threat and could not have known that beneath our cloaks we both wore mail shirts. They came at us. Henry the Luckless could have fled and, to be honest, I would not have blamed him, but he did not. He wrapped his arms around the man he had felled and wrestled him to the ground. As my sword clashed with Scarface, I heard shouts behind me and knew that Dai had fetched the watch. I saw my opponent's left hand move quickly and I knew that he had drawn a knife. I put my left hand down and grabbed his wrist, but he still managed to stab towards my middle. The edge of the knife caught on the mail links and the shirt, along with my left hand, arrested the movement. Our swords were locked, and our faces were close. I began to turn his left hand and I saw, in his eyes, what his next move would be. He tried to headbutt me. I did the only move I thought might save me. I lowered my head so that his forehead connected with the top of my head and he was hurt more than me. I did not intend it, but I was forcing his left hand up and the butt made him stagger. The sharp blade drove up under his ribs. As he sank to the ground, I heard a splash and turning I saw that Michael's opponent had been mortally struck.

The brands of the night watch illuminated the bloody scene and the three men pointed their spears at us. "Sheath your weapons and explain yourselves!"

I did so, sticking Scarface's dagger in my belt as I did so. "I am Captain Hawkwood serving the King and we saw this man being attacked by three men. When we asked them to stop, they attacked us, and we defended ourselves. It was I summoned the watch."

One of the watch knelt and examined the face of the man I had killed, "This is Bart the Scar."

The sergeant in command nodded and I saw that his spear moved away from our chests. He pointed to Henry the Luckless, "He is also known to us and has been warned about his vagrancy. I will take him to the castle."

I put my hand, still bloody, on the sergeant's arm. "I will take responsibility for him."

"Can you prove who you say you are?"

I took the parchment from my tunic and nodded to Michael at the same time. It took some time for the three men of the watch to read the parchment which Sir Walter had given me and in that time, he took the two swords from the two dead men.

"Very well, now begone. We will deal with these!"

I nodded, "Come Henry. It seems I am responsible for you now." He wandered over, bruised, battered and dazed.

As we headed away from the light Dai said, "What will they do with them?"

Just then I heard a splash, "They have done it. They took their purses, boots and anything else of value and dropped the bodies in the harbour. The crabs we ate in the stew were well fed. I am guessing that there are bodies aplenty at the bottom of the harbour."

"Captain, I thank you, but you need feel no responsibility towards me. I can look after myself!"

I laughed, "So I can see. No, Henry, I am responsible, but you can serve me if you will. I am commissioned by the King to fight for him next summer. The innkeeper told me of your prowess. It is but four years since the battle where you were rewarded. I do not think that you will have lost all of your skills. Would you join my company?"

"I would but I have no sword!"

Michael was like a magician and the sword appeared from beneath his cloak. "Now you have!" He handed the other to Dai, "And you might as well have this one too!"

The next day, with Dai and Henry riding double, we headed back to Southwark. I had two more men; an archer and a hobelar. My company was growing! Over the next month, I found two more archers. Like Henry they had fallen on hard times and, once more, I had to dip into the money I had taken from Basil to equip them. I kept telling myself that it was an investment. What it did do was make my new men both grateful and loyal. Peter the Archer and Joseph of Chester had both fought in Gascony and whilst no longer young were both good archers. We discovered that when we practised at the butts. We headed to Wynchchelse early. I knew we would be camping and did not know how long that would be. I wanted the best camp for my twenty men.

Chapter 11

Travelling the seventy miles or so to Wynchchelse was depressing as it took us through some of the most severely devastated parts of England. Here we saw the signs, even in small towns, of the empty and marked houses of the plague victims. We made the journey in two days with just one overnight stop. Thanks to our time in Southwark we were well equipped and those like Henry, Richard and the like who had lost almost everything now had clothes and boots. They would receive less pay until I had been recompensed but as they were all now well fed and well-shod they were happy enough and the prospect of a battle against pirates who were known to be rich and to keep their gold with them promised much.

When we reached Wynchchelse, I was pleased we had arrived early. The sites for the camp were marked and some had erected tents already. It was a damp and boggy area, and I ignored the instructions to camp there. Instead, I headed for the beach and the dunes. We would be dry and have shelter whilst still being close enough to the port to embark. Already there were some ships moored ready to board. While my men erected the tents which we were given I went to see whoever was in command. The old town had been destroyed by a flood and the first King Edward had rebuilt it in a very organised manner. The roads were all straight and the intersections were evenly distributed. The guildhall was the largest building, and I went there. I recognised the livery of Prince Edward and I approached the clerk who was outside checking off supplies which had just arrived by wagon.

I waited until he had finished before I spoke, "I am a vintenar, Captain Hawkwood and I have a commission from the King. Sir Walter Pavely commanded us to come here."

The man nodded and searched through the documents he held, "Ah yes. The number of men is not stipulated but you say there are twenty?"

I had no idea of his title and so I just said, "Aye, and a boy! We have camped by the beach."

He frowned, "But the campsites are clearly marked and designated!"

"And they are disease-ridden death traps! We will camp by the beach. What are the arrangements for food and cooking facilities?" I had seen few others and knew that this organised little man had been caught unawares.

"Erm, if you return at dusk, I will have some supplies for you. As for cooking…"

I saw a small stand of trees dotted along the higher ground to the north, "We will find kindling there." He might have been going to argue but he saw the look on my face and let it pass.

Until May there was just a trickle of men but suddenly a mighty host descended so that by the first day of June there was not only an armed camp but a harbour which was filling with ships. There were well over twenty and they varied from small ships to larger cogs. The Prince also arrived along with the knights he would lead.

I had got to know the clerk, Absalom, and found that he was not as officious as he had first appeared. He had been given a duty for which he had neither the experience nor the training. He was a scrivener by profession and wrote what others said. He was having to act as a quartermaster. Once I discovered that I was able to offer him advice. I realised that he had been the one who had chosen the campsite. He had done so because it was flat, and he had not thought about the issue of flooding. Between us, we found a better area so that when Prince Edward arrived, he was able to thank Absalom. I had made a friend and while I could not envisage a situation where I might benefit from the friendship of a scrivener it did no harm. It was Absalom who came for me one evening in the middle of June.

"Prince Edward wishes to speak with you, vintenar. Come with me."

He led me not to the town but the port and when I arrived, I saw him surrounded by knights, including Sir Walter. I waited behind the knights for I was a commoner and knew my place. Sir Walter spied me and shouted, "Come, Captain, for we need to speak with you."

The knights parted and I moved close to the Prince. I had not seen him since Crécy and now I saw the man. He was twenty

years old and looked like a warrior. He had led many men during
the great victory over the French and it had given him
confidence. He grinned when he saw me, "Hawkwood! It is good
to see you and I have heard great things of you from the
Archbishop of York as well as the Bishop of Durham and Baron
Mortimer! I am surprised that you have not sought your spurs!"

I said nothing for no matter what I wanted I could not make
that happen. Knighthood was the gift of those above me.

"Sir Walter here will be in command of my ship and your
men will be amongst the crew. This is my ship, Cog Richard.
Her captain is Richard of Rye. This will be your new home until
the threat from the Castilian pirates is gone. I return tomorrow to
Rotherhithe; Sir Walter will remain here. Address your questions
and requests to him, I pray you." He turned to the others, "Come,
gentlemen, while I allocate you your ships."

Sir Walter shook his head and grinned, "He is a young man
who knows his own mind. Come aboard. We climbed aboard the
vessel which had a single mast. It was one of the bigger ones and
was twenty paces long and eight paces wide. There was no castle
either at the bow or the stern and, while we had been at
Wynchchelse, I had spoken to sea captains in the harbourside
taverns and asked them about the enemy. The French, it seemed,
were not the problem. It was the Castilian pirates who were.
Since April they had been blockading the ports along the
southern coast and they had castles at the stern and the bow of
their ships. In addition, these mercenaries had bigger ships which
meant that they could tower over these small cogs.

The Captain was a small man with short legs. I later learned
that his stature, rather being a problem was actually a benefit for
with his legs spread wide he rarely took a tumble. He was at the
stern and I saw that unlike some ships, which had a steering
board, this one had a rudder.

"Captain Richard, Captain Hawkwood and his men will form
part of your crew."

He beamed and I saw that he had lost his front teeth. With all
the items which could fly around in a storm that was not a
surprise. He held out a hand and firmly shook my hand. This,
apparently, was a tradition amongst seafaring men. "None of this
Captain Richard and Captain Hawkwood. By the time we have

greeted each other, the Castilians will have taken my ship! I am Dick!"

I liked him immediately for he was an honest and open man. "I am John!"

"Well John, this vessel is an old one but is sound! We can turn quickly and there is no weed on her keel. How many men do you bring?"

"I lead eleven archers and nine men at arms. I have a youth who is agile and can use a bow and a sling."

Dick gestured with his right thumb, "Then he can be in the nest at the top of the mast. It is a precarious climb but once there a skilled youth can do some damage! Both sides will try to kill the enemy captains." He seemed unconcerned about the fact that he would be in mortal danger.

Sir Walter said, "Make no mistake Captain Hawkwood, if we are captured then we will simply be thrown overboard. The Castilians have done so already with the crews of the thirty ships they have captured!"

Dick nodded and his happy face became grim, "Aye, I have lost good friends! Still, let us be optimistic. I have met our Prince and he impresses me despite his lack of years."

I looked around the deck and saw that there were handles along the side, "They are there to give access to the hold?"

"They are. We lift out sections as and when we need them and you and your lads can use them to store your gear. Until the other fighting men arrive you have the whole of the deck forrard of the mast. There will be some room aft of the mast, but my lads sleep there. When we are at sea it will be a little cosier."

"And the food?"

He pointed to the stone quay, "We build a fire there. No fire on a ship as that would be deadly. We are well provisioned with salted meat. There is ale and those barrels are in the hold. Until the other fighting men arrive, we will leave them there."

I nodded, "I will fetch my men. We have had enough of sandflies!"

We broke camp quickly enough, but we had a problem for we had twenty-five horses and ponies. It was then that my new relationship with Absalom came to my aid. As we walked back to the harbour, I saw him speaking with a carter. I waited until he had finished and then said, "Absalom, we will be based on the ship from now on. What about our horses?"

He frowned and then said, brightly, "I should have planned for this. Others will be needing to leave their horses, and some will be coursers and destriers." He meant they were important and ours were not. "I will have to hire boys to watch them and erect a fence. We can use the place I planned on placing the camp. Could your men watch them this night?" I nodded. "I am grateful and yours will be given special consideration."

I nodded. I trusted the little man, "Then as part of that consideration I would have you guard a chest for me." I did not threaten for I did not need to and he nodded his agreement. My money would be safe, and I would reward Absalom when I returned.

It was a week before the rest of the men and archers joined us. During that week I got to know my new men a little better for we were closely confined on the deck of the ship and both Michael and I felt responsible for Henry. When you save a man, you take on the debt of his life. Henry was now luckless no longer, but he was lonely. Through his own weakness and fate, he had sunk to the bottom of a jug and Michael and I spent the evenings chatting to him. Robin and my archers did the same for the archers we had taken on. Henry was a man at arms. As a man at arms, Henry would regain his strength and skills faster than an archer when they ceased to practise. Fortunately, Luke, when he had worked for Basil of Tarsus, had managed to get to the butts once a week. The time in Southwark and on the beach had allowed Henry to become as strong as he had ever been. As we weaned him from his dependence on ale he became more open with us and confided in us that he had known what the ale and drink were doing to him but that he was powerless to stop it. I saw a way to keep his mind on the job and I asked him to take Stephen under his wing. He was the youngest of the men I had with me and despite having killed a man at arms he still needed experience. "I need you to become his shield brother so that you can watch each other's backs."

He nodded and smiled, "And while I worry about him then the demons of the drink will not fill my mind. I can see that you are a wise man, Captain."

It did not seem to matter that he had seen through my ploy. He did not resent it. At the end of the week, a colourful company of archers and spearmen arrived to take their place in the centre of the cog. These were from the Prince's own household and they brought news. The Pope had brokered a truce but all that it meant was that the pirates had thrown off all pretence of serving France. We had a war with pirates.

Life was not easy with the men who served Prince Edward. None of these had fought at Crécy. They thought themselves superior to us and that was a mistake. None would dare strike the Captain of the company, but they tried to bully my men. Each time had the same result. The Prince's men came off worse. Eventually, Captain Guillaume who captained them came to see me. Thanks to our early arrival we had the high ground, quite literally, and our camp close to the bow was the best on the ship. I waved my men away. Their murderous looks told me that they had endured enough of the harassment.

Captain Guillaume was a Gascon. I must have fought alongside him when I was with Lord Henry, the Duke of Lancaster, but I did not remember him. "Captain Hawkwood, this petty bickering must stop. It is not good."

I smiled, but not with my eyes, "Your men began this and cannot finish it. You have fallen short, Captain, of the standard a Captain should set. My men fought at Crécy and Neville's Cross. They regained Calais. What have your men done?" I had raised my voice so that it carried to the Prince's men. "I will tell you what they have done. They donned a tunic and paraded like popinjays. They came aboard this ship and they challenged my men and now that they have been, quite rightly, put in their place you complain! I tell you this, Captain, the measure of a leader is in the quality of the men he leads." I turned and glowered at the Prince's men. "Until these apologies for warriors show me that they know how to fight England's enemies then they are about as much use as the barnacles on the bottom of Captain Richard's ship." I stopped and smiled, "No, I am wrong. A barnacle has more use for you can scrape it off and eat it. The next time you come to speak to me it will be with an apology for your men's behaviour." I shrugged, "I may accept it, but I doubt it. Now unless you wish to draw a weapon then withdraw to your end of the ship!" I saw his hand go to his sword. I said, quietly, "Please draw it. It is many months since I hurt another warrior and you, I would cut down to size in a heartbeat."

I saw, in his eyes, that he believed me and more, that he feared me. He nodded and went back to his men. There was no more trouble, but I knew then that the Prince would be unhappy. I did not care for he needed us. I knew now that we were the best he had and that was why we were his first choice for his ship. He chose us before his own warriors.

It was July when we were sent to sea. Sit Walter returned from a meeting with the Prince and led the fleet in manoeuvres. This was not to fight but to practise the tactics we would use for the pirates had continued to take English ships and slaughter their crews. Surprisingly, the Prince was not there nor was the King, but Sir Walter gave the orders from our ship. When I had fought in the battle of Sluys I had just been an archer but now I was a vintenar who could use a sword well and I sailed on the flagship. I saw more of the plans which the Prince and his father intended to employ. It took five days for us to become familiar with the signals and the manoeuvres the Prince wished us to adopt. This was not like fighting on land. Here it was not the predictable hills, roads and woods. The wind and the sea were, by their very nature unpredictable and there were collisions and accidents. Men died but none on our ship. I concentrated upon looking to the way we would perform our task. Dai was in the nest and he was a quick learner. He could spot a potential accident before it could happen, and Captain Richard rewarded him with a shilling after two days for he was alert enough to shout and avoid us ramming Cog Thomas.

At the end of a week, we were better, but I knew we would struggle against men who fought at sea almost every day. If we were to win then it would be down to my control over my men. Some of my men were able to use the fore and backstays for support and release arrows. The four who could do so would target the steersmen and officers. The rest, I decided, would pick off the enemy crossbows and archers. My men at arms would be the ones to lead the assault and I reasoned that it was better to fight on an enemy ship than ours. We practised swinging from

ropes hung from the crosstree. We did this in the harbour and
without mail. The worst we suffered was a soaking!

The Prince arrived at the end of the first week in August. He
had news and as we were on his ship, we heard it first. We were
to rendezvous with other ships off Sandwich where the King
would join us. The King, it seemed, had learned of Charles de la
Cerda's plans. He knew where the Spaniard would make his next
raid and he intended to be there and bring him to battle. The
Castilian's spies had told him that the Prince was at
Wynchchelse and he planned on destroying the fleet at anchor.
The cog became almost unbearably crowded. Anticipating the
larger numbers, my men and I had taken our gear from below
decks and used our belongings to lay claim to a small area of the
deck that we had enjoyed when we had solitary use of the cog.
The Prince brought not only knights but also minstrels. It took
almost three hours for our part of the fleet to assemble outside
the harbour and then to sail along the coast to Sandwich. Banners
flew from mastheads and announced who we were. Some of my
men and I had done this before but for the likes of Stephen, Dai
and the Wigmore men it was a strange experience. It took longer
to reach Sandwich than they anticipated and when we reached it,
we had to wait a day while the King and his son conferred.

We sailed in the late afternoon and to my amazement we
sailed back the way we had come. Of course, the voyage back
was much quicker for we had the wind with us. As we sailed the
minstrels played airs and we heard singing coming from the
King's ship, cog Thomas. It was a strange experience. As the sun
set ahead of us and we headed west I spent the time with my men
going through our tactics for the battle, whenever it would be
fought.

"Dai, you will be the most important of my company." I saw
him swell with pride. "In your lofty nest you will see the enemy
first and when the battle is joined you will have the best
opportunity to slay the enemy. Go for those who steer the ship."
He nodded, "But you have a more important task for you will be
able to see any danger to the ship. You need to tell Captain
Richard and me!" I turned to the archers, "Like Dai you need to
use your arrows wisely. We are the best archers in the fleet, and
we do not waste them. We hit those who can hurt our Captain;

their crossbows and archers must be slain. As for the rest, use your shields to protect the archers and when I deem it to be right, then follow me aboard the enemy ships. The men at arms will be the ones who hurl the grappling hooks to bind us together. That is how we fight. We wear mail and if we fall into the sea it will be a quick death. Do not fall into the sea!" They laughed. "When we board the enemy ships then the archers can use their hand weapons." I lowered my voice, "Remember these pirates carry treasure! Let us be the ones to reap the reward and not the Prince's popinjays! We will be the first aboard!"

They cheered and I saw the others on the ship all look around. I smiled and shrugged. My company was in good spirits and that was all that counted. We would do the Prince's work, but we would also watch out for each other!

When we reached Dungeness, it was noon and we turned into the wind. Dick had explained to me, while we were in the harbour, how these things worked. While we could not sail directly into the wind we could sail at an angle. The slower speed, Dick had said, would help us to stay together. So as we bobbed, just keeping way, we were so close that I could hear the young Sir John Chandos singing on Cog Thomas which was next to us. We two ships would be the arrowhead of the fleet. Dai had a great responsibility, and it was his voice which stopped Sir John's singing.

"Captain, a mighty fleet heading from the east. I count twenty-five, no, twenty-seven sails. They are big ships!"

The Prince shouted, "A florin for your man, Hawkwood!"

The King's voice shouted, from his cog, "All ships take station on us! For God, England and St. George! Let us get amongst these murderous pirates and make England's seas safe once more."

Every ship which was close erupted in cheers. I donned my helmet and strung my bow. I then folded my cloak and gardyvyan. I wrapped and tied them around my body. The odds were we would leave the ship at some point and I wanted all of my gear with me added to which it would afford more protection for me. My shield rested against the gunwale. My archers copied me. Although it was uncomfortable to be so encased, we had more protection from enemy arrows and bolts. My men all wore brigandines, but a bolt could penetrate that. I selected a good arrow and held it next to the bow.

Being at the bows of the ship we had the best view and I clambered up to the bowsprit and forestay. Bracing myself I looked at the approaching fleet.

Dai's voice drifted down, "Captain Richard, there are another twenty sails on the horizon!"

While that was not a surprise it meant that we were evenly matched in numbers and as I gazed towards the Castilian fleet I could see, even at this distance, that all of their ships were higher and bigger than ours. They would have the advantage. Having the wind, they were approaching more rapidly but that meant that while we were together, they were spread out. However, the royal standards at our mastheads told the Castilians where the King and Prince were to be found. We would have the hottest part of the battle for they would come for us! We were the prize they sought!

I heard the Prince and his knights, including Sir Walter, toast each other. For them, this was still all about honour and glory. For my men, it was about survival and gold! It took an hour for us to close. We were running before the wind as were the Castilians for neither side wished to give the enemy the wind gauge, but we had shortened our sails and that would give us more control. There was little point in either side wasting arrows or bolts and so we watched the converging fleets for some time as we drew closer together. The closer they came the larger they appeared to be. It was like castles compared with cottages. The three which appeared to be heading for us were the largest in the fleet and they had two castles at the bow and stern filled with crossbowmen. That gave me some hope for it would take longer for them to reload than it did us.

I shouted, "Hawkwood, clear the castles first." The Prince's men could do what they wanted for we were at the bow and we would release the first arrows.

Dick was edging us as close as he could to the large ship on our larboard side. The King's ship, being the newer of the two was ahead of us and now was closing with the leading Castilian ship. I returned to the bowsprit. It made me a target and put me in danger of tumbling overboard but the extra height and view it afforded would help my strike. I balanced myself and it was the steady pace of Captain Richard which helped me. A bolt slammed into the bowsprit perilously close to my foot and I saw other bolts as they came towards me. That meant that we were in range and the six crossbows which had sent their bolts at me would take time to reload. The Castilians had hired Flemish mercenaries. They were known to be the best of crossbowmen and if we could kill them then the Castilian cause would be hurt.

As I released, I shouted, "Now!"

From behind me, I heard Dick shout, "John, get down for we are about to hit."

The Prince shouted, "Grapples at the ready!"

The crossbows in the sterncastle of the Castilian began to slam into us and some of the Prince's men were hit. My men were luckier. Too many of the crossbowmen had wasted their bolts on me and having missed they paid the price. I saw five men pitch overboard.

"Grapples!" My men knew the sound of my voice and they hurled the grappling hooks. The Castilian captain, knowing he had a larger and stronger ship, deliberately put his rudder over and as my men threw their hooks our ships collided with such a force that we were all thrown to the deck and none of our hooks managed to hold. Worse, the men in the castles began to drop rocks and lumps of iron on our decks. Looking ahead I saw that Cog Thomas, although tied to a pirate was sinking. We were about to lose the battle almost before it had begun. As our ships drifted apart, I was on my feet as quickly as I could. I nocked an arrow and drew. I saw a crossbow begin to rise and at a range of fifty feet, I sent my arrow into the Flemish head.

"Release!"

I slung my bow and slipped the guige of my shield over my arm. I picked up the grappling hook which lay by the body of one of the Prince's men. I found a space and whirled the hook above my head. My archers sent arrows at each weapon which looked like it posed a danger. I saw a huge Castilian raise an enormous iron bar above his head as we drifted closer together. It was Dai's arrow which struck him in the neck, and he fell back, his iron bar knocking three others to the deck of the bow castle.

As I threw, I heard Dick shout, "We have sprung! Make haste lest we drown!"

My hook caught and so did two others. I hauled as hard as I could, and we ground together with a terrifying crack and crunch. I tied the rope to a stanchion and shouted, "Dai! Get down here! Hawkwood's men, let us board!" I drew, not my sword but my hand axe and after putting the haft in my teeth I began to climb up the side of the Castilian ship. Thanks to our arrows and the collision I climbed unopposed. As I walked up, I saw that I was flanked by Stephen and Henry. Both looked determined.

When I reached the gunwale, a boarding pike was thrust at my face. It was lucky that I was strong for I held on to the rope with my right hand whilst pulling the head towards me. The pirate should have let go but he did not and he flew, screaming, over my shoulder to land with a sickening crunch on our deck which was already waterlogged. We were sinking! I sprang over the side and I just managed to grab my axe as a Flemish crossbowman raised his weapon. He was less than ten feet from me. I threw the axe instinctively and it split his skull. As I slipped my shield through my arm, I retrieved the axe now covered in blood and pieces of bone.

"Hawkwood to me!"

The enemies who were closest to us were the Flemish crossbowmen and their weapons had been discharged. When Stephen, Roger and Henry joined me I ran at them. There was no thought of quarter from either side. The losers would be tossed overboard. I punched a Flemish warrior with my shield and then hacked into his neck with the axe. The ship was too constricted for sword work. Michael brought the rest of my men at arms and we cleared the bow castle. I saw that it was mainly my men who had boarded but I recognised the Prince, Sir Walter, and the household knights as they clambered aboard. I also saw Dai reach down and pull Dick to the deck. I knew then that his ship had gone down. As the Prince, his knights and his men had only just made the deck, I led my men in a ship-wide wall down towards the mast and then the stern. A spear was rammed at me as a Castilian sliced down with his sword. The sword was more dangerous, and I blocked it with my shield. The spear hit my side but the mail held and I ripped the axe across the spearman's throat. This was not the weapon of a knight but it was effective. My archers had clambered aboard, and they had dropped their bows to draw swords. If the Castilian pirates thought that they were in for an easy time they were wrong for my men were deadly killers, even the new ones.

By the time we had reached the stern the fifteen survivors, they were mainly the sailing crew, surrendered. The Prince shouted, "Throw them overboard!" and his men at arms and archers obeyed. My men were busy stripping the bodies of their treasures and weapons before hurling them over the side. I saw that Cog Thomas had also sunk but the royal standard flew from the mast of the Cog they had captured. I saw three other Castilian ships were sinking while the rest were being grappled by our ships. The pirates had lost five ships and while we had lost two, we had captured two. The odds were now in our favour.

Prince Edward was in fine form, "Captain Richard, lay us alongside the nearest pirate! I have a mind to capture more of these sea dogs!"

I turned to count my men. All looked to have survived although two of my Welshmen, Siôn and Dafydd had suffered wounds. Already Robin was tending to their hurts. He had collected his treasure quickly. I had sheathed my axe and slid my shield around my back. I went back to the place I had boarded. Being at the prow the bodies had yet to be thrown to the sea. The sharks would feast well. I took a good dagger and a heavy purse. I opened it and saw golden coins within. I put it in the satchel I carried at my waist and then threw the bloody body overboard. I saw that King Edward's newly captured ship was being attacked by two Castilians and I wondered if we should go to his aid when I saw three more of our fleet, who were closer, racing to his aid.

The enemy fleet had not been together when they attacked and now it was too late for them to combine and use their weight of numbers. Some of those at the rear of the fleet were already turning and heading back to Sluys and Flanders. We had an opportunity to become rich men and hurt the pirates. Dick was keen to avenge his lost ship and his new vessel was fast. He had turned the rudder to cut off the large Castilian ship which the Prince had identified as our next target.

The Prince joined him at the stern, and I saw them talking. The Prince then cupped his hands, "Archers to the castles. Hawkwood's to the bow and the Prince's men to the sterncastle. We will attempt to cross his bows. Captain Hawkwood, your men did well before, let us see if you can repeat your success, I want your men to board first!"

I nodded and waved. I had been going to object when I saw that Captain Guillaume was no longer with us and less than half of the Prince's men had survived. They had been too slow to save themselves.

"Hawkwood to me." I took off my bow and bag of arrows and headed to the forecastle. Robin was there already. I handed Dai my bow and my arrows. "You did well today. Use my arrows. I fear my bow will be too much for you."

He nodded and held a sword up, "And I have a better sword as well as a purse."

"Aye, and I think you have won the favour of Captain Richard as well as the Prince. Your star is on the rise!" I turned to Robin. "I will lead the men."

He smiled, "I saw you wielding that axe, it was as though you were born to it!"

"The men did well from the corpses?"

"They did. The Prince's men were too slow and that is why they lost men and we did not." He raised his voice, "Hawkwood, when you board and fight, we will loose our arrows at those to your side. Trust us, we will not hit you!"

No one laughed because we knew it was not an idle jest. My archers would be no more than twenty feet from their targets. The practice at the butts had shown everyone the skill of Hawkwood's archers.

The Castilian ship was beating into the wind and was slow. Dick had used the wind well and we were flying. Most of his crew had survived and I heard him shout, "Shorten sail! Be ready for a collision."

Robin shouted, "Loose!" and our arrows slammed into Castilian flesh. The shields of our men came up as the bolts were sent back. As soon as we heard the crack as the bolts hit, the shields were lowered and while the cumbersome crossbows were reloaded, a second flight cleared the enemy forecastle.

I clambered over the forecastle and stood close to the bow. Dick was a good seaman, and we struck the Castilian a glancing blow which stopped her. I was braced against the gunwale and I leapt up, as we slewed around the bow of the Castilian which was still under full sail. "On me!" I grabbed the bowsprit of the enemy ship and climbed aboard. I was below the enemy forecastle but there were no men left there and I ran down the steerboard side, swinging my shield around as I did so. I chose this side as it allowed me a good swing with my hand axe. The first man I met rammed a boarding pike at me. I blocked it easily with my shield for it caught on the side of the forecastle. A boarding pike needed two hands and I hacked into his upper arm with such force that I severed the limb and blood spurted. His scream was short-lived as he fell to the ground and I ended his pain with a blow to the head.

Michael's reassuring voice was behind me, "I will guard your back Captain!"

The enemy sterncastle had not been touched and I saw crossbows levelled as men with swords, axes and spears ran at us. Robin and my archers did not miss. One bolt struck my shield with such force that the tip came through the wood, but the Flemish warrior paid with his life for that brief success. Prince Edward, Sir Walter and the household knights ran along the other side of the ship so that we had a two-pronged attack, and the knights were keen to show us that they were better. Protected by mail and plate the Prince and his knights sliced into the Castilians who were wearing, at best, mail. Some of those who wore no mail chose the sea. It would be their fate anyway and the wreckage of Cog Thomas was drifting by. With luck, they might be able to float to land. If they stayed aboard this ship, then they were doomed! As we passed from the forecastle to the belly of the ship so Roger and Henry, backed by Gareth and Stephen, joined us. We were not fighting knights. These were pirates who whilst well-armed had neither mail nor plate. Few had shields and our training began to pay off. I had practised with my men and we knew how to present a wall of shields and strike over them. Gareth and Stephen had each picked up a boarding pike and Stephen brought the axe head part down to split the head of the man I was fighting. Gareth rammed the spike into the face of Michael's opponent and when our foes fell then Michael and I were able to help to kill the men fighting Roger and Henry. By the time we reached the sterncastle, the battle was all but over. Robin and my archers killed the remaining crew who either tried to seek shelter or surrender.

Darkness was falling and further pursuit would have been in vain. Prince Edward shouted, "We have won! God save the King! Throw the dead into the sea. Captain Richard, send a crew aboard to sail us back to port. Sir Walter, you will command this vessel. The Prince's men and my knights let us return to our vessel."

My men were already stripping the dead and hurling the bodies overboard even before the skeleton crew came aboard. This time the bounty was all ours. It was beneath knights to strip bodies and there was no one else with whom we had to share. My satchel bulged and the weapons, helmets, and bits of mail we had captured would require a chest to hold them.

"Michael, when you have taken all that there is to take open the hold and look for a chest. While there is still light then see if there is valuable cargo!"

"Aye, Captain." He paused, "Dafydd is dead."

I nodded, "He had no need to fight with a wound."

"He was part of our company, Captain. He was one of us."

The death took some of the edge from our victory. His body would not be sent to the deep. We would bury him in the dunes at Wynchchelse.

Dai brought my bow and I saw that there were just five arrows left. "Well, Dai, your first sea battle!"

He nodded and I saw the joy in his eyes, "I was terrified and elated, Captain. I am glad that I came to war with you. Life in Knighton would never be this exciting."

It was like looking into a mirror which could look back through time. Was this the way I had spoken to Captain Philip after my first battle? I could not remember. "Go find us some food and ale. Fighting gives me an appetite and a thirst."

Sir Walter had finished speaking with the mate from Cog Richard and he joined me by the mast. "I do not think we lost above two ships." He swept a hand at the body filled sea. "All of those are our Castilian enemies. We have cleansed the seas of a disease, piracy!"

"And they will rise again!"

He nodded, "The Prince has asked me to sail to Gascony. He wishes to know how the land lies for another chevauchée. Would you and your men like to be part of the force I take?"

"The usual rate for service abroad?"

"I see no reason why not."

"Then we are your men!"

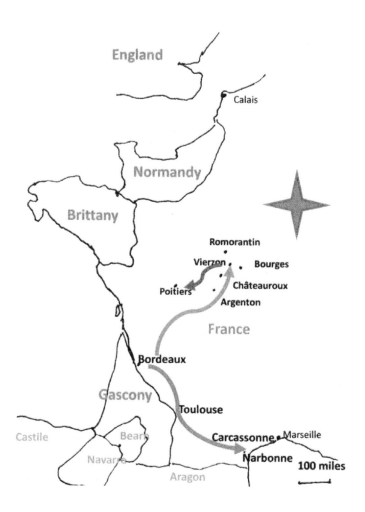

France in 1350
The red arrow is the first chevauchée in 1355
The blue arrow is the chevauchée in 1356
The shorter arrow is the retreat to Poitiers in 1356

Chapter 12

We were lucky for we landed at Wynchchelse and the first thing we did when we disembarked was to bury our friend. As was their agreement the other men divided his goods and money between them. We then recovered our horses and my chest. When other ships arrived, we learned that we had lost just two ships in the sea battle, the Prince's and the King's. We had sunk ten ships and captured seventeen. Captain William and the captain of Cog Thomas were compensated for the loss of their vessels with two captured ships. The rest were sold and after the King and his son had taken half, the knights a quarter, then the rest was divided amongst the ordinary warriors. It was unfair but we had already taken more from the dead and Michael had found a treasure chest and four barrels of Bordeaux wine aboard the last ship we had captured. We just smiled and nodded our gratitude when the Prince paid us off a month later.

I was tempted to return to Basil of Tarsus to invest it, but I decided that, as we had one spare horse now that Dafydd had been killed, that I would take it with me. I found a leatherworker who happily made me a pair of satchels which would fit across the spare horse's back. He was well rewarded, and he did a fine job. I also wished to buy some plate to go with my mail, but the town had suffered in the plague and there was none to be had. When I told Sir Walter he smiled, "Gascony will be a better place to buy such items. There is always war there and they have the best of weaponsmiths but why do you wish plate? You are an archer!"

"And I would better myself. Is that unreasonable?"

"No, and you are right. No matter what you do as an archer you will never be elevated, and Sir John Chandos showed the way to become a knight but it is a dangerous road, John Hawkwood. You have to attract the King or his son's eye in battle and do something so brave that death is a palpable risk!"

I laughed, "Sir Walter, when we boarded those two Castilian ships, I do not think that the pirates were trying to kiss me! They tried to end my life but I was too good. I will continue to risk all until I am so comfortable that I let others take the risk for me and by then I shall be leading armies!"

He looked at me as though it was for the first time, "You know that those who lead English armies are all of the royal blood or closely related?"

I nodded, "And who said it will be English armies that I will lead? Other rulers will happily pay for mercenaries such as me to fight for them."

"You are not a mercenary! You are an English warrior."

"I spent the plague in the north of England. When we were cut off, I spent many long nights thinking about that. I will always fight for England. I am an Englishman but if there are no wars with foreign foes what then? Will I sit behind a castle wall and grow old? Scotland, thanks to our victory at Durham, is a defeated foe. Wales is now a vassal. That leaves France, Italy and Spain. The Pope's emissaries have managed to negotiate a peace with France."

"You forget Gascony! There is a war for you."

"And when that war ends? No, Captain, I am happy to come to Gascony to fight with you and I will continue to do so but when there is true peace with France then I will take my men and we shall hire ourselves to whichever lord can afford us. If I am to lead my company then I need to be, at the very least, a man at arms. I will never forget my bow but I will choose, when I can, to use a sword!"

We sailed in Captain Dick's new ship, the first one we captured, at the start of October. The weather in England was changing and autumn was on the way. We went in convoy for although the Castilians were beaten there were still pirates out there and travelling together made sense. As armies go, we were small. There were just five hundred of us. Twenty were knights and the rest was made up of archers, spearmen, and men at arms. I was still paid as a vintenar, but I hoped to be given more men. There were already five centenars and so no place for me. That was despite the fact that most of the knights and all of my men thought I was the best man for the job. I was patient and I would happily step into dead men's boots.

We landed at Bordeaux which was, in reality, part of England. After the three week journey, our horses needed some time to recover and so we stayed close by the city. That allowed me to have the white jupons and cloaks made for my men and for me to buy the plate I would need if I was to become a gentleman and a man at arms. I was happy with my horse, but I knew that the next acquisition would be a courser. I bought a breast and backplate. This covered most of the upper part of my body and as I had a mail hauberk beneath the plate, I was happy. I also bought a pair of gamboised cuisse to protect my thigh as well as a pair of gauntlets with a gadling on the knuckle of each hand. This was cheaper than a full metal glove and yet the metal gave me protection while the leather gave me flexibility. Finally, I bought a mail coif. They were going cheaply for knights who could afford it were having helmets with aventails made.

Gascony had men who fought for England but had, in fact, never seen it. They spoke their own version of French and while most of my men could speak French, the exception were the ones who had come from Wigmore; to them, Gascon was a foreign language. Those first days, while we allowed our horses to recover, we tried to learn as many of the words as we could. I tried harder than any for I knew that while I would always be English, I would need to speak many languages. Robin and Michael were the same but most of the others concentrated upon the words for wine, ale, food, and doxies!

When our new jupons and cloaks were ready, I issued them to my men. Sir Walter was surprised for he said that they defeated the skill which my archers had, the ability to hide in woods and the like. I nodded, "Yet they each have their original cloak and if there is a need for such disguise then we can still adopt it."

"But white?"

"It is easier to keep clean and I remember when we were here with Lord Henry. This hot sun burned all the colours so that they faded. White can never fade. However, my lord, the real reason I wish us to wear white is to make us noticed on the battlefield." He gave me a surprised look. "I want men to fear the white of Hawkwood's men. Would you agree that my archers are the best?"

"Of course. You showed that when we fought the Castilians, and those who fought with swords were as good as any save knights!"

I did not argue with him, but I disagreed. My men were the equal of his knights as we had shown when we had captured the second pirate. "And while we are here, I intend to enhance that reputation."

"Do not worry, my friend. There is to be a tourney and then, when the weather improves, we shall venture forth and you and your men can show the French your skills. First, we have a celebratory tourney. The Gascon knights are keen to show us their skills!"

As usual, there were injuries which required healing and that delayed us, but I benefitted for one of the English knights, Sir Richmond Knolles, hurt himself so badly that he became crippled. He would have to return with his squire to England. The only ships which were sailing were the ones carrying wine and there was no room for their horses. I was one of the few men with enough money with me to buy them and I acquired a good courser, Roman, and a palfrey, Mary. Sir Richmond's squire was distraught to be leaving his palfrey and I confess that I became very attached to her myself for she had heart and such a pleasant nature that she was a pleasure to ride. Roman was a jet-black courser with a white blaze. The fact that I managed to buy both of them for thirty English pounds was a pleasant surprise but the injuries to the knight and the shame of his defeat meant he blamed his horse. I noticed that knights often did this. It was my gain, and I was happy. I know that, as we rode north to the border, I looked more like a knight than any other of those who were not for the white jupon and cloak, atop a jet-black horse made an imposing sight. I did not ride him every day and alternated with Mary. While I did not look as splendid on Mary, I found the ride more comfortable.

We were heading for Saint-Jean d'Angély which, despite there being a truce, was being besieged by a French army. Six hundred men were defending the town, but they were running short of supplies. Annoyingly we were just taking supplies to the town with no intention of raising the siege. We were led by the Seneschal of Gascony, John de Cheverston. He led five hundred knights and men at arms. With just a thousand men we could not possibly hope to relieve the siege for several thousand Frenchmen were surrounding the town.

Gascons were given the role of scouting and my company were with the baggage. As I had expected they complained. The centenar, John of Ely, did not like me. He had not been at Neville's Cross nor any of the other great battles. He resented the fact that men liked to ask me about those fights. He held his position because he served the Earl of Suffolk and there was a hierarchy about such matters. I would bide my time and it was not a problem to guard the baggage as that was the whole reason for this journey. We were there to deliver the supplies.

We were sixteen miles from the siege, close to the city of Saintes when the Gascon scouts returned to tell us that a huge French army was ahead of us and preparing for battle. There was no panic for the Seneschal was experienced. Sir Walter and his knights came to the rear and dismounted.

"John, dismount and leave your horses here with the carters. We fight on foot this day. John of Ely will command your company and they will guard the left flank."

I nodded and I tied my horse to the nearest wagon. I took a silver coin and flipped it to the carter and his son. "When I return if our horses are in good condition then there will be two further coins for you and your son!"

The man grinned. It would be the easiest money he had ever earned. I would make that with the first man I killed. I took my bow from my case and slipped my shield over my back.

"Hawkwood, let us go to war." I pulled up my coif and donned my helmet. It was an open-faced bascinet and I would have good vision.

By the time we reached the line, I could see that the French greatly outnumbered us, and they had also dismounted. The exceptions were two groups of knights. One faced our flank and the other faced the right flank. John of Ely shouted, "Come on, we await you! Were you waiting for us to die first?"

That was an insult, and my men murmured their anger. I turned to them, "I will deal with the slight at the end of the battle." I then raised my voice, "John of Ely, I would have thought that you knew we were given the task of guarding the baggage as it was you who ordered it. At the end of this, you and I will have words for no one impugns the honour of my men."

My men cheered and I knew that this was not the way to fight a battle. Once more I regretted my lack of position.

He scowled at me, "Place your men on the extreme right and keep our flank safe!"

Our knights were in the centre. My men at arms, for they were now so well-armed and armoured that they were the best equipped of any of the hired men, formed a line before us. I joined my archers and Dai stood behind with spare arrows and his bow. We were the only company to have a boy and I knew that when the battle was the hottest other companies would have to send an archer back for more arrows while Dai could fetch them for us. We had the most dangerous position. We were on the extreme left of the line and if the horsemen charged then we would be exposed.

"Michael, I want our left echeloned so that our side is protected."

"Aye, Captain."

It meant we had just four men covering our front while the other four protected our flanks. We had taken boarding pikes from the Castilian cog and they would present a serious barrier to horsemen.

The French began their advance. They had crossbowmen but once they had released their first bolts then we had grace before the next volley. We had to wait for the command from Sir Walter. He shouted, "Release!" when the enemy line was one hundred and eighty paces from us. He chose his moment well for he saw the crossbowmen kneel. It was a sure sign they were about to release, and we would be able to send our arrows a few moments before their bolts were sent in return. Three hundred arrows soared. The archers were all from the English contingent. We would continue to release until we either ran out of arrows or we were forced to use our swords. I heard thuds and cracks as bolts smacked into the shields of the men before us. Unlike knights, my men used old fashioned shields which, whilst being heavier, were also larger and now we reaped the reward. Most knights were so well protected by plate that they did not need to use a shield.

I had sent twenty arrows and shouted for Dai to fetch more when Henry shouted, "The horsemen advance!"

John of Ely commanded us, but these were my men. I
shouted, "Archers, turn and face them! Bodkins!" I had eight
arrows left to me and they were all bodkins. I nocked one and,
with Robin and Luke beside me I aimed at the line of fifty
knights who thundered towards us. They had spread out in a long
line. The eight pikes of my men at arms would protect us a little
but the other archers, to our right, had but a thin screen of
spearmen. Most of the spearmen had, at best, a mail shirt. If we
allowed the horsemen to hit then they would be swept aside.

My first arrow hit a knight in the right shoulder. The plunging
missile drove through the mail between two adjoining plates.
The lance dropped and I saw the horse veer to the left and when
the knight fell from his horse he was trampled by those
following. Robin and Luke both hit too. One killed a horse
which pitched its rider while the other hit the thigh of another
knight. Sometimes a battle is not decided by deaths but by
injuries and hurts which are not fatal. The three knights created a
hole in the enemy line, and we switched to those who were on
the extreme right of the French line. Our twelve arrows were
aimed at just twenty men who were there and ten of the twelve
hit true. When our next flight flew a heartbeat later the three
knights who crashed into us were easily stopped by the pikes. To
my right, the rest of our line had not fared as well, and the rest of
the French knights had charged through the thin line of
spearmen.

"Hawkwood archers, turn!" Although we turned and loosed it
was, perforce, a ragged volley. We still hit knights but not as
many as had we had time to aim. I sent my last bodkin and as
Dai had yet to return, I dropped my bow and, swinging my shield
around, drew my sword. "Michael, face the front and come to the
aid of our fellows!"

"Aye, Captain."

It was now a confused mêlée and French knights, Frenchmen
at arms and we English were now close together. It was then that
my choice of white came to my aid for we were recognised by
friends and I charged into the French knowing that I was
surrounded by my men. Robin and Luke flanked me with their
bows and as Ben and Edward swung their boarding pikes to
smash into the mail hoods of the French horses, their arrows,

sent from a range of twenty feet drove through plate and mail to kill the riders. The knights who remained turned and fled for they recognised the power of the bodkin. We were now fighting the French on foot and our bows were less effective. Luke and Robin dropped their bows and drew hand axes and swords. We had trained well, and my men were as confident in hand to hand combat as they were with their bows.

I saw a dismounted knight leading his personal retinue. I saw them slay with consummate ease two spearmen and three archers. Ben and Edward were still next to me and I knew that Robin and Luke were also close. I barrelled towards the knight as he brought his war axe down to split the head of John of Ely. As he pulled out the axe I gave him no opportunity to take the initiative for as Ben and Edward hacked across the front of his squire and the three spearmen next to him I sliced my sword not at the knight but the shaft of the axe he held. My sword had yet to be used and the edge was sharp. My arm was powerful, and I chopped through the shaft. As the head of the axe fell, I smashed my shield into the side of his full-face helmet. When he stumbled, I slashed my sword across the face of the nearest spearman. Ben ended the life of his squire with a blow from the pike to his head and the other three men who supported me killed another three.

As the knight tried to rise, I placed my sword close to his throat, "Surrender or die!"

He pulled off his helmet and I saw that his head was bloody, He shook his head, "No more, I surrender!"

Dai ran up with two war bags of arrows. "Dai, take this knight to our horses. He is our prize!"

He grinned and drew his sword. His French accent was deplorable but as he pointed with his sword the knight understood, "Come Frenchman, walk!"

The battle was not over for the French knights on our right flank had hurt the men there but we held. I shouted, "John of Ely is dead. Those with shields reform your lines and archers loose over their heads!"

That was easier said than done as some men were still fighting but those around me did as I commanded and with the extreme left solid once more we were able to help those to our left to stabilise the line. Robin and my archers had the advantage that they were loosing at the right side of the enemy where there were no shields. Of course, the knights with plate were protected from war arrows but enough men were killed by those self-same arrows loosed from twenty feet distance. They killed instantly and once the hundred warriors on our side of the field were solid once more then I was able to give the command, "Advance!"

The French had counted on their horsemen sweeping around our flanks and with those defeated, even though we had smaller numbers we were the ones in a position to outflank them. Even so, we might have struggled to end the day victorious but for the garrisons of Taillebourg and Tonnay-Charente, who small though they were fell upon the rear of the French. Horns sounded and the enemy tried to flee. The knights surrendered. Over six hundred were either killed or captured. For the crossbowmen and spearmen, the option of surrender was not open to them and they died in their hundreds. I killed so many that I blunted my sword. As the battle ended my men sought the treasure from the dead.

I found the knight I had slain with my arrow at the end of the battle. He was an old knight; I saw that when I removed his helmet, and he had good plate and mail. He also had a purse upon him. I found a wandering horse and used that to load the captured armour upon it. My men had been equally successful and as darkness approached, we made our weary way back across the corpse-filled field. All of us were laden. Dai would receive some of my share for he had guarded the knight I had taken. None of my men had died and for that, I would give thanks to God later that night. We had not been lucky but better trained. The men had obeyed my orders. Had I been in command then more of our men would have survived.

The knight looked sulkily at me until squires began to bring in more of the knights who had surrendered. I said to Dai, "Find a wagon and load it with our treasure. We did well and you shall be rewarded."

He grinned, "Next time, Captain, let me fight, eh?"

"Perhaps!"

The French knight said, "Who is the English lord you serve?"

My eyes narrowed, "What do you mean?"

"There will be a ransom for me and it will be paid to him!"

I laughed, "I defeated you and slew your squire and your men. It is I who will have the ransom!"

"But you are a commoner!"

"Your family will pay the ransom to me. Captain John Hawkwood!"

"They will not!"

I had the bodkin dagger out in a flash and held it to his throat. "Then if you are worthless to me I will end your life now and have your body burned with the commoners! Would your family prefer that?"

He looked terrified, "They will pay! They will pay!" Shaking his head he added, "You are the devil incarnate!"

We had begun to cook our food when the last knights were brought in and Sir Walter came to speak with me. From the blood on his jupon he, too, had fought and fought hard.

"Your men did well. I heard John of Ely was killed?" I nodded, "Then you become centenar and command his men and those of Roger of Tilbury for he also died. I am not sure how many men there are but I would have you as centenar."

I nodded, "And Robin as vintenar?"

"Of course."

That meant more pay for the two of us. The men from Taillebourg managed to get food to the garrison but the siege was not relieved. We retired to the town of Saintes while we awaited the ransom. The knight I had captured was angry when I took his mail, plate and sword. I think it confirmed in his mind that I was a barbarian. I cared not. We headed back, not to Bordeaux but south of that city for when the French army at Saint-Jean d'Angély was reinforced and King John himself took charge, the town capitulated, and the truce returned. We heard that there had been victories in the north around Calais for our forces and that told me that the war would return. We would spend the summer at the castle of Drax. We had money and we had time to train. More importantly, I had time to make the one hundred and twenty men under my command become as skilled as my men. We had lost the better part of ninety men in the battle and so, with just three captains, I led the larger contingent and the other two deferred to me. It was the largest number of men I had yet to command and although the appointment was temporary, I enjoyed it while it lasted.

It was while we were at Drax that I took up with a woman, my first real woman. Mary was Gascon and her father ran an inn. My men frequented it and I found myself attracted to Mary. Her father was a practical man and with four daughters and no sons, he turned a blind eye to their liaisons. Her sisters sold their services, but Mary did not, and it was a surprise to all when it was I whom she set her eyes upon. She hunted me with as much desire as I did her. I think she saw the potential in me and I had plenty of gold taken from the French. The fact that she was not a whore appealed but she was also the most attractive of the girls and that summer was idyllic and I learned how to be a lover. I had been with whores, we all had but that was not the same. Mary was a virgin and although she had flirted with men, that was as far as it had gone. I soon realised that Mary was not in love with me. She had seen her sisters go with men and take their money, but she wanted more and she knew, from my clothes and my standing amongst other warriors, that I was a catch. She would have me either as her husband or she would be my mistress. That became clear when she began to hound me to buy a house in Drax.

"I can find you a good house which will not cost you a lot of money, John. Then you would be more comfortable than staying with other soldiers."

I was not yet ready to throw my money at a house and so I prevaricated telling her that I had still to receive all of my ransoms. It was not true of course but it worked. And then, in November, she told me that she was with child. It was to be expected. Two of her sisters had given birth and their mother looked after them. The girls were fecund.

"So, you will marry me?"

I shook my head, "I am an Englishman, and this is not my land. It would not be fair on you. I go where the Prince commands. I will pay for my son's upkeep when he is born."

"And if it is a girl?"

I shrugged, "She will not go without."

She was not happy, however, it was a better arrangement than the one enjoyed by her sisters but events conspired to keep me from Drax when the child was born. Sir John Hutton arrived from England and sought out Sir Walter. The next day he came to see me.

"John, Castile is not far across the border from here. Prince Edward would like Charles de la Cerda punished for leading his attacks on our ships. He has an estate not far from San Sebastian. I am asked to lead a chevauchée to destroy it. I would like to use your men to help me."

"And the treasure we find there?"

"It is yours and your men's. I take five knights and we go to obey the Prince."

I nodded, calculating the profit. "The men will need to be mounted!"

"Of course!"

"And how many horses can you muster for the others?"

"One hundred and ten."

"That means I lead one hundred and thirty. Good. When do we leave?"

"In a week and do not tell your men until we are in Castile. It would not do to alert our enemies." He saw my questioning look and added, "It will not be so bad for the Prince of Navarre is an ally and we have a parchment to ask for help should we need it. We will not for although the home of Charles de la Cerda is well guarded, it is not a fortress. This is a message from Prince Edward that England does not forget hurts and although he may hide in Sluys, he cannot hide there forever."

Chapter 13

My men were all curious, but they obeyed me. The others had more questions. I simply said, "If you cannot trust me then I will not lead you. There are plenty of men for me to choose from." And so, the one hundred and ten men I took became like my Hawkwood men, obedient.

We had a long ride just to reach Navarre and I wondered if a ship might have been wiser and then I realised that the Castilians were pirates and that might prove to be more dangerous a route. Sir Walter took with us a Gascon knight, Henri de Grailly who was related to the Captal de Buch, one of the important Gascon leaders. We had forty miles to go before we struck the County of Bearn. The river Adour was a barrier but less so than the castle at Bearn. Henri knew of a ford and we headed for it. I had scouts out and they were my men. Robin led my archers along with another five who looked promising. I rode, not as an archer, but a man at arms. Dai rode with me and led Roman. I felt like a knight.

Henri was young but knowledgeable and keen. Sir Walter was desperate to do well for he hoped for advancement from Prince Edward. It was at the ford where we found our first fight. The ford was known to the French and was guarded. Had it been any other scouts than those led by Robin then we might have had more trouble than we did. As it was, Walter of Barnsley rode back and said, "Vintenar Robin has found French guards at the ford."

"Can he deal with them?"

He grinned, "Of course, Captain, but he just wanted you to know that he was about to break the truce!"

"Then tell him to break it." I sent another twenty archers with him and then turned to Sir Walter, "We had better hurry for no matter how good my men are the French will find their bodies and know that we have crossed. I would rather be in Navarre than France when they discover us."

Sir Walter nodded and said, "Let us ride hard!"

Henri said, "You have a sharp mind, Captain!"

"It has helped me live so long!"

Once we crossed the river our journey, for a while, was peaceful. I let the lords ride together and I rode with my new men. They had little experience of battle and chevauchée. I had to explain. "A chevauchée is little more than a raid on an enemy but, being sanctioned by a prince or a king it appears to have a noble function. We take whatever we can, and we hurt the enemy. We stop short of harming women and children, but I have known of chevauchée which have ignored that. We will not. We kill the men, take the animals and any treasure but we leave the women and children alone. Folk have a way of remembering such things. We wear the white of John Hawkwood; let them remember us as hard men but fair."

We crossed into Navarre and hardly noticed it for the people looked the same as did the dwellings. Henri shrugged, "There is no real border here. I confess that from now on I know little about the land."

Once we crossed into Navarre, Sir Walter said, "The estate is on the north bank of the Oiartzun Ibaia close to the village of Arragua I believe."

Henri nodded, "That is beyond the Bidassoa. Once we cross the fords there, we should camp for Arragua is just five or so miles from the ford. I have yet to make a raid such as this. How, Sir Walter, does a chevauchée work?"

"We ride in hard and fast. The element of surprise is the most important part for we need to eliminate any soldiers first and then we take what we can from the estate. What we cannot take we either burn or destroy."

"Then there is no honour in it?"

I laughed, "My lord, there never is. Prince Edward and his father usually use such a raid to weaken an enemy before taking land. This is more justifiable for it is for revenge. The Castilian soldier of fortune killed many sailors and he escaped punishment. That is the problem with fighting at sea. Unless you are our King or our Prince and hang your banners from the masthead then no one knows who commands each ship. The pirate de la Cerda had no honour for he fled before we could find him."

The Bidassoa was a wide river and we barely managed to ford it before the tide turned and darkness fell. Even had we wished to, we could not have attacked that night. While we made a camp I went with Robin to speak with Sir Walter. "My lord, if we wish surprise then we need to strike as soon after dawn as we can."

"Agreed."

"Then I will take my archers and Robin and I will find the manor of the pirate." I turned to Sir Henri, "How will we know the manor?"

The young knight rubbed his chin as he gave thought to the question, "The road to Arragua leads to the ford over the Oiartzun Ibaia. There is nothing else which is close to the village that is as large. From what I was told it is close to the river so that Charles de la Cerda can land from his ships close by to his home."

Robin nodded, "Then that should be easy. We find the village and head towards the sea."

Sir Henri asked, "But what if the villagers should see you?"

Robin smiled, "If I do not wish them to see us then they will not."

We found the road easily enough and headed for the village. Robin smelled it long before we came close to it and he took us off the road and we travelled through scrubland and then trees. Robin seemed to sense where the water was, although even I knew that we had to descend rather than climb and we found the water to the west of the village. We dismounted and leaving our horses with half of my men I went with Robin, Dai, Walter of Barnsley, Alan of the Woods, Ned and Jack to scout out the walls. These were my most experienced archers and Dai had shown himself to be both agile and resourceful.

The river was easy to spot for it was noisy and we soon spied the walls. They were more substantial than I had expected. They were made of stone and eight feet high. A path ran along the river next to the walls. The sound of the water hid our whispered words, "I will take Dai and clamber over the walls, Captain. If this pirate lands from the river then there should be a dock or quay. Why don't you take the lads and find it? We will meet you back at the horses."

I nodded and pointed to Ned and Walter of Barnsley who stood with their backs to the wall and cupped their hands. Robin

Goodfellow and Dai ran a few steps, put their right foot in the cupped hands and were boosted to the top of the wall. While they did so Ned and Jack had nocked arrows in case a sentry showed up. Dai waved from the wall and they disappeared. I nocked an arrow and headed along the path. Even in the dark, I could tell that it only carried men on foot. I saw no hoof prints. The wall to my right was not crenulated and the mortar was old showing that the manor's defences had been made for many years. I saw the wooden dock and a small boat was tied up to it. The vessel was just twelve feet long with a single mast. I saw the gate which was substantial and closed. There were no towers there. I had seen enough, and I led my men back. There was no sign of Dai or Robin where we had left them and we went back to the horses and mounted.

Dai and Robin ghosted up, unseen, a short time after we had done so. Dai was learning and soon we would have two scouts who would be will o' the-wisps. We waited until we were back on the road north of Arragua before we spoke.

"They have sentries on the main gate and that has two small wooden towers. There were just two sentries and they did not look up to much. Inside there is an enormous hall and it is made of stone. They have what looks like a warrior hall and there is a stable, a large one, and it has many horses inside. There were two large buildings. We did not get close for they had dogs, but they seemed to me to be warehouses."

"Good, then that should be simple enough. Alan, you will take Ned, Jack and Walter of Barnsley as well as Stephen, Edward, Ben, Siôn and Henry. Secure the river gate and destroy the boat and the quay. Robin, you will take the rest of our archers and the other men and clear the main gate. I will lead the rest of our band."

"It sounds easy!"

I turned to Dai, "They always do when you plan them, Dai, but the reality may be different. This has more chance of success because it is our men who do this. I trust them and it is why I will lead the others, the ones I do not know. There is less for them to do and less risk to the enterprise."

Alan chuckled, "And that also means that we have the first choice of any dainties we might find!"

There was food ready when we reached the camp, and I went to the knights to explain the plan. One of them, a young knight freshly out from England with new plate armour which had yet to suffer a scratch said, "Why does a mercenary tell nobles what they are to do? Surely his job is to tell us what he has seen and then we decide."

Sir Walter shook his head and although he spoke patiently to the knight, I heard an edge in his voice, "Sir Robert, Captain Hawkwood has more experience than any six knights here on this raid. It will be his archers who will clear the walls and gain us entry. The Prince himself asked for Captain Hawkwood to lead this raid. We are here to support him. Do you understand?"

I knew the other knights with us, and I had spoken enough to the Gascon knight for him to be of the same mind as Sir Walter. Sir Robert was not convinced but defeated, he nodded.

We did not have much sleep for we left before dawn. I had not noticed the brooding cliffs of the Pyrenees the previous night, but I saw them to the east as the sky there began to lighten. This time we did not avoid the village, but Alan and Robin led my men to gallop towards the manor while it was still dark. By the time the sun came up, we would be close enough to it that we would be able to gallop through the gates which, hopefully, would be in our hands. As we passed through the village, I shouted to one of the vintenars, "Peter of Lincoln, take your men and secure this village. Take whatever they have and any animals. If the men resist, then slay them otherwise drive them away!"

It was cruel but de la Cerda needed to be punished and this village would both support the pirate and be rewarded by his ill-gotten gains. I had not seen the gates the previous night but, as the sun suddenly splashed its light from behind the mountains, I saw that they were open. My men had taken them already and I saw four bodies lying close by. None wore white!

Sir Walter drew his sword and shouted, "For England and those sailors drowned by this cruel Castilian!" It was justification for our attack but as every sailor taken by any side was thrown overboard it was a debatable point!

My bow was in a case on the back of Mary which was led by Dai at the rear where the knight's servants led their spare horses and so I drew my sword and dug my heels into Roman. I was soon next to Sir Walter and we galloped through the gates. I saw, towards the river, smoke rising and knew that Alan had set alight the boat and the quay. The wind was from the south-west and the gates would soon catch fire. Men raced from the warrior hall. They had armed themselves, but none wore mail. The rest of the archers had dismounted once we had entered and now their arrows slammed into men who ran from the warrior hall. If I had counted to twenty it would have been too long a measure for the fight. They surrendered. I do not think I had ever been in a raid which ended so quickly.

My men were already in the main hall and I saw women flee, screaming. My men would not have harmed them, but they would have presented a fearful sight. The women ran towards the main gate and none were stopped. The men, on the other hand, were stripped of their weapons and their boots and I saw Sir Walter commanding men to bind their hands. I rode towards the two buildings which Robin had identified as being warehouses. He was right and when we opened them, we saw the barrels of wine they had taken from the ships sailing from Bordeaux. The two buildings were packed with the loot and booty taken by the pirates. None of it was perishable, that had already been consumed, and we could take it back.

I waved over one of the vintenars, "Find wagons and horses. I want the buildings emptied and whatever they contain taken!"

He grinned, "Aye, Captain! We shall all be rich men!"

"That we will!"

Even after the Prince's share had been taken every man who had taken part in the raid would receive a share of the sale of the goods we had recovered.

By noon all was packed in heavily laden wagons and carts. The manor was on fire and the bound men branded with the letter P for pirate and set free. Charles de la Cerda might be safe in Flanders, but his family had been punished! The village of Arragua was also set on fire. The fact that there was a river close by meant that any pursuit would not reach us until we had crossed the Bidassoa and we had timed our crossing to coincide with the tide. While we would be safe on the northern side any Castilians who sought to catch us would have hours to wait.

We camped safely in Navarre and Sir Walter opened one of the barrels of wine. That, along with the food we had taken meant that we ate better than well, we feasted.

The next day would be the hardest part of the journey for we would have to cross French territory and the river Adour. While we had raced across on our way south the journey back would be slower, and the French would have more opportunity to fight us. We had slain the guards at the ford and this time they would be in greater numbers. I sent Robin and my archers to scout it out. Dai was disappointed that he had to lead Roman! We rested our draft animals a mile from the ford and awaited the return of Robin. His grim face told me the story before he even reached us.

He addressed Sir Walter, "My lord, there are sixty men at the ford. They have erected shields for their crossbows and placed stakes in the water."

Sir Walter looked at me, "It seems that this is a task for archers, Captain."

I nodded, "I will leave all but my archers here. There are fifty men I will take upstream." There was an island in the middle of the ford we had used, and it meant that the convoy could rest there and draw the attention of the crossbows. "If you take the wagons to the island and then have the men with shields march to the edge of the water with their shields before them then the French might think we are foolish enough to try to force the crossing. I will attack them when they have sent bolts at our men.

Sir Robert said, "You would use your own men as bait?"

"Of course, and they do not see it that way. They know that by drawing the enemy bolts they have less chance of dying." I smiled, "Consider this lesson as a gift, my lord, but further lessons may be expensive!"

I saw Sir Walter grin, "Go then, Captain, and God speed!"

As we rode, I hoped that there was another ford, but we would be able to swim our horses across. I might lose some of the archers I did not know but mine could all swim. We found a shallow crossing a mile upstream from the defended ford. Robin and I led them. Most made it but Walter of Barnsley had to pull from the water a clumsy archer who lost his saddle. He coughed and spluttered his thanks when we reached the northern bank.

We headed away from the river and used the cover of the trees until we found the road which led to the ford. We stopped when we heard the sound of bolts hitting wood and dismounted. We tied our horses to anything we could and with nocked arrows followed Robin through the undergrowth to the river. I saw that they had twenty crossbowmen. There were horses there and that meant it was likely that they had sent for help once they had seen the wagons. We would not have much time! I saw that at least one of our men had been hit and he was being dragged to the rear. We had only brought one healer with us and he could be busy. We advanced as closely as we could. We each had an arrow nocked but not drawn for I wanted to be as close as we could before we released. The crossbows were slow but if the man with the shield was in the slightest bit careless then they could be deadly. Their steady rate led me to believe that they had sent for help. We were sixty paces from them before we were seen and as soon as a face turned, I released and nocked another arrow. We were at a ridiculously close range for such powerful weapons and soon weapons were dropped. We had no time for prisoners, and they were all killed.

I shouted, "Search and clear the bodies. Remove the stakes from the water!" Sir Walter had seen our success and the wagons were moving across even as we began to recover arrows and take weapons and purses from the dead. There were two men at arms who wore mail and we recovered those and put the weapons and mail on the horses which were obligingly tied up.

Sir Walter rode up and I pointed west, "Tracks are heading west and I think they have sent for help."

"We will wait for them here. Have half of your spearmen accompany the wagons and the rest can wait here with the archers."

I nodded and as the men came across, I chose the ones to stay and fight and the ones who would escort the wagons. I chose the wounded men and the weaker warriors. The French had sent sixty men to guard the ford. They would send at least twice that to hurt us! By the time the last heavily laden wagon was across, the first wagons were half a mile along the road to Gascony.

163

With Roman tied to a wagon, Dai was able to fight with us and I had him issue the bodkins we would need. Sir Walter dismounted the knights and men with shields. My own men did not really need shields for all had mail and some had plate armour, but it presented a more solid front and they would be on the flanks of the knights. I had the archers behind.

Dai said as he handed me a sheath of arrows, "What if the French do not come, Captain?"

"Then our horses will have had a good rest, but they will come. Why else leave men to guard the ford?" He nodded as he digested that information. He was a quick learner and reminded me of me! "Fetch ale and any food the French guards had!"

We had just emptied the wine and ale skins when we heard the thunder of hooves as the French approached. "Robin?"

My little scout knew the unspoken question, "Knights and mailed men at the fore. Perhaps twenty of them. The rest of them are light horsemen."

"Bodkins!"

The bodies had been cleared from the ford and most of them lay on the road from the west. It meant that the French would have to ride over them. The archers who had moved them there had not done so deliberately but the French would be angry and that would make them reckless. I saw the leader raise his lance and shout something. The knights and mailed men lowered their lances and spears and charged at us. Michael and the rest of Hawkwood's men had boarding pikes to defend themselves. With their arms through the guige straps of their shields they had some protection and could hold their pole weapons in two hands. The other men would have to brace their spears against their foot. With just one second rank there was a danger that the French could simply ride over them. The only thing in our favour was the fact that there were only twenty of the French thus armed. The light horsemen were not as much of a problem as they were armed with spears and javelins.

The plate and mail worn by the twenty men who had now spread out into a long line would be hard to stop. The knights' horses had a shaffron on their heads and some had mail protecting their necks. They also had a caparison. The men at arms had no such protection and their horses could be targeted.

We needed to use our bodkins well. When they were just one hundred and fifty paces from us, I shouted, "Loose!"

For Sir Robert and the other new knights, the line of men, horses and steel approaching them must have been a terrifying sight. Our arrows soared. Each one was a bodkin but the archers who were not Hawkwood's men would have fewer available. It was why I had waited until they were so close. I nocked a second and after adjusting my aim released. I sent a third before I looked up and saw the devastation we had caused. Only four horsemen were still unharmed although more than half were still mounted. I saw that four lay on the ground and that four of the horses of the men at arms had been killed. The arrow storm had halted the charge and now the light horse joined the remaining heavy horsemen and advanced. It was harder for us to hit them now and only the best archers could thread the arrow through the gaps between our men. I sent a bodkin at an eye hole in a helmet. Considering that it was an instinctive release I surprised myself when I saw that I had hit the target. That did not mean that I had hit the eye or even killed the knight, but I would have hurt him. I saw one of Martin the Fletcher's arrows drive through the side of the helmet of an unlucky man at arms who had turned to bring down his axe at the head of Sir Henri. Such was the force that it threw him from his saddle. The arrows had slowed the charge so that the horses which made our line were not travelling at speed.

Then the two lines met, and horses and men died as the French tried to avenge their dead. I saw the boarding pikes of my men rise and fall while the spears of the others jabbed upwards. Our arrows were now sent on a flatter trajectory and, inevitably the French broke. It was the light horsemen who turned and ran and then the men at arms and knights who had survived also fled.

We had taken so much booty from the estate that we headed, not to Dax but Bordeaux. We had a longer journey, but Sir Walter wished to impress the Seneschal. It meant I did not return to Dax for six months. We did not reach the most important city in Gascony without losses, but they were equine rather than human. I was lucky and I had two horses which I could ride but some of the knights had only brought one horse. Some died on that long ride. It meant that, when we reached Bordeaux, most of the knights chose to return to England. They had done what was asked of them and now they wished to return home. Many of the men who had come with us also chose to return to England. Their share of the booty we had taken made them rich men and another outbreak of the pestilence further to the east of France and Burgundy worried some. Eventually, the ones who had remained in Dax rejoined us and by the turn of the year, most had decided to go back home.

It was one of the last to return who brought me the news that Mary had died in childbirth and the baby, a boy, had lived but for an hour. I do not know why but that changed me. I wept like a baby and determined that the next time I lay with a woman it would be because I intended to make her mine. If I had another child, then I would be there for them. My men and I had been contemplating travelling back to England. Alan of the Woods put it in perspective for me, "Captain, the death of the woman and your unborn child is a sign. Let us return to England."

I nodded, "I will sleep on it and pray to God for guidance." In the end, I did not even get to pray and ask for divine help. Sir Walter came to see me for he came to me that evening before I had retired for the night. He was in low spirits for so many men had returned to England that he felt abandoned.

"I confess, Sir Walter that I am considering a return to England." I did not tell him my news.

"John, I pray you to stay. You and your men are the best I have seen and if you go, I am left with a force of little more than ten men at arms and ten archers. We can do nothing."

I shook my head, "We merely double those numbers. What can we do?"

"I know that the King and his son wish to retake France. The Duke of Lancaster is in Brittany and the King is in Calais. Once Prince Edward persuades Parliament to fund us then he will return here with greater numbers than ever before. What we can do is to be so familiar with this land that we know more than the Gascons. You know that some Gascons doubt that we can hold on to Gascony. Sir Henri was forthright on the matter. If we can bloody the French noses, then it will make it more likely that when Prince Edward returns, he will have support for those Gascons who waver."

He was so earnest that I believed every word he said. Perhaps I could atone for the two innocent deaths. None of my men blamed me for the deaths, but I did. I was the one who had taken Mary's maidenhood and I had made the child. Had I not done so then Mary would be alive. I agreed. When I gave him the news, he was like a child being given a sweetmeat! In the end, however, it was not one year before the Prince returned; it was three!

Chapter 14

Those three years were not wasted years. Not only did my men and I become better soldiers we also increased the men who followed me. Soldiers of fortune made their way to Bordeaux and I took them on. Castles and towns on the borders fell to the French and some of the garrisons who escaped also joined us. Taillebourg, Saint-Jean d'Angély, Tonnay-Charente and twenty others fell to the French and rather than our presence stiffening Gascon resolve, we saw it weakened. That is not to say that we lost, far from it. We became the masters of the chevauchée. We learned how to use the back roads and forest trails to appear like ghosts well behind the French lines. The white surcoats and cloaks added to the illusion that we were supernatural. We never took on a castle for that would have been suicide, but we did fight against superior numbers. It was Robin and my archers who were always the deciding factor. Perhaps, I am being too modest. Robin and my archers allied to my skill as a leader made all the difference. Sir Walter was a good knight but more often than not the plan which brought us success was mine.

I used my bow less frequently these days. I wore good plate, and I had a sword I took from a dead French knight which even Sir Walter envied. I had a number of helmets and used whichever I thought was most appropriate. I had taken several swords and I kept three of them. I had become not just a good rider but a great one and that was down to my horses. Roman and Mary were good horses; I become a better rider and whichever horse I rode became an extension of me. I had made sure that my original spearmen were now all men at arms. They were equipped with mail and plate. Whilst not as good as mine they were not the ragtag group who had begun life at Knighton Castle. They wore helmets with aventails and had good protection for their horses. We had moved out of Bordeaux to the walled town of Saint-Émilion although we only lived there in the winter. When Spring and Summer came then we would raid. My original Hawkwood men seemed to bear charmed lives. We lost men both archers and spearmen but Dafydd remained the only death. Dai had grown and now wore mail and was as good a swordsman as Roger of Norham or Michael. We had a house which had been loaned to us by the father of a young man we had rescued from the French. While we did not own it, the dwelling, nonetheless, felt like ours.

Our last task was not one of battle but of intrigue. Jean, the Count of Armagnac, was ostensibly loyal to England having been given Quercy as well as Armagnac by the King. However, he was seen as a possible weakness for he had been speaking with both the Duc de Berry and the King of France. Sir Walter received missives from Prince Edward each month. Sir Walter enjoyed the letters for they confirmed the likelihood of betterment. As the raiding season drew to a close and we looked forward to a winter in Saint-Émilion where we could enjoy some of the profits we had made, Sir Walter sent for me. I had got to know his squire, Richard, quite well and unlike some of the other squires, he did not look down on mercenaries such as we.

"Sir Walter has had another letter from the Prince?"

Richard laughed, "You must be a seer, Captain, aye. How did you know?"

"We have finished campaigning for the year and the only time Sir Walter needs to speak to me is when he needs my sword or the bows of my men."

Richard feigned ignorance although I knew he would have been told my task. "I know not, Captain, I was just sent to seek you out."

Sir Walter had done as well from our raids as any and was reflected in the house he had bought. He liked comfort and there were plenty of servants. His standard, a golden cross patoncé on a blue background, fluttered from the top of the house. His steward, Raoul, took my cloak and ushered me to a well-padded chair.

Sir Walter smiled, "Wine, John?" I nodded and took the proffered goblet. "That will be all Raoul. See that we are not disturbed."

I drank the wine. They produced good wine in the wineries around the town. It was red, rich and heavy. I would have just the one goblet for Sir Walter had given me his best wine and that meant he wanted something from me. I knew from his plea for me to stay, years earlier, that he was more dependent upon me than I was on him. I had thought back to Calais and my conversation with the Italian mercenary, Giovanni d'Azzo, when we had discussed my fighting for some of the princes in Italy. Now that I had more men under my command it was a prospect worth considering.

"Prince Edward has sent me a letter, John." I nodded. "He knows that we have done well and when we return to England, we will both be rewarded for our services." I knew that he had already received one reward for he was the first Knight of the Garter, the most prestigious order of knighthood. Did he hope to become an earl? As for me, I dreamed of becoming a knight but thus far the only hope I seemed to have was to be made a gentleman at arms. That would be a start and was the reason I had stayed so long as I had. "He wishes us to speak with Jean, the son of the Count of Armagnac."

I frowned, "They are allies, are they not?"

Sir Walter lowered his voice, even though we were alone, "The Count is in communication with the Duc de Berry and the King of France. His son, the one they call the hunchback, is seen as someone more sympathetic to England and Gascony. We go to speak with him, privately, to ensure that he supports our cause. The Prince is coming here next year, and he will bring with him a mighty army. Armagnac guards our right flank, and the Prince cannot risk a knife in our back!"

"Will this not be more likely to turn the Count against us?"

"You misunderstand the Prince's intentions. He does not want Jean to usurp his father but to use his good offices to persuade the old man to aid us and not the French."

I finished the wine and put the goblet on the table, "Which begs the question, why all the secrecy?"

"Arnoud d'Audrehem. He does not like England and fought in Scotland against us. He is close to the Count. Jean, the son, spends the winter at Aire de l'Adour just one hundred miles south of here and that is many miles from his father. If Lord d'Audrehem gets to hear that Englishmen are attempting to speak with the heir to Armagnac, then he will send men to stop us. So, you see I need a small group of men who are resourceful and can protect themselves in case of danger."

"And you need small numbers so that they can move across the land unseen."

He nodded, "I need the ones the others call Hawkwood's men. Of course, you will have to go in disguise. The white surcoats and cloaks will tell the world who you are."

I nodded. Now that I knew what was required, I could turn this to my advantage. I rose and went to the jug of wine. I topped up Sir Walter's goblet and then half-filled my own. I sat and drank a little.

"Well, John? What say you?"

"You know me well, Sir Walter, do you not?"

"I believe I do." I heard the edge in his voice.

"Then you know I am ambitious, and I have, like all men, dreams."

"Of course, and you have done well in the service of the Prince."

"I would do better. Both you and the Prince have benefitted from the skill of my men and my leadership. I would be rewarded for that."

"How?"

"Spurs." I watched him drink. "He has done so before. Sir John Chandos reaped that reward, did he not?"

"That was in battle!"

I laughed, "And my sword has remained sheathed since I have served you?"

"I tell you what, John, and here you must trust me for I have never lied to you. I will not put that request on parchment but when the Prince comes I will plead your case. I can do no more than that."

It was not what I wanted but it would have to do. I tried another tack, a veiled threat, "When the Prince comes next year then we go to fight the French and retake the towns and castles we have lost?"

"Yes."

"So he will need my company, will he not?"

"Of course, and you will be here, and your experience will help us."

"Then when the Prince comes and you apprise him of my request, I will decide if my company serves the Prince or travels to Italy to seek an employer there."

He looked appalled, "But you are English!"

"I believe that there are Englishmen who fight there, and they pay well for English archers. We both know that I have the best."

I saw that he was worried, and he nodded, "I am certain that I will be able to persuade the Prince for he knows your value."

"Good." I stood, "Then I will need to tell my men that their rest will not begin immediately. We will be paid for this quest for my men are worthy of their hire?"

"Of course." He patted a purse on the table and that told me the coin would come from Sir Walter himself. He could afford it.

"Then we will need new clothes which I will acquire. When do we leave?"

"In two days."

This was not England if it was then in late October we would be lashed by autumn gales and torrential rain, but it was autumn and by the standards of the land the weather was chilly, to say the least. My men all wore plain cloaks and jupons. Even Sir Walter did not wear his liveried jupon. His squire, Richard had that on the sumpter which carried his baggage. Sir Walter and Richard, along with the two servants he brought, rode in the middle of our party. Robin and four archers rode half a mile ahead of us and the rest rode at the rear behind the servants. My men at arms surrounded Sir Walter. Our helmets hung from our cantles and we had not brought our shields but with plate and mail as well as mail coifs we were ready for any danger which came our way. My archers just had their hauberks and helmets. The one-hundred-mile journey would take three days. If I had just had my men, then it would have been completed in a hard two. Sir Walter, however, wished to husband our horses for we would need them when the Prince came and so we stayed at the castle at Langon and later at Captieux.

Langon was a powerful fortress which guarded a crossing of the Garonne. We were welcomed by the castellan for while we might disguise ourselves on the road, here we were known and Hawkwood's men were welcomed. I was unhappy, however, for the castle had too many people inside for my liking and I had no way of knowing if news of our journey would leak out. However, we were still close to Saint- Émilion and as we had not disclosed to any of our intended destination then I hoped we were safe. When we left it I was relieved and we headed to Captieux which was more to my liking for it was a small castle and there were few fighting men within either the walls or the town. When we left there we headed for the Count's son.

It was fortunate that my men did not relax for a moment. Robin and my scouts had the ability to sense danger before they saw it. This was a beautiful land, but the road rose and fell through slight dips and inclines. It wound its way through forests which were hunting grounds of the nobles and it was perfect country for an ambush. I was constantly aware of my scouts and I saw that Robin and my scouts had reined in where the road twisted, turned and descended to another curve in the road.

Sir Walter looked puzzled, "What is it, Robin? Is there an injured horse?" We had already had to replace one sumpter and Sir Walter thought another had become hurt.

He shook his head and although he spoke to the knight his words were addressed to me, "No, Sir Walter, but as we came over the rise a flock of carrion birds took flight. It was not us who startled them for we were too far away. There are men down there, about a mile away."

Sir Walter dismissed it with an airy wave of his hand, "It is probably the local lord who is hunting."

I shook my head and spoke, "My lord, Robin knows his business and I have been uneasy since Langon. Too many men were asking questions of us and a spy would have had time to ride to Lord Arnoud d'Audrehem and tell him that Sir Walter and Hawkwood's men are on the road."

The use of that name made him more serious about the threat. "And what can we do?"

I smiled and nodded to Robin, "We can walk directly into their trap."

Robin dismounted, as did my other archers, and began stringing their bows. He spoke as he did so, "Alan of the Woods, take half the men and ride along the eastern side of the road. I will take the west."

Alan merely nodded and pointed to the men he would take. He chose those he shared a fire with. It is in the nature of soldiers that they fight better with those they are closest to. The two groups took off and used the woods. I dismounted and adjusted my girths.

Sir Walter looked puzzled, "That is all?"

I shook my head and remounted Roman, "No, Sir Walter. They will dismount and tie their horses up. Then they will stalk the hunters. If the enemy soldiers are any good, then they will have men on both sides of the ambush. They will be attacked in the rear."

"But there may not be anyone there. They could be genuine hunters."

"In which case, Robin and Alan will meet us and Robin will be embarrassed and endure the ridicule of the others, but I would wager that there will be an ambush."

Sir Walter looked at my other men at arms who had donned their helmets and begun to slide their swords in and out of the scabbards. "You, too, believe that we will be ambushed?"

Michael grinned, "If you would wager a mark, my lord, I will make the easiest of money from you!"

That convinced him and he donned his helmet.

"Richard, you and the servants stay in the middle. My lord, if you ride next to me for that is who they will expect to see at the fore. When we were in Langon they only saw Hawkwood's men. They did not see our bows. They will expect any archers we have to be guarding the baggage. Robin and Alan should be in place. Let us ride. If we can take a prisoner then so much the better but we take no risks."

As we rode down the incline the hairs on the back of my neck prickled. Robin was right and whilst I could see nothing ahead of me, I knew that the ambush was in place. It would be a hired company such as mine. I doubted that there would be knights and it would be hard to trace back the blame. Arnoud d'Audrehem could deny all knowledge of the attempt. There would be crossbowmen, perhaps archers, although I hoped not and there would be men at arms. I doubted that they would have plate armour but whatever they had would be good. The only sound I could hear was the noise of the horses breathing and their hooves clip-clopping on the road. The noise would reassure the ambushers for if we suspected danger then we would be galloping. Our very lives depended upon my archers.

The first we knew of the attack was when my armour was tested. I was on the right and the crossbow bolt slammed into the spaudler plate on my shoulder. It hit so hard that it forced my shoulder around and dented hard into the metal, but the coat of plates and mail beneath easily held it. I drew my sword and wheeled Roman to the right. A second bolt struck a glancing blow to Sir Walter's helmet, but it was an expensive and well-made one and held. He would be dizzy and that showed in his reaction. He was slower than the rest of us who drew our weapons and charged towards the danger. I saw men in the woods, and I went for the one with the pike. He wore a good brigandine over mail and had a bascinet helmet. I could hear the sound of arrows flying from ahead of me and as I jinked towards the pikeman, I saw a crossbowman in the process of reloading his crossbow fall with a goose feathered arrow in his back. The pikeman was between two trees and must have felt confident. He was protected on both sides and my only approach was directly at him. The mail hood which Roman wore and the caparison would give some protection, but it was possible that my horse could be seriously hurt. I did not intend to give the pikeman that opportunity. In the last two or three years, I had learned much about fighting on horseback and I feinted Roman to the right and then jerked his head to the left. The pikeman took the bait and lunged at where he thought I would be. I rode around the tree and his pole weapon was his undoing. To bring his pike around he had to step back and, as he did so, I brought my sword to smash into the back of his neck. He had a mail coif but there was no padding beneath and my blow broke his neck.

I whirled Roman around and saw a man at arms fleeing for, I presumed, his horse. A sprung ambush is a death trap and the arrows flying from their rear had shown these mercenaries that they had gambled and lost. I fully intended to obey my own orders and smash the flat of my blade on the man's helmet but he turned and swung his sword two handed at me. I had good protection for my legs and thighs but Roman just had a caparison. I could not replace such a fine horse and so I swung

175

his head around and slashed my sword down across the man's head. His sword collided with my greaves and whilst it hurt and scarred the metal it did not break flesh. My sword, in contrast, tore through mail links and across his throat.

My archers were now in their element and having disposed of the crossbowmen first were able to pick and choose their victims. They had not been there when I had asked for prisoners and every arrow was mortal. I kept searching for killers, but I saw none. I do not think we slew them all but the ones we did not, fled. I shouted, "Hawkwood!" My men answered one by one. "Meet on the road and fetch anything which is useful!"

When I reached the road, I found one of Sir Walter's servants tending to the wounds. Dai only wore mail and a bolt had penetrated his short mail shirt and hit him in the side. While not life-threatening it was a wound which would leave a scar and make life hard for him. The other servant lay covered in a cloak and when I lifted it, I saw that he had been struck by a bolt.

"Apart from Dai was anyone else hit?"

Siôn complained, "I have a dent in my new helmet!"

Roger of Norham laughed, "If that counts as a wound then we are all injured, including the Captain!"

"Did we take any prisoners?"

Silence greeted me. Alan of the Woods wandered over to one of the men at arms and now that his helmet had been removed, he was able to see the face. "I may be wrong, Captain, but I think that I saw this one at Langon. The reason why I remembered his face was that he turned away when I smiled at him. I thought it strange."

"Then I was right. Load the animals with the weapons and armour and leave the bodies where they are. This is not our land and if their friends do not return to bury them then the wild animals can have them." I knew that we had become even more callous over the years, but it was the nature of this war and reflected the views of the men who commanded us. We took with us Peter, the dead servant.

The rest of the journey was uneventful, and we reached the castle just before darkness truly set in. Sir Walter gained us admittance and I must confess that the castle did not seem to be on a war footing. There was a little scrutiny of us. It was not a large castle, in fact, it was more of a large hunting lodge and there was no room for me or my men in the main building. We had to sleep outside the hall in what looked to be a feasting hall used for the hunting season. We did not mind for we were well fed and left alone. Sir Walter, his squire and his remaining servant were feted in the castle. Jean d'Armagnac had his servants send us not only good food and wine but also some of the spirit for which they were becoming famous. Once we had eaten, drunk all the wine and each had a good beaker of the spirit we began to talk of our future.

I spoke first, "I had been thinking of leaving Gascony for I tire of these piecemeal raids which offer little reward,"

Ben said, "Compared with the earnings from Wigmore I am a rich man."

Robin shook his head, "There are greater riches to be had. Italy, Captain?"

I nodded, "But Sir Walter tells me that next year Prince Edward brings an army to make war on the French. He thinks it is right for the plucking."

Michael was the most thoughtful of my men. He waved a hand around, "Here there is little sign of war. We eat the finest of food and enjoy good wine. There must be places like this behind the French border. If they are as lax as this noble…"

"Aye, you are right, Michael. So, as we are all alone here with none to listen in on our words, what is the opinion of you all."

Henry said, "But you are our Captain. We owe to you and you should decide."

"Thank you, Henry, but I know that individually we are nothing. It is when we work together that we are unbeatable. I will listen to your opinions about the direction we take but once the horse is on the road then you shall heed my commands."

In the end, it turned out that all were happy to serve for another year in Gascony and equally happy to try a foreign field. We stayed for two more days and it was the easiest money we had ever earned. We were invited to hunt. For the nobles who hunted with Jean d'Armagnac and Sir Walter, it was a pleasurable activity. For my archers, it was a way to hunt meat which we could eat. While the nobles almost sang ballads about their blows and strikes with spear and arrow, my men just killed quickly and with deadly efficiency. We ate well while we were there and even managed to take back with us a couple of haunches of venison. We would let them hang for a while and enjoy much more succulent meat.

The only eventful part of the journey back to our home was the weather. A storm blew in from the west and we were battered and soaked for two of the three days we journeyed. Had any attacked us then surprise would have been on their side but as they would have not been able to use either bows or crossbows then it would have been a short but bloody encounter. Perhaps our slaughter of the mercenaries had made the French think again. Sir Walter and I spoke at night. The Prince would be pleased for Jean d'Armagnac had agreed to use his good offices to ensure that his father did not change sides. The Count, it seemed, was an old man. The son was eagerly anticipating the title and, for the time being, Armagnac and Quercy were safely held for the Prince.

"I will, when I communicate with the Prince, tell him of your part in this mission. You have served both him and England well. He will not forget."

I remembered the men maimed and killed in the two battles eight years earlier, not the handful of nobles who fell but the spearmen and archers. When I had been in the north of England, I had seen some begging. Those who lived in Durham were luckier for the Bishop gave them alms and in times of bad weather shelter but the King and Prince who had been so grateful for the victories, did nothing for the ones who had achieved it. That was one reason why my men and I ensured that we profited from every battle. When we drew our weapons or nocked an arrow, we wanted a reward and that reward would be for the time we could no longer ply our trade.

Chapter 15

Dai's wound took until February to heal properly. The healers in Saint-Émilion were clever men and although it cost us coin, they removed the piece of wood which threatened to poison the wound. It was a lesson he would carry with him for the rest of his life. I went with Robin for they had knowledge which we could use. I saw him watching the healer and knew that the knowledge would benefit my men.

We had been lucky with our horses when we had sailed from England, but we knew that many horses would die from what was called '*shipping fever*' or '*the strangles*'. I had deduced that it was nothing more than poor care on the voyage and riding animals too hard once they had landed. Nonetheless, I knew that when the army came, sometime later in the year, they would need horses. We bought every suitable horse we could. A courser or destrier would be too expensive but there were palfreys, hackneys and sumpters which would be needed. The price would rise when the army landed, and we would be assured a profit. Sir Walter had elaborated, as we wintered on the river, about the Prince's plan. It was nothing more than a huge chevauchée. For it to be successful we had to be highly mobile and that meant horses.

The other preparation we made was in both bows and arrows. Martin the Fletcher had proved to be an invaluable member of the company for he was not only a skilled archer but also a craftsman and he happily shared the secrets of his craft with the others. Making arrows and bows was a long process but by using others to do the simpler tasks and by sourcing the wood and feathers locally, he was able to speed up the process. The result was that we had more bows than we would need as well as more arrows. We would never run short and if Prince Edward's army needed replacements, we could sell them, at a profit. We found a local weaponsmith and in exchange for the poorer quality mail, weapons and helmets we had taken in our raids, he provided us with bodkins and war arrows at a much-reduced rate.

It was not until August that we heard that Prince Edward was finally on his way. Being close to Sir Walter meant I was privy to knowledge denied to others. King Edward and the Duke of Lancaster had each led a chevauchée around Calais and Brittany respectively. Both had been failures; the Duke's because Charles of Navarre did not provide the help which was needed. The result was that Prince Edward had been starved of the horses, men and arrows which he would need for his raid. He had been required to impress more archers from Cheshire, bows and arrows from Lincoln as well as horses from Cornwall. All of that took time. We learned this when Robert Pipot of Broukford came to assess the availability of resources in Gascony. He returned to England and had to order a thousand bows, two thousand sheaves of arrows and four hundred gross of bowstrings. Martin and my men used the time well!

The Prince arrived first at the end of August. Sir Walter travelled to Bordeaux to meet him from his ship. He came with his senior earls. I was with Sir Walter not in a position of authority but, with Hawkwood's men, as bodyguards. I received a nod of recognition from the Prince and was then forgotten.

"I have, Sir Walter, one thousand men at arms and their horses sailing from Plymouth. With them are three hundred and fifty archers as well as one hundred and seventy Welsh spearmen. My father has promised me a further four hundred and thirty men at arms and four hundred mounted archers, with their horses as well as three hundred archers who will fight on foot. That is not enough for what I intend. What of the Gascons?"

"They might be able to match those numbers for there are at least ten mighty Gascon lords who will provide men to serve under you. The best of their leaders is Jean de Grailly, the Captal de Buch."

I was close enough to see the Prince frown. "Just ten?"

Sir Walter shrugged, "Towns have been lost, Prince Edward, and while we have been able to prevent the French from raiding, we have been unable to resist their armies which took castles and towns."

The Prince seemed to see me for the first time and noticed that I was wearing plate, "Captain Hawkwood, do you no longer use your bow or do you have dreams of becoming a man at arms?"

I bowed, "My lord, I can still draw a bow but our efforts in this land mean that I often have to fight as a man at arms."

He nodded, "I believe that you still hope for spurs?"

That was a clear message. Sir Walter had said that by staying in Gascony I might receive a knighthood. The Prince was still dangling the hope before my eyes. "Aye, my lord. I was at the battle where Sir John Chandos achieved that honour."

Prince Edward had become a man since that day and his smile was cold, "Then impress me when we battle the French." He turned back to Sir Walter, "I shall need you close by me for your local knowledge may prove to be invaluable. We need lodgings and camps for our men. Where do you suggest?"

"Saint-Émilion, La Réole, Sainte-Foy, and Libourne are all close to the river and have grazing for the animals."

"Good, then you shall allocate the men to their places when they arrive. I wish to begin the raid in September!"

Sir Walter asked, "Will you not allow time for the horses to rest, my lord? If we are to raid, then we risk shipping fever."

"We strike now, and we hit them hard. We will drive where they least expect it." He lowered his voice, but I still heard his words. "They will expect me to drive north to join up with my cousin, but we will head to Narbonne. The harvests will be collected, and we can reap the reward whilst hurting our enemies." He waved a hand at me, "You may send your men back for you shall not need them."

Sir Walter turned to me, "John, have my people and my goods sent here. You may use my house if you wish."

I shook my head, "I am comfortable with my men and my home, lord."

As we headed back, I spoke with the others about the profit we might make. We had hired a couple of servants and the house we had taken over had stables. Robin had a sharp mind, "It seems to me, Captain, that when we return from this raid, then there will be those who have lost horses. If we have Charles and Pierre watch over the horses and fatten them up, then we will achieve a higher price than if we try to sell them now."

He was right. The Prince would have men appraise the animals he was to buy, and we had the opportunity to have them in prime condition. Now that the Prince was here then if horses were hurt on the campaign the Prince had to replace them or compensate us. I would ride Mary to war and leave Roman at our quarters.

We left so soon after the men and horses were disembarked that I knew horses would suffer. Men were more resilient. We were placed under the command of the Earl of Warwick. There would be three columns which struck south and east towards Narbonne. As I was familiar with Armagnac then my company was designated as the vanward of our band. Sir William, the Earl of Warwick, was with the mainward and another company of mounted archers was with the rearward. We were lucky in that we had no infantry to slow us down. Even though I led just twenty men I was paid as a centenar. The Earl of Warwick knew my worth and it was comfortable to be riding with men I had known for so many years. I would say that he rode easily but that would not be true, for we were still alert and unlike many others who might be in our position there was no need for idle chatter. We had spoken enough around the campfires so that we could focus on the task in hand and, once we had cleared friendly territory, we were able to find targets for the army to attack which were both rich and easy. If we saw a castle, we led the army away.

We devastated a large swathe of land and encountered no opposition until we reach Auch. This was a walled town and there would be knights. I rode back myself to report to Sir William. Already the effects of the sea voyage from Plymouth were beginning to manifest themselves. Some horses had become so unwell that they had to be destroyed. We had taken some horses but none of them were suitable for what we had to do. They would just mean that fewer men had to walk.

"This is a large town ahead, lord, Auch!"

"Could we take it, Hawkwood?"

"We could but you would lose many men and there is no need. The River Gers can be forded further south and there are more towns there which, whilst smaller, will not provide much opposition."

"Then lead us to the ford."

This proved to be our first battle, for the men of Auch saw us spying out their town and when we left they must have mobilised their men for in the time it took to find the ford they had assembled a force to face us and dispute the crossing.

"Dai, ride back to the mainward and tell the Earl that we are opposed. We will test their fortitude with arrows but as there are more than four hundred men that I can see I doubt that a shower of arrows will deter them."

"Aye, Captain."

"Robin, dismount the archers and tie the horses to the trees. I will test the depth of this ford. Try to avoid them hurting Mary."

My horse had a mail shaffron and caparison, but it would not do to lose her so early in the campaign. He nodded and I pulled up my coif and donned my helmet. I was wearing my kettle helmet with bevor. It gave me good protection and yet afforded me excellent vision. I had my shield and as I could see crossbowmen across the river, I hefted it before me and stepped into the water. The ford was identifiable by the hoof, wagon and footprints. The footprints told me nothing for men could have walked into the water and then hung on to horses or clambered on wagons. The wagon tracks suggested that horses did not need to swim. I would discover that for myself. The river was just over fifteen paces wide. There was no cover at either side and, as I stepped into the water four bolts came my way. These were neither Flemish nor Genoese crossbowmen. These were garrison soldiers and not very good ones at that. They were more used to using their weapons where they could rest them on the battlements. Only one of the bolts came close to me and that ricocheted off the angled face of my shield. The eleven arrows from my men were sent towards the four and the others who had yet to release. As five Frenchmen fell the rest hurried back to the protection of the men at arms and spearmen. They had shields for protection. I reached the middle of the river and the water came up to my knees. We could cross it easily and the bottom of the ford appeared to be covered in flat stones. I turned and rode back. The bolt which hit my backplate had been sent from extreme range. It was not an isolated bolt as I saw others splash into the river. The bolt cracked as it hit the metal. It did not hurt but I cursed. That was another dent which would need to be knocked out. Some of the tools we had acquired over the last years had been weaponsmith's tools taken on a raid. The dead weaponsmith would no longer need them. I would repair it that night.

Robin shook his head, "They know your white cloak now Captain. There must be a price on your head!"

I laughed, "And as all of you wear the same then all is well!"

I turned to face the French. I saw that just twenty men at arms and knights were mounted. The rest of the men at arms, forty or so, were on foot. The bulk of the men who faced us had no mail and they carried pole weapons, some of them improvised. I saw homemade wooden shields; planks nailed together. We had thinned out their crossbows now and the five by the water's edge could not be recaptured. Archery duels were largely about confidence and belief. Thanks to a single volley the initiative lay with my men.

Dai galloped up and shouted, "The army comes."

I heard the hooves as Sir Thomas Beauchamp brought up the mainward. There were four hundred men in our column and only twenty made up the rearward. The French outnumbered us but not where it counted, in quality.

The Earl had yet to don his helmet and he reined in next to me. "How deep is it?"

"Chest high for a man on foot."

He turned, "Captain Robert, bring up the archers. I want the French moving out of range so that we can cross."

The Captain of Archers turned and shouted, "Archers, dismount! Horse holders!"

The Earl said, "I will lead the men at arms across the river when they fall back. Come with me and then find us a target we can raid and a place where we can rest."

"Yes, my lord." I waved a hand, "Hawkwood, mount. We will go across behind the men at arms!"

That suited my men. We would conserve our own arrows and be in a position to loot whatever place we found before the rest of the army. Already the leather satchels we each carried on our horses were bulging.

Captain Robert knew his business and he lined his men along the riverbank and they loosed their arrows at the French. Even while the arrows were in the air, he had half of his archers walk towards the middle of the river and holding the bows horizontally loose a volley. While not as effective as the normal method and only sending the arrow half the distance, it still allowed a shower to descend and the other half of the archers waded across the water to stand on the other bank. There were casualties but not as many if we had not thinned out the crossbows. When all the archers were on the other bank then Sir William waved his sword and the men at arms and my archers galloped across the now muddied water. While Sir William and his men charged directly at the French we headed obliquely off to the right. The road led to a small town or large village we could see in the distance. The roofs and the smoke marked it. All the attention of the men of Auch was upon the horsemen who were charging them, and we escaped notice.

Pessan was just three miles from Auch and as we neared it, I could see that it was undefended. There were no walls and as I dug my heels into Mary to increase her speed the villagers began to flee. They knew what was coming. Our job was to secure the place and ensure that nothing was taken from it. We needed to hurt the French and destroy their will to fight.

I shouted, "Michael, take half of the men and get to the far end of the settlement. Kill any men you find but let the women and children go."

"Aye, Captain!"

He took four of the archers with him and I drew my sword and waved it, "Spread out!" The archers left to me would use their swords to drive the people from their homes. The sound of our hooves made those who were in their houses flee outside. I knew that my men would have been tempted to retrieve their treasure, however small it was from their hiding places but that was better done with an empty village. Some would have buried them while others would have made them inaccessible, close to the roof. The people who came out empty handed or clutching children we let go. The ones who grabbed small chests and boxes were slapped on the back of the head with the flat of a sword. We knew our business and within a short time, the place was ours. Only one man had fought, and Henry had slain him.

"Dai, ride to the ford and tell the Earl of Warwick that we have Pessan. You may take your time and rest your horse."

He grinned for he knew we would loot while he took the message to the earl, "Aye, Captain for we are tired." It would not take us long to search the houses and retrieve the coins and jewels which the people had hidden. In most cases, it would be copper and silver hidden to avoid taxes while others would have gained loot in the same way as we had. There would be Gascon and Navarrese jewels hidden away. By the time the army arrived there would be nothing of value except for the food and we would share that with the rest of the army. The men who were fighting would have the dead defenders of Auch to loot. We would all profit. The knights who were taken prisoner would be ransomed and our nobles would profit.

As we watered our horses and listened for the arrival of the rest of the raiders Robin said, "This will be a more destructive raid than the one we made with Lord Henry."

I nodded. The legendary raid by the man who was now Duke of Lancaster and fighting in Brittany had been one which brought almost as much ransom, gold and treasure we received after the battle of Crécy. "And that is simple, Robin, numbers. Even with the Gascons, we have less than three thousand men and we cannot assault walls. This is a three-pronged attack and, it is my view that the King and his son are probing for weaknesses or, perhaps, prodding a sleeping France with a stick in the hope that they react."

"Then it is expected that we will fight a battle with the French?"

I could hear the hooves approaching from the direction of Auch, "That must be what the Prince hopes."

Robin stirred the pot filled with the hunter's stew we had concocted, and he shook his head, "This army is not enough to fight the French! We would be doomed and the deeper we go into France the more dangerous it will be."

My archer was right. Narbonne was on the coast. We might get there without too much harm but getting back would be much harder and the time that the Prince had chosen for this chevauchée whilst a perfect time in terms of reward also brought us mightily close to the winter. I hoped that we would complete our task swiftly. I was not really worried about my men. We were well mounted, and our horses had been seasoned. We were also self-contained. Having both archers and men at arms meant that we could fight off most enemies and had the ability to flee. Already knights and men at arms in other lances and conroi were losing horses. The fight at the ford might yield a couple of replacements but I doubted it.

The Earl was in an ebullient mood when he arrived. The French had been soundly defeated and driven back into the walls of Auch. We had lost few men and they had been spearmen and archers. I knew that the nobility regarded such losses as acceptable. There would have been an angry mood amongst them had a noble suffered.

"A good day's work, Hawkwood and the hunter's stew smells good. We shall join you!"

"And welcome, my lord." Deeper into Pessan, Alan of the Woods and the rest of my men were busily cooking a second batch. This had happened before and Robin and I would take just one platter of food and then excuse ourselves. The wine and the ale we had taken were with Alan of the Woods. We might share that with fellow archers and the Earl was welcome to this tempting cauldron of food.

As we had with the other thirty towns and villages we had taken and robbed, we burned Pessan before we left. The people would have to rebuild and starve while they did so for there was not an animal left alive nor an ear of wheat left for them. Our horses ate well on the oats we took.

Prince Edward had thought this out well and the three columns of warriors all met up at the banks of the Garonne just south of Toulouse. That was a fortress city, and we would not assault its walls. It guarded the safe crossing of the river and the Prince was gambling. His Gascon allies knew of a ford but this was not the ford close to Auch. This was at the confluence of the Garonne and Ariège rivers. Here we had to negotiate almost four hundred paces of water, small islands, and treacherously hidden rocks. Its only saving grace was that it was undefended. It was hard to see how any could defend such a wide piece of water and, once again, it was my men, augmented by the rest of the mounted archers who, quite literally, tested the waters. We had taken enough wagons for the men on foot to have transport

187

across the white flecked and rushing waters which headed to the sea.

I allowed Robin to ride slightly ahead of my line of men. We rode gingerly into the waters which were higher than they would have been in the summer. There were dangerously deep potholes and Walter of Barnsley, riding just behind Robin Goodfellow was almost pitched from his horse when it found one. We were all skilled now and he managed to avoid a soaking. He waved to his right as his horse swam him to a solid footing. The waters rose as high as Mary's bridle, but my clever horse could always find a safe passage. Behind us, the rest of the mounted archers followed and tracked our movements. Further back the men at arms and wagons formed an even narrower front as they used our passage to ensure their safety. Robin's horse rose from the eastern bank of the Ariège and he raised his arm and gave a whoop! One by one we all scrambled up the bank which would become a muddy morass by the time the wagons had passed.

We did not make it completely unscathed. While my men all reached the eastern bank four archers and their horses were swept away, north, towards Toulouse. Once again, the Prince and his senior nobles regarded such a loss as acceptable. I saw their reasoning for thus far we had yet to fight a battle and yet we had taken more than two hundred settlements. Blackened shells of homes, houses and businesses marked our passage towards the sea.

I was too lowly to be privy to the council of war; We camped at the burning remains of the village of Vigoulet and used the fire to dry our clothes and cook our food. I was, however, summoned as darkness fell to the presence of Prince Edward and the Earl of Warwick. It was there that I met the famous Gascon, the Captal of Buch, Jean de Grailly. I saw Sir Walter in the background. He was a good friend of the Prince but here there was a hierarchy! The Prince, as one might expect, was in a good mood, "Hawkwood, the Earl speaks highly of you and your men. They must be lucky for today you were the first across the foaming waters and yet you lost none. You either have skill or are the luckiest of men."

"I believe we have the former skill, but I will take all of the latter I can!"

That made both the Prince and the Earl laugh, "A good answer. We drive now as one mighty chevauchée towards Carcassonne. If you can find us a way into that city, then you will be richly rewarded. It is sixty miles hence and we will burn every place twixt here and there, but I want you and your men to ride ahead. Remain unseen, scout out its defences and report back to us." He smiled, "Look for the pall of smoke in the sky. The Captal here tells me that it is impregnable and while I do not doubt his veracity, you and your," he paused as he chose the apposite word, "skilled burglars, have the ability to inveigle their way into the most difficult of places, eh?"

"Yes, my lord."

He lowered his voice, "And you shall be rewarded."

Once again, he was dangling hope before my eyes. I knew it for what it was and yet I had set my course and would have to follow it.

We headed east along roads which already knew of the imminent arrival of the English and Gascons. Mothers would be terrifying their children with tales of Englishmen who ate children. There was no danger to us for over forty miles and it was not until we came to the small, fortified village of Bram that we had to deviate from the road. There were no knights within its wall but its gates could be slammed shut and its walls defended. I noted its position.

We saw the huge fortress of Carcassonne long before we were close. Rising high above the river Aude it was the largest castle I had ever seen, and I wondered why Prince Edward had even bothered to send us here!

Once we had passed Bram we stopped. We found a deserted farmhouse. The Crusade against the Cathars during the time of Simon de Montfort had wiped out whole swathes of the population. The plague of eight years earlier had merely finished the job. I hoped that the pestilence did not linger for eight years. With sentries set I laid out my plan.

"Tomorrow we don the plain cloaks and surcoats we wore when we went to Armagnac. We will ride to within two miles of the walls. I will ride with Michael and Roger of Norham. If the French even suspect there are English archers then the game will be up. Our French is better than the rest of you and I intend to pretend that we have fled the English. It must be common knowledge what Prince Edward is up to for you can mark our progress thus far with the fires of burning towns and they will be just waiting for our arrival. If we can we will pass through the town and over the bridge. If we have not returned by dark, Robin, then you and the others will head south along the banks of the Aude and watch for us."

"You seek a ford?"

"Or a crossing of the river, aye."

"Suppose you are taken?"

The idea had not crossed my mind. I had not fought in this area and there was no reason to fear discovery. The fact that I was a clean-shaven man at arms might make a highly suspicious person wonder about me but other than that I had few fears. The French were worried about armies and not three spies!

"Robin, you know me. I shall try to affect an escape. However, if the worst comes to pass and you do not find us then ride back to Sir Walter and tell him what you see."

The next day we rose early and headed to the main road into the Cathar Castle. We rode as though two separate groups and that we were unconnected. As we neared it, I saw that the castle had a wall, and the main town was surrounded by another wall with huge towers along it. The road led through one gate, but I could see that even the suburbs had a high wall surrounding it and a solid-looking gate. Robin dismounted his men at a roadside stall selling jugs of the local red wine. We carried on towards the gate.

We were greeted by two men in the livery of the town; I saw the same livery on the standard fluttering above the castle. "What is your business, friend? You are travelling along the road which the God Damns will be using."

I nodded, "I know better than any. My friends and I were caught by them close to Auch. They attacked us without provocation. Two of our company perished despite the fact that we were on our way to Holy Crusade."

His eyes narrowed, "I see no sign that you are Crusaders."

"And that, my friend, is because we are meeting others of a similar mind in Avignon. We seek the Pope's blessing and then we will don our crusader garments. We thought that the fact we said we were crusaders would help. I fear for you when they come."

I saw his features relax; my thin story had worked, "Do not worry, unless they bring a mighty army and siege engines then they will fail. We have two hundred trained men to man these walls and many others who will defend it. Even if they cut us off then help will come for King John has promised us that he will come to our aid."

"I am relieved. May we pass through?"

"Of course. The alternative is a five miles ride south to the ford and that would be a truly wet crossing. The river is rising!" He pointed to the sky. The skies were black and foreboding, "And clouds like that mean a week, at least, of rain!"

The first obstacle overcome, we headed through the gate, towards the barbican which led to the inner city and through to the bridge gate. I saw that these were all dwellings. The business area was outside the barbican defended wall. The town itself did not look busy and I wondered if that was the pestilence or if it was simply that people had fled. The latter made little sense for whence would they flee? The diseases which had begun, as far as France was concerned, at Marseille, had caused much damage. We stopped in the main square where we watered our horses and paid for some food and drink at a stall set up there to catch those who used the square. There were other travellers and we shared experiences of the dreaded and evil English. They were all fleeing and trying to get to Narbonne. That did not bode well for Prince Edward. It suggested that Narbonne was even stronger than this citadel. We saw the actual citadel rising high above the town; this city would not be easily taken. No one seemed to question our motives for going on a crusade. Until the plague had hit Marseille that had been a popular place to take a ship to Cyprus but now most went overland, through Italy. They told us that Marseille was no longer the place to embark. I stored that information. When my service to the Prince was done and peace descended on England I would head to Italy. We did hear some news which the Prince would need to hear. King John had ordered a general mobilisation and the men of Carcassonne were hopeful that a relieving army would soon drive the English into the sea.

After we had eaten, we mounted and headed out of the gate and across the bridge. As we left the gate a sergeant at arms warned us, "Do not expect to get back in when the English and their Gascon lapdogs come. If you wish to be safe, then stay now and use your swords on the walls. We can do with men like you who look like they know how to defend a wall!"

I shook my head, "I am sorry, my friend, but we have a higher calling!" It sounded pompous but he believed me, and we headed south and east. Once we were out of sight of the gate we turned and travelled along the narrow river road. We now had knowledge of the ford and, when we reached it, although it was higher than I would have liked, we crossed.

"I thought we were going to meet Robin here?"

I shook my head, "There is no need now, Roger. We will head along the river and when darkness falls Robin will find us."

He gave me a sceptical look and Michael laughed, "I would wager you a gold crown, Roger, but I do not like to take money from my friends. He will find us." We stumbled into Robin and the others just three miles north of the ford.

Two days later we reached the vanward of the army. They were less than forty miles from Carcassonne. I saw that the horses looked weary but there were even more wagons following the mailed snake that was the English army. This time I was whisked into the presence of the Prince. He came directly to the point, "Hawkwood, can we take the prize that is Carcassonne?"

"Prince Edward, even had you the armies of the Duke of Lancaster and your father the King you could not make a dent on the walls of the fortress." He looked disappointed. "You can, however, raid the houses and business which lie outside the city wall. There are walls around them, but the gates could be easily taken, and the warehouses emptied. They have enough men for the castle walls, but I counted more than twenty towers around the walls," I shook my head, "it would be a waste of men to assault them."

"You and your men could take the gate?"

I hesitated briefly and then nodded, "We could, Prince Edward!"

That was the answer he sought, and he beamed, "You are the best of fellows!"

Chapter 16

It took three days to reach the city. We threatened Bram and they surrendered to us when we allowed them to leave. I knew that they would flee to Carcassonne and the city would have a warning of our approach but that did not worry me. We could still take the gate guarding the suburbs. As the vanward, we were the first into the village of Bram and we chose only the best and easily transported items of loot. The Prince allowed us to do this as he needed us to be his key into the city.

The Prince did not ask me how I intended to gain entry, but the Earl of Warwick did for it would be his men who would be the first through and he needed the signals.

"There is no ditch before these walls, my lord, and the gate is just ten feet high. We will find an undefended part of the wall and scale it. The inner walls are thirty feet high with towers which are forty feet. These walls are there to keep out horsemen. My archers will slay any curious guards and even if we are spotted then once we are on the walls, they can do nothing. I have a horn and when we have the gate and it is opened, we will sound it. You need to have the rest of the men within fifty paces of the walls. Even if they see you it matters not."

He shook his head, "You are confident, and you believe you can do this easily. How is that?"

I smiled, "I know men. You and the Prince deal with nobles, princes, and kings. You can deduce their plans and motives. I was brought up with the common folk and I know what drives them. The men who stand a watch are not real warriors. If they were, they would earn greater pay as a crossbowman or man at arms. These have, normally, an easy job. It is only the presence of us which makes it a threat. I will take no pleasure from killing them, but it is my job, and they will die."

I saw the Earl shiver a little, "I believe you and I am glad that you do not hunt me!"

We did not bother with cloaks nor shields. We had swords and hand weapons as we headed to the wall. Robin and the archers would eliminate any sentry who came too close to us. There were houses outside the walls but, as they knew the

English were near, then they were abandoned having been emptied by their owners now inside the fortress. We left our horses tied to the fences around the houses. The wall was in darkness, but we knew where the sentries were. We counted just three of them for a four hundred pace section. That was not enough, and we knew that they were just the town watch, men paid coppers to walk the walls at night. We heard them chatter when they met and saw that each pair of two would linger and talk at the end of their section. As we made our way forward, I saw that they were not doing their job. Their lighter faces barely lingered on the ground we crossed. They needed to stare for minutes rather than moments. They ought to have kept their head still but they did neither. They merely looked up and saw what they expected to see, darkness.

Having identified the three, Robin silently allocated their killers and Edward and Ben put their backs to the walls and cupped their hands. We could have used shields to lift us to the top, but it was unnecessary. Michael and I ran at the two of them and in one slick and practised move we were boosted so that our elbows and forearms easily made the top of the wall. First I heard a bowstring thrum and then heard a body topple to the ground. One of my archers had decided that a sentry was too close. The other two said not a word and Michael and I pulled ourselves over the top. I was on my feet and had my sword and dagger drawn before Michael had even tumbled over. I ran along the fighting platform towards the gate. It did not matter now if the sentries raised the alarm. Two of my men were inside, and the others would be moments behind. I heard a strangled cry as a sentry saw us and was hit. This time the last sentry tried to raise the alarm, but an arrow slammed into the side of his head and he fell, with a crash, onto a small wooden lean-to next to the wall. This time the noise was loud, and I saw lights as doors opened. It mattered not for I ran down the stone steps as the two gate guards came from their cubby hole to see what was the matter. One was slain before he even saw me and the other merely had time to put his hand on the hilt of his sword before I sliced my dagger across his throat.

Michael, Richard, and Gareth were with me and I said, "Gareth and Richard, get the gate!"

Michael stood beside me and we waited while the huge bar behind us was lifted. As I heard it lifted, I put my dagger in my belt and put the horn to my lips to sound a couple of blasts. My other men at arms had reached us before the alarm raised enough interest for men, with lighted brands, to investigate the noise. When they saw us then the alarm was raised in earnest. Men began to pour from houses and buildings; in their hands they held weapons. By then it was too late for the foxes were in the coop and the hens had nowhere to go. It was in our interest for them to open the gate to the city and the castle, but they were not foolish enough to do that. As the gate behind us was opened my archers ran with nocked arrows and it was they who sent war arrows to knock down the ten men who advanced to see what was the danger. The rest fled for safety and then horns sounded from inside the citadel.

As I heard hooves I shouted, "Stand aside lest we are ridden down by our own men."

We just made the shelter of doorways as the Earl and the Prince galloped in. We waited until all the horses had passed us before we ventured into the houses closest to the gate. All had fled, presumably to attempt entry to the citadel but they would not find sanctuary. There were screams and shouts as men and women were ridden down and killed. To be fair to the horsemen it was hard to discriminate in the dark between a threat and an innocent. We methodically searched every building and found some treasure in most of it for it was a rich city. By the time dawn broke and the defenders had enough daylight to use their own missiles, the buildings within range of their weapons had been sacked and emptied.

By then we had found a house with good food ready to be cooked and an obliging fire. When Sir Walter found me, I had eaten one platter of victuals already. "Captain, the Prince desires conference with you. He is pleased."

I nodded to Robin, "Make sure there is food ready for when I return."

The Prince and the Earl, along with his other leaders had taken over a warehouse which was in the process of being emptied. The wagons the spearmen had found were being loaded with mainly grain but also barrels of salted beef and lamb.

"Well done, Hawkwood. This bounty will feed us over the winter."

At that moment I heard the rain which had been threatening for the last day or two begin to hit the roof and I felt I had to pass on the local knowledge which I had gained, "Prince Edward, the locals say that this rain can last for weeks. And we heard that the French King has mobilised his army and mustered the levy! Perhaps, now is the time for a withdrawal!"

"Nonsense! We are not far from Narbonne and perhaps you can work your magic there too." He threw me a small purse of looted gold, "Here is for your pains. Eat well tonight and I want you to scout out Narbonne. See if we can repeat this trick!"

Even though I knew that it would be futile and we would not be so lucky again I took the commission for we had been paid well and with our gains from the suburbs of Carcassonne, we were becoming richer with every mile.

God aided us on this scouting expedition for the rain came down for most of the morning and we were forced to ride hooded. There were no travellers heading in our direction and the odd refugee we passed headed off the road when they heard our approach. We reached the great walled city in less than a day but we did not see much for darkness fell before we could complete our task properly. Once again the houses which were close to the city had been abandoned or, in some cases, were still derelict after the pestilence. We chose one off the road and set amongst a stand of trees almost a mile from the city and while the food was prepared Robin and I headed across the fields to view the walls. The ground was not yet sodden but soon it would be, and I feared for our already weary army.

The walls were just as imposing as Carcassonne but here there was no easy entry to cause mischief. The walls around the city were the same height as those around the citadel of Carcassonne and the towers were just as imposing but the city had not spread beyond them and there were no houses we could loot nor warehouses which could be emptied. Presumably, they were closer to the harbour. The darkness and the slight mist which resulted from the rain, allied to our dark cloaks enabled us to get to the gate and see that it would take siege engines to reduce and we had neither the machines nor the time to build them. Even worse was that we could hear their sentries on the walls and there were more of them than at Carcassonne. There would be no repetition of the sneak attack. We trudged back to the camp and the next day we rode to view the walls in the misty dampness of a dank and dismal day. They were every bit as imposing as they had seemed in the dark. I wasted no time in turning our horses and heading back to Carcassonne.

The Prince and his army were still emptying the area around the great walled city of anything which could give them sustenance. Black towers of smoke rose all around from the burnt buildings and further afield I could see that every farm had been put to the torch. We squelched through the mud to reach his headquarters where I gave him the truth.

"You cannot take Narbonne, my lord. The walls are as high as here and there is no way for my men to repeat their trick."

His face showed his disappointment and yet I did not know why. His aim had been to devastate the land and he had done that. His success, it seemed, had made him believe that he could do more! While he considered what to do, the Earl of Warwick said, "He is right, my lord, and we are seriously short of horses. The long journey has meant we have lost good mounts. We should withdraw back to Bordeaux where we can winter."

The Prince nodded and I thought he was going to agree and order a withdrawal, "You may be right. We will ride to Narbonne and raid around the city. When all is destroyed, we will head back to Bordeaux."

He would not be dissuaded, and we marched along roads which were increasingly muddy to Narbonne where knights and men at arms posed and paraded around their walls while the archers were led to raid the land for twenty miles around. When the rains came again then even Prince Edward agreed and we began the march back to Bordeaux. It was over two hundred and fifty miles through a land we had already robbed of anything which could be eaten. I suppose it could be argued that we ensured the French would suffer even more but the truth was it took from us many of the horses and men we would need when we went to war again. I blamed the lack of rest when they had been landed for the deaths of the horses while the men died from the inevitable dysentery. Once again it was not the nobles who suffered. Added to that the ford across the Garonne and Ariège rivers was now a raging torrent. We had little choice but to cross and this time we lost men. We managed to save some for we had men downstream with ropes to catch those swept from their horses. We saved some of the men, but their horses were lost.

When we reached Bordeaux, we might have been victorious, but we looked like a muddy rabble. The chevauchée had been an undoubted success but Prince Edward had pushed us towards a city too far. As we wintered in Bordeaux, we spoke of this, warm in the house we used. Had we stopped at Carcassonne when the rains began then we would not have had a river crossing which took some of the shine from the victory for it cost us good men we would need in the next campaign!

Robert Pipot of Broukford was sent back to England for more horses and we sold our spares to him before he left. He readily paid the higher price we asked for he knew the horses would not have the sea voyage from England which might result in weaknesses later on.

We had two months of rest. My men had lived here long enough to form liaisons with local women. My chastening experience with Mary meant that I was wary of such relationships. Ben, Edward, Peter and Joseph had actually married Gascon women and girls. Others, like Robin, had taken up with either widows or women who were less desirous of marriage. There were already a couple of babies and the winter saw others become pregnant. It would tie at least four of my men to Bordeaux, but the others would still be able to follow me if and when I left the Prince's service.

The Earl of Warwick sought me out in early January. My men were still well mounted, and the Prince of Wales had commissioned him to raid the Garonne Valley. I was content to do so for the Earl was a pragmatic and practical man. He did not readily waste men.

Our first target was the town of Tonneins which lay eighty miles south-east of us on the northern bank of the Garonne. It was a walled town, and I knew that we would need to assault it. We headed down the road to the town. The land along which we rode was controlled by us and so we could not take from the people who lived there but the north was different. It was

French-controlled, and I led fifty men, mainly mounted archers and my men at arms, to subjugate the villages and towns without walls and take from any farm which resisted us. It was not war, it was legalized banditry but it was necessary. All of the settlements: Saint-Martin-Petit, Castelnau-sur-Gupie, Mongauzy, Virazeil and Longueville fell quickly to us without losing a man and the leaders in the villages happily swore fealty. We gained no horses, but our own animals were well fed on the oats the farmers had kept for winter bread.

When we reached Tonneins they were ready for us and the walls were manned. The main gate guarded the bridge over the river. The Earl had sent men to blockade the other two gates so that the French knew they were trapped. The Earl rode to speak to those manning the walls and he had me with him. The reason was simple, he wished my opinion. It was obvious that they would resist us for they had known of our advance down the river road and had they wished to, could have opened their gates to allow us in. The closed gates and armed men on the walls showed that they were belligerent, and I knew why. Over the last few months, the King of France had been recapturing the towns taken by the Gascons in the autumn raids. The men of Tonneins were hoping that the French King would come to their assistance. While the Earl spoke, I listened but my eyes were assessing the weaknesses of the town.

"Prince Edward will offer you his protection if you open your gates to him. You will be left alone and enjoy peace. What say you?"

"I am Gaston de Cardaillac and while your offer is generous, we are French and wish to remain so. You do not have the forces to take our walls and King John will soon come to our aid. It is you, Englishman, who will be driven back to your cold little island."

The Earl had expected nothing less, but he continued to speak to allow me to search for defensive frailties. "Know that when we do take your walls, we will take all that you have. Any nobles will be held for ransom and any soldiers can expect harsh treatment."

The French knight nodded, "And when we defeat you then your archers will all lose two fingers from their right hands and we will impoverish the families of every noble who falls into our hands."

I looked at the knight. His words suggested that he expected help sooner rather than later for the only way he could capture nobles and archers was if an army came to relieve it.

The Earl glanced at me and I nodded. I had seen enough. "Very well. Then consider us at war!" As the two of us and the herald rode back, he said, can we take it?"

I nodded, "Our archers can clear their walls for there are no hoardings to protect the men on the walls. The men there will not be able to use their weapons effectively. The wooden gates are old, and a ram or fire will be able to destroy them."

"Fire arrows?"

I shook my head, "Too unpredictable. Men with axes and protected by shields could attack each of the gates. There are, as far as I can see, no defences around the gates. These walls are not even as secure as the outside walls of Carcassonne."

"Then we will let them wonder what we do this night and attack on the morrow."

"Perhaps the French King will come to their aid as the knight implied."

The Earl shook his head, "The Gascons under Captal de Buch are to the east of us and raiding. The French would have to come through them. I fear the men of Tonneins have been misled."

I was given command of the archers while the Earl organised the men at arms who would attack the gates simultaneously once we had cleared the walls. Although fire arrows would not work the Earl had men collect kindling and oil taken from the farms we had raided. They would be used first. His Welsh spearmen would be the ones who would race in and place the kindling at the gates.

We were all in position by dawn. I had spoken to all the vintenars and they knew their task. When I blew three blasts on my horn then they would each send arrows until the walls were cleared. A shipment had arrived from England with the replacement horses and we could be profligate with them. We would be using war arrows rather than wasting bodkins. I had my archers and men at arms with me along with twenty other Cheshire archers; I gave myself the harder task for the better-

defended gate was the main one which protected the river
crossing. We had crossed the river by boats we had captured, and
my men clambered up the side to secure this end of the wooden
bridge. With the men at arms protected by shields, we advanced
to the town end. The French sent crossbow bolts at us, but the
shields stopped them and all that it did was to allow my archers
to see where the crossbowmen lurked.

Robin said, "All ready, Captain!"

I lifted the horn and blew three blasts. Even as the last note
echoed off the walls the arrows soared. I knew that there would
be a delay from the other archers for the sound would have to
travel but I was encouraged when I heard screams and shouts
from those on the walls before us. I saw few men hit but as most
of the arrows were plunging almost vertically then we would be
hard-pressed to see their effect. Behind us, the spearmen with the
kindling and the men at arms who would assault the gates were
all ready and eager to charge. Here they had the shortest
crossing.

Robin said, "I would give the command now, Captain, we can
move forward behind Michael and the others. I cannot see much
movement on the walls."

I turned to the Welsh Captain behind me, "Are you ready
Captain Iago?"

"So long as your men can keep the walls clear then, aye."

My archers were still releasing but the rate had slowed, and
Robin was targeting those he could see moving.

"Michael, are you ready to move?"

"Ready!"

"Robin, arrows, Michael, run!"

This attack worked because it was led by my men. The
archers were protecting their own. As we ran Robin and the
archers sent another shower of arrows to keep down the heads of
the defenders.

"Robin, move!"

With my shield held before me, I ran with Robin and then
passed the archers to add my shield to the wooden wall
defending my archers. The Welshmen were fast, but they wore
no armour. One French crossbowman saw what was being
attempted and he raised his crossbow. The first arrow sent in his

direction slammed into the machine but the second drove into the side of his skull. The Welsh spearman, his mission completed, hurried back to the protection of the bridge. Captain Iago held the burning brand, and it was as he was lighting the kindling that a spear jabbed from one of the murder holes in the side of the gatehouse. He was a tough man added to which the spear struck his upper left arm. He used the brand to hit the spear to the side. I saw blood spurt from the wound, but the Welshman stuck to the task and ignited all the kindling. The spear was pulled back, presumably to strike a second time, but the Welsh Captain dropped the brand on to the kindling, drew his sword and rammed it into the murder hole. He withdrew the blade and ran back behind me.

As one of his men tied a crude bandage around the wound to staunch the bleeding, he grinned at me, "When we enter the gate, I will know the bastard who wounded me! I scarred his face!"

The Earl and the nobles had one plan, but we had another, more personal one. When we entered the town and enter we would for the flames were already licking at the ancient wood, then we would slay all those with weapons before we robbed the town of all that it possessed! I could hear cries from within the town and knew that they were calling for water.

"Robin, shower the area behind the gate. Stop them from dousing the flames."

Robin gave his orders and the arrows rose high above the gate and descended blindly. It was hard to tell if they had an effect for the cacophony of noise from within the walls was too great. The knights and men at arms who were behind the Welshmen were just waiting for the first sign that the gate was damaged enough to force. The breeze from the river fanned the fire and the smoke billowed from inside the walls. The flames took hold of the lintel and then began to set fire to the wood beyond the gate.

Sir Jocelyn, who led the men at arms, could wait no longer, "Charge!"

The men at arms had axes and they sprinted towards the gate which was now an inferno and they began to hack at the centre. The breeze took the flames within the town and allowed them to hack and chop. Suddenly I heard a cheer as the gate gave way and the men at arms charged through the flaming gates which looked like the entrance to hell. The Welshmen followed.

I shouted, "Hawkwood, to me!" With drawn sword and shield around my back, I followed the Welshmen.

Once inside I saw the effect of Robin's arrows. There were bodies indiscriminately laid on the ground pricked by arrows. Some had been struck after they were dead. I saw Captain Iago skewer a scarred French soldier. He had vengeance for his wound. Those who could, were fleeing for the centre of the town. They had nowhere to run for the other gates were also under attack. I pointed my sword to the large buildings which lay to the right of the street leading from the gate. They looked to be worth ransacking. My men ran within while I looked around for other targets. The men at arms and the Welshmen were rampaging through the streets seeking men to slaughter and women to take. In my mind that was a waste when there was treasure to be taken!

I entered another house on the opposite side of the road. It looked as though it belonged to a rich merchant for it was well furnished. The furniture would be destroyed for it was not portable. With a drawn sword I ran up the stairs and it was as I reached the landing that a sword darted out at me. Two things saved me, my lightning reactions and my armour. I flicked up my left hand and that forced the sword down and along my side. My surcoat was torn, and I heard the rasp of sword on plate. I pulled my hand back and drove my sword into the face of the fat merchant clutching the small chest under his left arm.

He was dead before he hit the ground, "Silly man!" I retrieved the chest and took the rings from his fingers and the golden chain from around his neck. He had been a person of some importance. His sword was a good one; it had just been used badly! I entered the room the man had hidden within and saw that there were goods worth taking. I went down the stairs as Henry and Roger entered. "Upstairs there are some fine furs and good bedding. Find a chest and take everything!"

They both grinned and Henry said, "Michael has found a wagon. He is loading it with the barrels of wine we found!"

While many soldiers would simply gorge themselves on the wine, we knew its value and we would sell it! Once I was on the street, I saw that the fire at the gate had burned all of the wood and was now a glowing reminder of the foolishness of the men of Tonneins. The screams in the distance told me that some men had found women. There would be few who would survive the mayhem. It was dark before the Earl managed to restore some sort of order by which time four of my men were on their way back to the home we used with the wagon filled with our loot. None saw them go and the Earl would never realise that I was four men light. He would assume they had been hurt. When this war was over, we would all be richer men.

We spent the next day taking the rest of the treasure of Tonneins and then headed not down the Garonne but the few miles to Clairac on the River Lot. Prince Edward needed control and his fast-moving columns were spreading out across the French border to seize towns, destroy farms and impoverish the French. Clairac was close enough to have seen the effect of our attack. I suspect that the odd survivor from Tonneins had fled there and told them. When the Earl made his demands, they opened their gates, and we took it without any effort at all. Their lives were saved but their warehouses and homes were emptied.

We spent another month along the river taking, not towns, but farms and wineries. Before our horses could be exhausted, we headed back to Bordeaux for this was just the prelude. The Earl confided in me that ships were coming from England with more men, horses, and arrows. Encouraged by his winter success the Prince intended a summer raid deep into the heart of France itself. We would head to the Loire and the riches of that untouched land. Once it had belonged to the Prince's Angevin ancestors and he would take it back!

Chapter 17

It was August by the time the Prince had gathered his army for the raid. The army had just eight thousand men. Almost four thousand were men at arms and a little over three thousand were archers. This time they were all mounted. The rest were Welsh spearmen and they walked. The Earl of Stafford had reached Bordeaux by June but the Prince had learned his lesson and both men and horses were given six weeks to rest and it had been July when Prince Edward ordered his men to gather at La Réole on the Garonne for that would be where we would begin our raid. This time I was given a larger force for the vanward. Sir John Chandos and Sir James Audley along with four household knights and ten men at arms joined Hawkwood's men. I liked Sir John Chandos for he was brave and not afraid to lead but I preferred to be my own master. I rode Roman and left Mary behind this time. I did not wish to overburden Roman and so instead of the mail shaffron, I had a leather one riveted to his caparison. It gave him some protection and meant he would not become as exhausted. I also changed my helmet. We had taken many helmets and I chose a bascinet with an aventail. It meant I did not need a coif and yet I was still well protected. My men at arms all made similar choices. The kettle helmet I left in the wagon which accompanied us.

We left La Réole in the first week of August and rode to Brantôme which we reached on the ninth. It was undefended and, being the first in the town, we took advantage. The vanward this time was led by Jean de Grailly, the Captal de Buch, and his Gascon knights. He was closer on our heels than when we had raided the south-east. I was quite happy about that as it meant we had a large number of men at arms to support us. We only had my archers and that, I believed, was a weakness.

We found a strongly defended castle at Quisser and so we simply went around it. We were looking for loot and easy victories. The chevauchée which had worked so well the previous year was being repeated! There were brief hold ups but nothing that delayed us for too long. By the time we reached Bellac, we had travelled ninety-three miles in ten days, and we rested at the manor of the widow of the Earl of Pembroke for two days. The horses needed the grazing and the Prince and his senior lords were entertained by the lady whose lands, of course, were spared.

In those two days, I was sent out with just my men for a longer reconnaissance. It was we who found the castle of Argenton which was ready to fight and had men on their walls. This was the first time I had been without supervision on this raid and I was enjoying myself. We had found and raided a large manor house. The inhabitants fled when they saw us approach and we were able to take oats for our horses, a couple of jugs of wine not to mention fresh bread, a ham, and a box of coins. When ee saw the castle across the river we halted and while Robin and I rode a little closer to inspect its defences my men took the opportunity to water the horses and have some of the bread and ham. The castle did not look as formidable as Quisser.

Robin rubbed his chin, "I think we could take this one, Captain. They have allowed some of the houses to be built too close to its walls and they would give our archers cover."

"You are right. We have seen enough so let us return to the Prince."

Perhaps it was the sight of our men, some two hundred paces from us, enjoying bread, ham and wine which maddened the defenders of the castle, I know not but suddenly, the gates opened and two dozen horsemen galloped out. They were led by a knight, but they were mainly light horsemen. I drew my sword and Robin whipped his horse's head around and shouting, "Archers! Ware your front!" he galloped back to them. My men did not panic. They put the food and wine back on their saddles, donned their helmets and drew their swords. As I trotted back to meet them Robin and the archers each nocked an arrow.

I could hear the hooves behind us, and I shouted, "Give way!"

My men at arms knew the command and digging our heels into our horses' flanks we rode to the side of the archers and wheeled them around. The horsemen were so keen to get at us that they fell into the trap easily. My archers sent two flights of arrows into them. Eight men were knocked from their saddles. They were using war arrows and so the knight was not harmed.

He reached us, however, with just a wounded squire for company and Michael and I surrounded him. He clashed his sword against mine and then Michael had his sword at the knight's throat.

"Yield or die!"

Henry and Roger had taken the squire and as more arrows were sent at the light horsemen the survivors headed back across the bridge. I heard a horn sound in the castle. "Just fetch the horses and leave the bodies. There will be little enough on them in any case." Michael and I flanked the knight while Roger and Henry did the same for the squire. The knight had surrendered but I was taking no chances.

The Prince was delighted with the capture of a knight for it gave him a prisoner to question. The knight was still my prisoner and so I was allowed to stay while he was questioned. He learned a number of things which were useful. The Count of Poitiers was in Bourges and King John was mustering a large army to meet us and bring us to battle. The former news was more welcome than the latter although I had learned from Sir John Chandos that the Duke of Lancaster was heading through Normandy to cross the Loire and to join us.

"Thank you, Hawkwood. Enjoy this ransom for you have earned it!"

"Thank you, my lord."

The squire, his wounds tended to, was sent for the ransom and the knight was left with the widow of the Earl of Pembroke at Bellac. I knew not when I would be able to collect my ransom, but it was safer with the lady than on the road with me. The Captal de Buch and his men now joined us as the scouts and we swam the river to cut off the town. The Prince then arrived with the mainward and began the assault. We were spread out across the road to Châteauroux. As soon as Prince Edward arrived then the populace fled. They headed straight into our arms. We took every horse and wagon. The men who resisted, there were just two, were slain and the rest allowed to trudge the seventeen miles to the next citadel, Châteauroux. Once again, my men took only those things which we could carry easily and yet were valuable.

We heard the fighting and the sound of battle as the castle was assaulted. It fell in less than half a day and that impressed me more than anything. It was our archers who achieved the victory for it was their shower of arrows which decimated the defenders. While half of the army rested for a day the remainder were sent out to devastate the surrounding area and bring in supplies. The town would be burned when we left.

Two days later I was sent with Sir John and Sir James with a large force of men, two hundred in total, and all of them mounted, to ride to Bourges. It was hoped that we might capture the Count of Poitiers. This time Sir Walter came with us. Once again, we had too few archers for my liking. Sir John sent my archers and me to scout it out. When I saw its defences, I knew that we were too few to seriously threaten the defenders. The Roman walls had been added to and towers built. This was clearly stronger than Tonneins. The town had a wall around it, but they had built houses, warehouses and businesses beyond the walls. I saw that they had not evacuated the suburbs. We had approached so carefully that we had remained hidden. Leaving all but Robin half a mile from the suburbs we walked our horses along the main road. There is something less threatening about a mailed man walking a horse rather than riding it. I saw that the buildings outside the city walls were largely made of wood. I did not think that we would be able to take much loot, but we could do mischief. We turned around, mounted our horses and rode back to the others. Sir John and the rest of the men at arms were waiting a mile from the city.

"We cannot take the city, my lord, the walls are too high, and it is well defended but we can destroy many houses and businesses which have been built beyond the walls."

"We cannot take the Count of Poitiers?"

I shook my head, "We would need a full army and not just a raiding party."

"Then let us cause some mischief." After shouting his commands, he wheeled his horse and charged off towards Bourges.

This time we were seen and horns sounded a loud alarum. People ran screaming for the open gates. Sir John and a handful of knights outrode the rest of us and closely followed them. I thought it futile for knights had emerged from the gates and were duelling with Sir John and our knights. I heard the clash and din of war, but I knew that it was unlikely there would be deaths for both sides were well armoured and I had learned that to be effective on horseback you needed a lance. I dismounted my men and set them to burning the buildings while Robin, Michael and I searched the nearest buildings for treasure. As I came out of one with a purse of coins I saw Sir John leading his knights from the gates which were now closed. Fewer than a hundred people had found sanctuary and the rest were fleeing what they saw as the wrath of the English.

Sir John grinned as he stepped from the horse, "So close, Captain and yet so far. I see you have found treasure!"

"A little my lord. My men will begin the fire and with this wind, we might even make life uncomfortable in the city itself!"

We left two hours later with the buildings ablaze and threatening the very walls of Bourges. We headed back to the main army.

Five days later we were again sent with Sir John and Sir James to raid Aubigny-sur-Nère. After the excitement of Bourges, this was almost an anti-climax and we met little opposition. The French knew when we were coming. The fact that this settlement had neither castle nor wall meant that the inhabitants fled, and we were able to loot at our leisure and then burn the town. We were less than sixteen miles from the Loire.

As we rode back, I chatted to Sir Walter, "The Prince has achieved all that he intended then Sir Walter?"

The knight shook his head, "His goals have changed a little. The supplies and loot we have taken, not to mention the towns we have burned, have emboldened him. I think he would go to Paris and fight the King of France."

I knew that this would be a mistake for our army had shrunk. There had been deaths. Inevitably there was also disease and, as poor men became rich in the blink of an eye, desertions. The Prince had also used some of the spearmen commanded by knights to garrison a few of the castles we had captured. "With this army? We both know, Sir Walter, that it is too small!"

"Until the Prince sees the size of the French army then he will continue to believe that we are invincible!"

Any further discussion ended when Robin and my archers galloped in, "My lord, there are two hundred or more French horsemen ahead! They didn't see us, and they are riding in a column of fours!"

We had found a French version of us! Sir John did not flee from a fight and he turned to me. "Have your archers support us but you will need to keep them out of the way."

I nodded, "Robin, dismount and support us. If things go against us, then get back to the Prince with the news!"

"Aye, Captain. There are some big bastards with the French. You watch yourself! Right lads, dismount and get out the bodkins!"

I donned my helmet and pulled my shield up to protect my left side. The knights would go in first and I wanted my men at arms to fight with me. "Michael, I want our men in two ranks. You and Roger flank me!"

Sir John did not wait for us to organise. Our scouts had given us the edge and he wanted to slam into the enemy while they were in a column of fours. If we could hit the head of the column and hurt their leaders then we might turn the tide in our favour. He and the knights were ahead of us and I rode just behind with the other men at arms. They knew me and they formed up on me. We were travelling through open fields which had been harvested but there were hedges. The slight ridge ahead hid the French from us and we from them. The first that they would know would be when they crested the rise in the road and would then have to deploy. Sir John was trying to hit them as they crested it. God smiled on us that day and the trotting horses of the French were suddenly engulfed by the galloping horses of Sir John and his knights. We were on the French so quickly that some of them were knocked from their horses before they could draw a weapon.

As is the nature of such skirmishes our line, which had been somewhat ragged to start with, disintegrated into little battles and duels. We had the initiative, however, and my men and I galloped to attack some men at arms and light horsemen towards the rear of the column. Robin had disobeyed me and followed, with my archers, closely on their horses. I knew that for arrows suddenly began to pluck light horsemen from their saddles ahead of us. I rode at the knight who led the men at arms. I had taken a ransom of one hundred florins for one knight and I relished the prospect of a second. Protected by Michael and Roger I was able to urge Roman towards the side of the knight. His shield still hung over his leg, but he had his sword out and, standing in his stirrups, he brought it down to split my head in two. I had my shield ready and I lifted it as I slashed at his unprotected middle with my sword. He had a breastplate and a corselet beneath it. My sword did not break the plate, but I hurt him. I heard the grunt from beneath the visor. Raising his sword to strike again allowed me to hit his boar's snout helmet with my shield. I never liked the protruding visor for when I hit it the whole helmet was jerked back, and his already limited vision became worse and I was able to bring my sword down hard on his shoulder. There is a bone there which even though protected by plate, mail and gambeson is susceptible to damage. I knew I had hurt him when his sword fell, and he grunted.

"Yield, for you are weaponless."

We had been fighting but briefly and yet the combat was almost over. The French, surprised and hurt, were fleeing back towards the Loire. A dozen or so light horsemen lay dead or dying. They had been slain by my archers and my men at arms. Already the horses they had ridden were being collected.

The French knight pushed up his visor. I saw blood on his face. The blow from my shield had hurt him. He nodded, "I yield." He seemed to see me and my white jupon for the first time. "You are the one who fights as a knight, yet you are an archer; the white one."

I nodded, "Captain Hawkwood."

"You shall have ransom. If I give my word to send it to you will you let me go?"

"I would trust your word but first we must take you to Prince Edward for he will have questions for you."

The knights had taken other prisoners and we were in a good mood as we headed back to the main army. The Prince was resting at Vierzon which had been taken by the Captal de Buch. Our raiding parties had burned every town within twenty miles and, I think, that the Prince hoped we had hurt the French enough for them to fall back to Paris. His plan was still to cross the Loire and link up with the Duke of Lancaster. It was our prisoners who ended that hope. Once again, as I had a captive, I was privy to the questioning. We learned that the French King was at Chartres and that the bridges across the Loire were either destroyed or heavily guarded.

He turned to me, "Hawkwood, take the captives and see that they are fed. My knights and I will hold a council of war."

I took the captives from the huge hall he was using and led them to the small hall in the castle of Vierzon. As a commoner, I always found it strange that when taken prisoner and having given their word then knights would behave as though it was all a game. For the likes of me and my men if we were taken there would be no ransom and, at best, we would be incarcerated. The French had given their word and I knew that they would keep it. They had promised ransom and it would be delivered. Sir Geoffrey, the knight I had captured, promised me a ransom of one hundred florins. When he realised that I intended to keep his horse and his plate he raised the ransom to one hundred and fifty if I let him keep his horse and armour. I agreed. Some squires had been captured and, as the other ransoms were agreed then they were sent off to fetch the money. The knights all lived close to the Loire and they were eager to be ransomed so that they could rejoin King John and then fight us once more. They would hope to regain their ransom from us! Such was war in those days. As they ate and talked, I realised that the French thought that they could defeat us. Crécy was still a raw wound and they wished a victory to take away the shame of that defeat. They would pay the ransoms for they believed they would take it back tenfold when they defeated us and took ransoms for the likes of the Prince and his earls.

We stayed for three days at Vierzon. All the ransom was delivered within two days which told me much about the riches north of the Loire. Sadly, those riches would not be taken yet for the Prince decided to make a strategic withdrawal and head along the southern bank of the Loire, taking all that was there.

We left after making the castle indefensible and burning the town. This time we were not the vanguard. Two of the knights closest to the Prince, Bartholomew de Burghersh and Edward Despencer wanted the glory of leading the Prince's army. I thought it an unnecessary risk, but the Prince acceded to their request. We were still attached to Sir John Chandos, but it was Bartholomew de Burghersh and Edward Despencer who led the two hundred men at arms and knights towards the castle of Romorantin. They had no archers and, as far as I knew, no experience of riding through wooded land which was perfect country for an ambush.

The three hundred French who ambushed them were clever. They allowed the knights and their men to pass and then, with levelled lances, led by the Sire de Craon, Boucicault and the Hermite de Chaumont, they charged the rear of our vanguard. Sir John saw them ahead in the distance, and he wasted no time in ordering the charge. He and the knights had lances, but my men and I did not. As we charged down the road, I saw how knights fought one way and my men and I another. Bartholomew de Burghersh and Edward Despencer turned their knights to face the charging Frenchmen. The French were travelling so quickly that when our vanguard opened their ranks to allow them through the French could not stop in time. By the time we clattered into the rear of them, it was a confused mêlée and lances were inappropriate. Little damage was done by either group of knights. When we hit them, we had swords and axes. My archers dismounted and began to use bodkins to pick off the knights. Stephen and Ben had acquired maces and they were deadly with them. As Prince Edward brought up the mainward the survivors of the ambush fled back to the castle which lay just a mile or so up the road. The gates were slammed shut as the last of them galloped over the drawbridge and we had a siege.

I had my archers dismount as soon as we reached the castle and town walls on the River Sauldre and even as the French were trying to man their walls, they were sending arrows at the battlements. As the rest of our archers galloped up, I deployed them too and that allowed Sir John as well as Bartholomew de Burghersh and Edward Despencer and their men to cross the river and begin to attack the gates. Such was the arrow storm that we managed to take the outer gate of the town and enter. The keep, however, was another matter. Prince Edward decided that he would take the castle and the town even though it required war engines to throw stones at the mighty keep. I thought it a mistake and said so to Sir Walter as we toiled to make stone-throwers.

"The Prince believes that the Duke of Lancaster will be able to join us. King John's army outnumbers ours but when the Duke joins us then we will outnumber the French. We do not want the French to have the garrison of this castle to swell their numbers. It makes sense to me, John."

Once again it showed the difference in the way we thought. I disagreed but I was just a man at arms.

Thanks to our archers the walls of the keep had few men trying to hit the mangonels and rams. We spent two days trying to breach the walls but, in the end, the defenders capitulated, and they surrendered. After burning the town and taking the much-needed supplies we pushed along the Cher towards Tours. All the time we knew that the French King and his armies were coming closer, but Prince Edward clung to the hope that the Duke of Lancaster would join us. This time I was selected to scout out the town. This was a mighty fortress and the bridge across the river was heavily guarded. We rode back to tell him that we would have to force a crossing of the bridge. Messengers had arrived to tell him that the Duke of Lancaster was still seeking a crossing of the Loire. We were sent to raid and this time it was not for mischief. Thanks to the siege of Romorantin we had eaten all that we had collected. Most of the food had been perishable. There were few animals to be had as they had been driven across the river to the safety of France. We would go hungry. We were good scavengers and we found farms where the occupants had not had the good sense to flee. We took what they had and returned to the main army.

As we headed back to the army with the meagre supplies we had found I confided in Robin, "I fear we are about to be trapped, as we were all those years ago at Crécy but the difference is we have no suitable hill to defend and the coast is too far away for our ships to take us off. I do not think that the Prince knows where the French army is to be found and, even now, they may have blocked our escape route."

"We thought the same all those years ago, Captain. As I recall we were contemplating a retreat when we managed to turn the tide of battle." He hesitated and then said, "Captain, you have changed. You now fear for your position. This is the same Prince who led us, along with his father at Crécy. The men are the same warriors. Have faith in us."

I looked at Robin and realised what a rock he was. He knew me better than I knew myself. I nodded, "You are right and what shall, shall be. We are a clever company and even if disaster strikes us then we can escape whatever fate throws our way."

We waited for four days and our supplies continued to diminish. Some archers, spearmen and men at arms deserted but none of mine did so. While we had eaten our supplies, the coins we had taken were still a temptation and those who deserted thought we might lose and left us. It soon became clear that the Duke would not be able to cross the Loire and join us. The Prince decided upon a retreat and we headed south towards Châtellerault. Scouts were sent west in case the Duke had managed to cross the river. My men and I were sent east towards Loches. Our task was to find the French.

Our horses were now beginning to suffer, and it was fortunate that my men had managed to capture some. We took them with us so that we could swap horses. I was aware that we would be in constant danger and so we used woods and forests as much as possible. We had left the road south-west of Loches to change our horses when we heard, coming down the road, horses. We withdrew a little way into the forest and then Robin and I, after discarding our white cloaks and donning our brown ones, headed back to the eaves where we hid in the undergrowth. It was clear that it was the French army which was passing. In the time it had taken to hide our horses and return the vanguard had passed us, but we now saw and heard the main body. I recognised the standards not only of the King and his son Charles but also that of the Constable, the Duke of Burgundy, and the Duke of Bourbon. It took some time for the main body to pass us. There was a gap and then the rearguard came along the road. It looked to be as large as our whole army! I saw the standards of the Seigneur de Craon and the Comte de Joigny. I estimated that the army which had passed us exceeded ten thousand men.

Robin and I turned to leave. On reflection, we should have waited until the baggage had passed us, but I was keen to get to the Prince. By my estimation, they could catch us within a day or so. The four-day delay waiting for the Duke might have hurt us. There was a shout from behind us and I heard hooves. We did not turn but I shouted the order to run loudly. I drew my sword. My men were veterans and well trained. They heard the noise and knew what to expect. Even as we fled, I knew that they would be dismounting their horses, nocking arrows, and drawing weapons. The sound of horses drew closer and Robin, who had a strung bow and an arrow ready suddenly stopped and whirled. I could not let him face danger alone and I whirled around too. A dozen light horsemen, Bretons by the look of them, were chasing us and the leading rider was less than twenty paces from us. Having already dismounted, I stepped behind a tree. Robin's arrow plucked him from the saddle. As Robin moved towards our waiting horses and as he nocked a second arrow the next Frenchman levelled his javelin at Robin. He had not seen me, and I swung my sword at his leg as he passed me. I hacked through the breeks, muscle, bone and into the side of his pony. He crashed to the ground and that made the others who were following, veer to the side. Robin managed to hit a third man and then we both raced back to our men.

Michael had taken charge and he had brought our horses and the others towards us. I saw my archers with bows at the ready. Behind us, the survivors of the light horsemen were thundering to get at us, their shouts like angry wasps. My archers' arrows silenced them, and we swung ourselves into our saddles. Digging my heels into Roman's sides and holding the reins of my spare we rode deeper into the forest. If there was a pursuit, then it would take some time to organise and with our spares, we would evade them.

We rode into the camp at La Haye after dark and I went directly to the Prince, "My lord, the French are less than a day behind us and they outnumber us." I told him what I had seen.

He called over his senior commanders and I heard their debate. "If we are to be caught then let us find somewhere we can fight him. Where is there?"

The Captal de Buch said, "South of here at Châtellerault, the river forms a good barrier, and we could use your archers to thin the enemy out."

It seemed like as good a plan as any and the Prince agreed, "Hawkwood, tomorrow you will shadow the French and let us know where they are."

I nodded, "We will hide close to here, my lord and use the forests for cover. We will let them pass and follow them. I will send a rider if they deviate.

"Good. You shall be rewarded for all of your work, Hawkwood."

I did not relish the prospect for the French would be more alert having had the noses of their light horsemen bloodied. While we ate, I told the men what I intended. "Michael, you will lead the men at arms and stay with the rearguard. I will take just archers. You can take the spare horses."

Dai said, "Is that wise, Captain? You were nearly caught today."

I smiled, "Today was a warning from the Almighty that I am mortal. I do not need a second one. I will take my bow with me tomorrow. You take Roman and I will use one of the captured horses."

The army left well before dawn and I took my scouts to the woods south of the bridge. The main road headed south down the Vienne and the road to Châtellerault was a smaller one which passed close to the woods in which we hid. My decision to use just archers and only take one horse was based on the assumption that the French army would need to camp at La Haye, and we would be able to use the woods to shadow them. We were in a position to see the village which lay on the eastern side of the Vienne. This time we would follow the vanguard. It was the middle of the afternoon when they arrived in the village. Of course, the locals lost no time in pointing south and west to tell them the direction our army had taken. Although we had taken their food the Prince had not burned this village for he did not want to alert the French army. Perhaps he should have burned it! I saw the main army arrive and they camped. As the rain began to fall, they erected tents. We were not so lucky, and we had to use our oiled cloaks and eat cold fare. The cold camp ensured that we were awake early, and we heard the French as they broke camp while it was still dark. We saddled our horses and watched the bridge. The French did not cross it but headed down the Roman Road along the river. What was the French King up to?

I had been told to follow the French and follow we did although it was hard for we were travelling along a river trail, across the river from the French, while they enjoyed a good road. By noon it became clear that the French were trying to get ahead of the Prince for they were moving quickly along the road. This was a clever King. He knew how long it would have taken his army to cross the narrow bridge at La Haye, indeed it had taken our army, a much smaller one almost three hours to cross it. I disobeyed my orders and we headed through the woods and across the country to get to our own army. I expected to find them on the road south of Châtellerault but to my horror, we found them still in the village. The Prince continued in his belief that he could bring the French to battle. I was ushered directly into his presence.

"Prince Edward, the French are heading south to cut off our retreat," I told them of the road they had taken,

Jean de Grailly, the Captal de Buch nodded, "Chauvigny! They can get ahead of us there and we will be ambushed. My scouts reported a French column heading south from Saumur and they will be able to join King John at Poitiers."

We were trapped and I saw despair on the faces of the earls. The Prince shook his head, "They think they have us in the net, but we will show them our guile. Lord de Grailly, your men will lead us tomorrow and take us as fast as they can down any secret roads and trails that you and your men know of. I wish to get ahead of the French! Hawkwood, you and your men will accompany our Gascon allies."

I did not mind working with the Gascon. He had shown himself to be a cunning and resourceful leader. His knights and men at arms were well trained and reliable. Equally, the Captal de Buch needed my archers. The next day, he detached me, my men and forty others to be the advance scouts. I rode at the head of the small column with two Gascon knights, Sir Eustace d'Aubrecicourt and Jean de Ghistelles. They knew the area well. It was getting on to the evening when we crossed the Chauvigny to Poitiers road and I drew their attention to the many horse droppings on the road.

"My lords, the feet which marched through this dung were heading west." They both nodded but did not make the connection. "A large force of horsemen and foot soldiers marched from east to west along this road. Perhaps it is the French army."

Jean de Ghistelles nodded, "Perhaps, but, equally, it might just be a party of raiders, but we will proceed carefully.

A mile or so later we were passing close to the manor of La Chaboterie when we suddenly came upon French knights and barons. It was clear that they outnumbered us many times. I said, "My lords, we should get back to the army. My archers will delay them!" Without waiting for a response, I shouted, "Robin, dismount and give them two or three flights!"

The French reacted and I heard horns sound. My men were fast, and they had dismounted and nocked an arrow almost before I had drawn my sword and hefted my shield around. They sent three flights so quickly that the French had barely travelled thirty paces. As Robin and his men mounted their horses, my men at arms prepared to fight any of the French who closed with us. The arrows had only felled three men, but two horses had been pricked by arrows and their wild rearing disrupted the others. We galloped through the woods as fast as we could. Sir Jean and Sir Eustace had alerted the Captal and the Prince. They left a gap for us to gallop through before they closed and presented a hedgehog of spears backed by archers. We managed to kill or capture the whole of what turned out to be the French rearguard. It was a victory and an unexpected one at that but it told us that the French army was ahead of us and we were now trapped!

We took valuable prisoners: the Seigneur de Craon, the Comte de Joigny, Vicomte de Breuse and the Seigneur de Chauvigny. When the Prince questioned them, he learned the whereabouts of the French army. It was ahead of us and close to the town of Poitiers. The French nobles, even though they had been captured, arrogantly suggested that we should surrender as we were so seriously outnumbered.

I was close to the Prince. I knew that now he would have his battle but unlike at Crécy, he would not have the luxury of choosing the battlefield. The French would soon know where we were and, the next day, we would have to give battle against an army almost twice the size of ours! We would have to move silently and do so without any food to eat knowing that there were more than twice our number ahead of us!

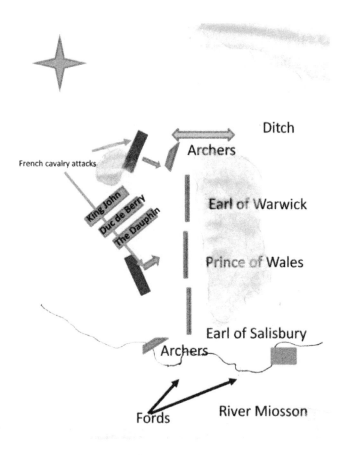

Poitiers: the French attacks and the initial Anglo-Gascon positions

Chapter 18

We camped knowing that the French army was close and we kept a good watch that night. Foragers went to the nearby monastery to try to find some food. At dawn I was sent, on foot with my archers, to find the French. The rest of my men were placed with the Earl of Warwick. We headed through the Nouaille woods and headed north. When we came to the edge of the woods, I saw a large open area which I did not relish crossing. However, it proved unnecessary for we saw, just beyond the crest of the higher ground the French banners and even a tent or two. We made our way back and found that the Earl of Warwick and the vanguard had moved north crossing the ford and was following the ancient trail. I reported directly to him. He had one-third of the army, the Prince had a third and the Earl of Salisbury had the rest, minus the two hundred men led by our only reserve, Jean de Grailly's Gascons.

"My lord, the French are camped about a mile north of us."

"Were you seen?" I cocked my head to one side, and he smiled, "Of course not." He turned to his men, "Dismount and hide the horses in the woods. We may need them if we have to leave in a hurry. I want a defensive ditch with stakes digging across the north of our position. Hawkwood, have your archers protect the men while they dig."

"Aye, my lord."

"I will go to speak with the Prince!"

I took my bow and strung it. While my men at arms laboured at the ditches I would not sit idly by and do nothing, with the incentive of a French army seemingly oblivious to our presence, the men worked hard. With a thick wood at our back the Prince, when he brought up the other two battles, deployed them ready to fight and Captal de Buch's men guarded the baggage. It was then that we heard the trumpets and horns of the French. We had been seen and, with the ditch almost finished the Earl had us stand to. We were facing west. Prince Edward sent some of his own knights to place themselves between the two armies. It made sense for if this had been lightly armoured archers or spearmen then they could have been run down by horsemen.

It was these horsemen who brought the Cardinal of Périgord with some other churchmen. He came to offer a truce and a slightly more peaceful end to this conflict. He spoke to the Earl of Warwick and I was close enough to hear the words. They were suitably romantic and impractical!

"I suggest, Earl, that one hundred knights from each side should fight here between the two armies and their joust should determine the outcome. Think how many lives that would save!"

The Earl smiled, "I fear, Cardinal that only the King of England could make such a decision and he is not here. I think that the men you see before you will have to fight, and I trust that God will be on our side!"

I did not know if the cardinal had been sent by the French King but if he had then the French King was in for a disappointment. We watched him return to the French banners. They had the Oriflamme next to those of the French King and the Dauphin and that showed us that they intended to give battle. They debated for a while and then began to array for battle. It was at that moment that I remembered it was Sunday. There were no rules about fighting on a Sunday, but I knew that the French King was a religious man. Would he delay for a day? It would not help us over much as we were all starving, even the Prince!

The earls were summoned to the Prince's council of war and that left me with my men. Some had fought at Crécy and Neville's Cross, but the majority had not been involved in a major battle. I sensed that they were nervous for the French not only outnumbered us they were, in the main mounted on large war horses and wore good plate and mail. Robin and I did our best to allay their fears.

I looked at them and wondered at the difference the years had made. The young Welshman, Stephen was now a seasoned veteran who along with his shield brother, Henry, would be a rock the French would not pass. The old and the young had bonded and that was good. Michael, Gareth of Chester, and Roger, too had become so skilled that I had seen earls look at the feet to see the spurs. Even those archers who had come from the Bishop of Durham, Martin and Peter Longbow were unrecognisable. Either of them could have been a vintenar. The most transformed of all was Dai; the slinger from Knighton had become the bowman on the cog and was now a man who would soon be a man at arms! I was lucky to have such men but this day would be the severest of tests.

"Here the ground rises and whilst not a hill will be hard for the French to ascend. We have behind us, a wood. That is the same as Crécy. This battlefield does not suit the French."

"But Captain, they have large horses and wear good plate." Siôn tapped his mail hauberk. "I confess that when I first wore this hauberk, I thought that I was invincible, but I have seen others, like Michael and Roger with plate and know how good that is at protecting a man."

Robin laughed, "Then when this battle is over, and we have won!" He paused to let his words sink in, "Then you shall take good plate and weapons from the French that you will kill." He nodded to the archers, not only our archers but the ones from Cheshire who were listening. "And you archers, keep your swords, axes and knives ready for a knight who is afoot is easier to slay and we are unencumbered by metal." He took out his dagger and as he said the action he mimed it on his own body, "Under their armpits, their eyes, their jewels! They are soft targets and when they have bled to death you take their iron!"

I saw that Siôn was not convinced but some of the others were smiling.

I pointed to the woods, "Don't forget to water and feed your horses. They are in the woods now, but we need to let them graze if we can."

Dai came over to me, "I have watered and fed Roman and Mary already, Captain."

"Good, and are you worried about this battle?"

He smiled, "I get to fetch arrows and tend the wounded. I doubt that I will have to fight."

I shook my head, "There are no such bystanders in a battle, Dai. Robin is right we should win but if we do not then know that your youth will not spare you. Wear your mail hauberk and do not put down your weapons for an instant. Keep your wits about you and if you have to fight then make each blow you strike one which will kill the enemy! This will not be like using a bow. Here you will be close to your enemy who will be trying to kill you. We have trained you well, but no man knows what he can do until he faces another man in battle and it is kill or be killed! As well as arrows keep pole weapons to bring to the men at arms should ours be damaged."

The Cardinal's visit allied to the councils of war mean that time passed. As the afternoon wore on it became clear that there would be no battle that day. Neither leader relished the prospect of a battle fought at twilight when chance would play a great part. There was little food to be had and so we improvised. We still had the bone from the ham we had taken. We put it on to boil and found some greens. Robin and my archers went into the woods to hunt some birds. The few they killed padded out the thin soup. We had barely finished it when the Earl returned.

He waved for his centenars and leading knights to come close to him. His face was grim. "We are to change positions with the rearward. The baggage will return across the river."

One of the other centenars, Richard, shook his head, "My lord, surely we do not retreat before these poxy Frenchmen?"

The Earl gave us a strange smile, "Captain Richard, do not presume to tell the Prince of Wales what he must and must not do. Obey your orders!" The archer, chastened, nodded.

We took our horses and marched south. The Earl of Salisbury and his men passed on the other side of the Prince's battle as they took up our previous position to the north. I confess that I did not mind either way. The only problem with our new camp was that it was muddier having been trampled over by our whole army. We stood to and faced the French. This was a formality, of course, we all knew that we would not be fighting that evening. I wondered if the move had been made in the dusk to confuse the French. I learned a lesson that evening; do not make judgements unless you know all the facts.

It was pitch black when we were woken. The Earl of Salisbury and some of his men had been forced to skirmish all night but we had managed to get some sleep. Sir Walter came to fetch me not long after I had made water and dressed for battle. "Prince Edward wishes to see you, John." Like the Earl the previous evening the knight had a whimsical look upon his face. It was as if those around the Prince were involved in some huge joke; they were in the know and we were not. I saw there were bishops as well as our leaders with the mainward and they were holding a Mass. Religion was always important both before and during a battle. The skirmishing had ceased, and the French were also holding a Mass. It did not do to die without confession! I wondered at the invitation for me to join them. The service was longer than I had expected, and dawn broke just as it was finishing.

I was about to head back to my men when the Prince's herald read out a list of names. There were eight of them and one was mine. When he had finished the list, he ordered us all to come to the Prince and to kneel. I did not recognise any of the others although from their garb they were gentlemen. The Prince had his sword in his hand. "All of the men before me have shown to me that they are not only loyal and brave but also worthy of knighthood. Today the Prince of Wales will dub these soon to be heroes. This day we fight the French. These men have the opportunity for glory."

He came along the line and lightly touched our shoulders with the sword. I heard no other names all I heard were the words he said to me, "Rise, Sir John Hawkwood!"

I desperately wanted to shout and cheer. I wanted Robin and my men around me so that they could share in this glory, but I was before the great and the good, the bishops and the lords, the Prince's family and so I stood.

A wagon was fetched, and the Prince stood upon it. "Today when we fight, we fight to win. We take no prisoners until this field is ours. All my lords know my mind and my plans. Every man will follow those orders and if they do as they are commanded then we shall win. God is on our side for what we do is right! We are here to return the land that was stolen from us in times past. I do not doubt that each and every man here today shall do his duty!"

Sir Walter and Jean de Grailly were both on hand to congratulate me as was the Earl of Warwick, Sir John Chandos and Sir James Audley. I was now a member of the elite and who knew what my future held? I had achieved all that I had set out to do and now I was a knight. All that I had to do was to survive this day! I made my way back to my men who had breakfasted on the meagre rations left from the night before and confessed to the priest who was with our battle. They were now in position, viewing the French. The French, for their part, were forming up in their battles. They had three enormous battles one behind the other as well as two forces of mounted knights on their flanks. The knights who were our scouts and would give advanced warning of an attack were trotting towards the ground which separated us. I noticed that they had lances. The Earl of Warwick was still in conference with the Prince. I realised as I neared my men that the land had hidden the fact that I had been knighted from my men. The Prince had performed the ceremony in a slight dip. Some of his speech might have been heard but they would not know of my knighthood. Sir James walked back with me for he and Sir John Chandos would fight in our battle, the vanward.

Michael greeted me with a beaker of the last jug of wine we had taken, "Well Captain, do we fight this day?"

I took the wine and smiled, "I fear you are wrong in the title you afford me."

Robin growled, "They have not demoted you, have they?"

Shaking my head, I said, "No, for I am now Sir John Hawkwood!"

The cheer was so loud that not only did the rest of the battle stare at us but also the knights who were scouts. Robin grinned, "So, the Prince kept his word! Then there is hope for us all, eh, Sir John?"

I nodded. I confess that I had been promised a reward for so long that I thought it had been an empty promise. I was not a fool and I knew that there had been a method behind the Prince's actions. I did not doubt that the ones who had been knighted were chosen from as wide a range of lances as possible. All who heard of the reward would fight even harder in the hope that at the end of the day there might be similar rewards. Knights would die and it was in the Prince's power to replace them!

The Earl of Warwick returned and gave us a command we were not expecting. It took all the joy from the knighthood from us and made us wonder at the Prince's state of mind.

"Fetch your horses for we are the advance guard, and we cross the Gue de l'Homme ford."

There were grumblings and mumblings but not, I am pleased to say, from my men.

"Do as you are ordered and trust to your future king!"

Dai said, "I will fetch Roman, Sir John!" He grinned as he said it and seemed to enjoy the words in his mouth. I looked towards the French and saw that they were forming up for battle. There was a large body of horsemen at their fore although the rest of the knights and the men at arms appeared to have dismounted. Already our battle was heading towards the marshy ground which surrounded the ford. Already churned up, by the time the Earl of Salisbury's rearguard crossed it then it would be a truly muddy morass.

As I mounted Robin said, "This was a good position! Why does the Prince abandon it so readily?"

I shook my head, "I know not but let us not judge hastily."

Behind us, I heard French horns, as we moved off towards the ford. The French had seen our movement. The rest of our army was still in position and facing the French. It was as I looked back that I saw two knights, one English, Sir Eustace d'Aubrecicourt, with whom I had scouted, and a French knight, lower their lances and charge each other across the open ground between the two armies. It was at that point that one of the Earl of Warwick's subordinates, the Earl of Oxford, shouted, "Horses to the woods. Archers nock arrows and face the enemy."

Was this part of some plan the Prince had concocted or was it a disaster waiting to happen? I dismounted and handed Roman to Dai, "Fetch me one of the pikes we took from the pirates. I think it will be of more use against these horsemen." As I dismounted, I saw the two knights collide and so violent was the collision that horses and riders fell to the ground. Only Sir Eustace stood but some of the Frenchman's companions rode up and took him prisoner.

That was the point when Marshal Audrehem led his mounted knights to charge us. We must have looked a ripe target and the hundreds of horsemen who charged towards us must have thought that the battle would be won in the first encounter.

"Hawkwood's Men, form up behind me!" I slithered across some muddy ground to a slightly firmer piece. The rest of the archers followed me, and their captains deferred to me for I was now a knight. As Dai handed me the pike, I saw that the Earl of Salisbury was also being attacked. He was in a better position than us for he had not been on the march and his archers were in the woods. The earls of Warwick and Oxford had their men at arms before their archers. My men at arms were the only ones protecting the archers on the extreme left of our line, but we were at an oblique angle. The muddy ground would channel the French across our front.

I heard the Earl of Oxford give his order to loose. It was too soon and so I shouted, "Hold and await my command! Have bodkins ready!"

The archers who heard me obeyed. If we lost because the archers under my command had not released when ordered, then I could be in trouble. There was vindication for me, however, for the arrows, sent at extreme range did no harm to plated knights and men at arms not to mention horses whose heads and chests wore mail. As I had anticipated the horsemen avoided the muddy ground and, turning slightly, headed towards the Earl of Warwick and the centre of our battle.

As soon as I saw the horses were almost side on to us, I shouted, "Archers of England, release! Pour death into them!"

This time the arrows were effective and horses which were struck first stumbled and then, as more arrows hit them, fell throwing their riders to the ground. My handful of men at arms were all that stood between our archers and the French on this flank, but the Earl of Warwick had a solid line of men before the bulk of the archers. I saw the French Marshal fall from his stricken mount and, as he rose, he was taken by Sir James Audley. The attack had failed but now the French men at arms chose an honourable end to their doomed attack. They turned their horses and rode at their attackers, us. Once more the arrows failed to be as effective when sent directly at the front of horses and mailed men. My men at arms would have to face and fight the enemy.

The first knight who rode at me had a horse whose caparison was covered in arrows, but they had not penetrated. His shield also was pricked by arrows. I swung my boarding pike, not at the mailed head, but the unprotected legs of his mount and the sharp head sliced through one leg and bit into the other. I stepped aside as the horse's head crashed to the ground and the rider flew over its dying head. My archers would finish him off. I presented the spike to the next horse and the knight, seeing the fate of the first rider, veered to his left to avoid the same fate. He tried to pull his lance around to spear me, but I lunged with the pike's head and the spike found a gap between his plates for I came from underneath them. I hurt him and he wheeled his horse around. An arrow from Martin the Fletcher slammed into his back where the plates were thinner. He rode off but he was out of the battle. Michael and the rest of my men at arms were also using pole weapons. Michael was now the equal of any knight I had ever seen. He had a large frame, and he knew how to handle his weapon. With him on one side of me and Roger of Norham on the other, I felt as safe as any man on the battlefield. Roger's spear rammed into the leg of a man at arms who turned to flee. That was the last of their attack and arrows thudded into his back and the others as they struggled across the muddy ground. The man at arms I had speared fell from his horse thirty paces closer to his own army. The first attack was defeated but now I saw that their other battles, dismounted, were advancing.

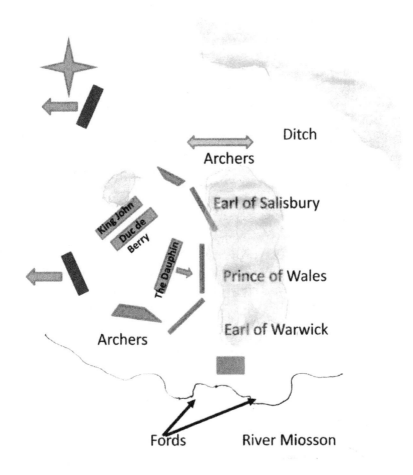

Poitiers: the Dauphin's attack and the second position

The Earl of Warwick shouted, "The vanward will march north and rejoin Prince Edward's battle."

This made perfect sense for if there was a gap then the French could exploit it. It was at this point that I saw we had lost men. Ben, Edward and Siôn lay dead. French men at arms lay dead close by the three of them but I now had three men fewer. They would have to stay where they lay. We had the battle to fight and they would understand. We hurried back up the muddy trail to where we had begun the day.

The hedge which protected our front was still in place, but it was damaged for horses had charged through it. The hedge had slowed their attack and, until it was totally destroyed, would continue to do so. Our archers stood behind the men at arms taking advantage of the slightly higher ground while I joined the other men at arms as a screen through which the French would have to fight to get at our archers. My shield hung from my arm as did those of my remaining men at arms. Other knights and men at arms flanked my diminished company and, through the broken hedgerow, I saw the advancing French battle. It was led by the Dauphin of France, Charles. To the left of the advancing three battles, I viewed the crossbowmen as they formed up to protect the flank of the French and their German allies.

The Earl of Oxford had taken it upon himself to command the archers although he may have been ordered to do so by Prince Edward. It was clear to me that the feigned retreat had been deliberate to draw the French on to us. They knew we were surrounded and starving. The battlefield suited us and so long as we stayed there, then they need not attack. I wondered what other plans he had put in place. I could not see our mounted reserve and they were, perhaps, the reason why the French had deployed their crossbows on their right. I saw that the Dauphin's attack would not strike directly at us for it was aimed at the centre battle and our right flank. The French had a problem for the horsemen who had survived the failed attack now disrupted the advancing battle which was being showered with arrows. Every one of our archers sent their missiles at the French and men began to fall. The French had good plate and mail, but some arrows still insinuated their way into flesh. When they reached the hedge, it became even worse as they had to fight their way through the diminishing barrier and archers given a flatter trajectory could not miss.

As soon as the French were through the Earl of Warwick ordered the men at arms to advance. I led my five men, along with Dai who was behind us with spare weapons, to attack the French knights and men at arms ahead of us. The French had cut down their lances so that they were six feet in length. They were, compared with our spears, poleaxes, and pikes, clumsy and ineffective. The French were, however, eager and when they finally extricated themselves from the hedge they rushed at us. These were the Dauphin's personal knights at the fore and they were desperate to impress their leader and their king. My handful of men and myself had not been trained as men at arms. We had merely been men with skills so that when we fought, we did not know the names of the blows we struck but we were all effective fighters and there was one rule for us, win at all costs. While the French might still hope for prisoners they could ransom, we would see who survived before we took any captives.

I swung my pike at the first knight and used an upward blow. He was not expecting that and, as he hurriedly blocked it, I stepped forward to swing the butt end of the pike into his side. He had a visored helmet while I wore the bascinet with the aventail. I had better vision and the knight did not see the haft of the pike coming around. Overbalancing, he fell, and I hacked into his helmet with every ounce of strength I possessed. I severely dented the helmet with the boarding pike. He was stunned but he tried to rise. I rammed the spike from my pike up into his groin. His body contorted briefly and then as blood oozed from between his legs, he became still. As men had forced their way through the hedge so they had widened it and now more men than ever were pouring through but many of them had arrows sticking from them. An arrow, even if not mortal, can make a man lose blood and become weaker.

A lance was rammed at my face but thanks to my open helmet I saw it coming and knocked the lance upwards. Michael had broken his spear and he now had a war axe. He swung the head at the helmet of the knight that I was fighting. From the way the man fell, he must have died instantly. I saw that neither knight wore spurs. That was wise for a battle fought on foot.

"Thank you, Michael!" There were, for a few moments, no enemies close enough for us to strike.

"We could not have our new knight die so soon after knighthood."

Five knights burst through the hedge at the same time and rushed at us. This time I brought my pike overhand to smash into the boars' snout bascinet of the centre knight. The head of the pike embedded itself in the helmet and he crashed to the earth. I whipped out my bodkin blade and forced it into the eye hole of the helmet. I think he was dying already; the bodkin merely hastened it. One of the Earl of Oxford's men at arms had fallen and I grabbed the poleaxe he had been using. I rejoined the others just as the last of the five Frenchmen fell. I saw that it had not all been one-sided. Gareth of Chester lay with a lance embedded in his chest. He was not yet dead but soon he would be, and we could do nothing to alleviate his suffering. I saw Michael lean down and give him a crucifix to hold. He whispered something to him and then I saw the next wave race at us.

"Michael!"

He stood and swinging his shield around blocked the strike from a lance. He was angry. I knew that from the force he put into the blow which almost took the arm from the man at arms. The knight I was fighting had no lance, but he did have a mace. With no protection for my face, a blow from the mace would end my life. He also had a short sword in his left hand. He lunged with the sword, but I blocked it with the haft of the poleaxe. His short sword bit deeply into my haft but it held. I saw arrows fly perilously close to our heads as Robin and my archers protected us as best they could. Many of the Earl of Oxford's men lay dead but so far Gareth had been our only casualty in this part of the fight. The French knight took his chance and swung the mace at my head. I was too close to both Michael and Roger to be able to move too much and I simply swung the poleaxe at the knight's head. I kept my eye on the poleaxe as long as I could and, when I thought it was going to hit, I turned my head. The mace struck the side of my bascinet at exactly the same moment the axe head hit the knight's helmet. I staggered to crash into Roger, but he had just wounded his opponent and he held firm. The French knight had no one next to him and he fell. I thrust with the spike at the end of the weapon and drove it through the eyehole in the helmet. The man screamed and I pushed and twisted harder. It proved too much for the haft of the poleaxe which broke. I would have to use it one handed.

I pulled my shield around and prepared for the next wave. I could now see the Dauphin. His standard marked his position clearly and he was surrounded by his bodyguard. He was fighting someone in the Prince's division. They had not yet pushed us back! I would have to use the pole axe one handed. Had I not been an archer I might not have had the strength but after drawing a longbow for so many years I did not find it hard. All the enemy lances had now been discarded and most held their swords which they used one handed. Thanks to the casualties we had taken we now had more room to swing our weapons. It meant that any blow which was struck was more likely to result in a serious wound. It is strange but I was detached enough to be able to watch the knight in the dark blue jupon with four stags' heads upon a yellow band coming for my men, as well as Lord Douglas the Scot who fought with the French. He was roaring some Scottish war cry and advancing towards Roger of Norham. Roger had no love for the Scots and if I was to put money on one of them, it would be Roger.

The knight with the dark blue jupon ran the last few steps as he swung his sword from behind him; using two hands it would be a powerful blow. If it had been me making the strike I would have made it a backhand blow for my shortened poleaxe had no metal to protect the shaft and a good blow from the sword could shatter it. He chose the predictable forearm swing and aimed it at my left. I was swinging my poleaxe overarm as his sword smashed into my shield. It jarred and briefly numbed my arm as well as cracking the shield, but he had left himself wide open to a strike down at his shoulder. The poleaxe bit and he reeled. I lifted my arm again and struck a second time even as he was swinging his arm back for a second strike. This time I hurt him, and he had to let go of his sword with his left hand. As I brought up the poleaxe to finish him, he shouted, "I yield! I yield!" He dropped his sword.

Prince Edward had said that we take no prisoners, but I could not begin my life as a knight by slaying one who had surrendered. "Dai! Take this man away!"

I saw that Roger of Norham had severely wounded Lord Douglas who was being dragged away by his oathsworn. I also saw knights in the King's livery speaking with the Dauphin. They dragged him away and soon it became clear that we had defeated the first battle and that they were withdrawing. The second battle was commanded by the Duc de Berry and, to my amazement, when the Dauphin and his men began to leave, they followed.

Prince Edward pushed up the visor on his helmet and began to shout, "Stand firm! Do not pursue!"

We were still outnumbered but we had some respite. I turned to my men at arms, "Take Gareth to the woods, we will bury him later. Robin, retrieve arrows!" I said this because other archers were racing through the hedge to pull arrows from the dead and wounded alike as well as those which had embedded themselves in the ground. I knew that they would also search the dead and the wounded for treasure. It was second nature to them. I picked up Gareth's shield. It was in better condition than mine.

Dai returned with a flask of wine. He grinned, "I found it on the field. Have we won?" He added cheerfully.

"Not yet but it is less likely that we will lose now that two-thirds of their army has left the field of battle!"

My archers returned and from the expressions on their faces, they were all richer. The Earl of Warwick waved me to him, "Come, let us see what the Prince has planned."

I wondered why I had been singled out and then I saw the bodies of knights who had been killed and wounded being taken to the healers in the woods. I might be a new knight but I was one of the more experienced healers. I saw that the Earl of Salisbury, looking bloodied but unbowed was with the Prince as were his friends, Sir John Chandos, Sir Walter Pavely, Sir James Audley, the Earls of Suffolk and Oxford were also there as well as the Captal de Buch and the captains of archers."

The Prince had taken off his great helm and I could see that he was sweating. He had been in the thick of the fight. "Thus far it is going well. Keep the men on a leash for I do not wish them to become wild and chase after the enemy."

Sir John Chandos said, "Ride forward for the day is yours! God will be with you today. Let us make straight for your adversary, the King of France, for it is there that the battle will be decided. I am certain that his valour will not allow him to flee!"

The Prince smiled, "Sir John, as much as I would like to do as you say, the battle hangs yet in the balance." He gave a knowing nod to the Captal de Buch. "We have time enough to do as you say and when you see my standard go forward then you will know that is the time. Sir James I would have you mount a body of good horsemen for if I see the opportunity, I will seize it. Await my command. Until then we hold them. We use our archers to hurt them and we preserve as many of our men as we can. God be with you!"

We had all heard the same words, but I wondered if we would all heed them.

The pavesiers and crossbowmen who advanced towards us were the first sign that the French still intended to attack. They were fresh men as were the elite who followed King John. I turned to the men around me, "We will have to endure a storm of bolts, but I trust in our archers, our shields and, most of all, God!"

The bolts began to descend, and our archers had to be frugal in their reply for they had fewer arrows now. The nature of the crossbows flight and the pavise held by the pavesiers before the crossbowmen meant that there were not as many wounds as might have been expected. I saw the Oriflamme come to the front of the King's line and knew what it meant.

"Stand to! The French King advances!" Others had also seen the sacred French flag and the message was passed along the line. I had picked up the French mace in place of the poleaxe. I determined to use that. The crossbows and pavesiers moved out of the way and the storm of bolts ceased. Our archers had to wait until the French knights and men at arms closed with us. They needed their arrows to penetrate plate and mail! As they came, I saw more than a dozen men dressed in identical armour and jupon to the King. It was a clever move although as the Oriflamme and his banner were close together it would not be hard to work out the real King! It was then that I saw two things; firstly, from behind the French, I saw the flag of Saint George waved and then before the French could react Sir James Audley charged the German element of the French army with his mounted men. Sir Jean de Ghistelles was with Sir James and his knights. They charged for Sir Eustace who was still a prisoner of the French. The Captal de Buch leading horsemen and mounted crossbowmen attacked the rear of the French line and as the Germans were driven from the field, Prince Edward ordered our archers to send the last of their arrows into the French. As the goose fletched missiles descended, he had his standards signal the advance.

I led my men at arms and archers in a wedge formation. Michael and Roger flanked me and, having discarded their bows, the archers had swords, axes and spears taken from the French. The French King could have fled but he had courage. The knights who were before him were honour bound to die to try to save their king and the Oriflamme. They were fresh and they were good.

We passed through the hedge and found a sea of bodies before us. It would be hard to find a clear space in which to actually fight and those with experience and open helmets would have the best chance to do so. Prince Edward was heading for the King along with his household knights. I took my men towards a band of knights who all wore similar colours, yellow and green. The white surcoats of my men at arms and the white jupons of my archers also marked us out and the yellow and green knights made directly for us. These men were armed with war hammers, poleaxes, glaives, and long swords. They did not carry shields and we did; this would be an interesting battle.

Poitiers: the attack of the Anglo Gascon horse

Their war cry was, "God, Saint-Denis and King John!" Filled with religious and patriotic fervour they ran at us. Robin and our archers had practised with us when we had wintered on the Garonne. They knew to put their bodies behind ours to make us a more solid line of steel. My remaining men at arms kept enough of a gap between us to allow us to swing and with the spears of our archers protruding we were able to give the French a shock. Those archers who still had missiles now rained death upon the French and the range was close enough for them to be more effective and they broke up the French formation.

The green and yellow knight leading his familia ran at me and swung his sword from on high. Raising my shield, I felt Robin and Dai lean into my back and their spears came out on either side of me. My shield partly blocked the blow, and the blade jarred my arm which was still numb from the last attack, the long sword slid down the side of the shield. The two spears arrested the French knight's charge a little and I used the mace for the first time. I pulled back and hit it against the side of the visored helmet. It rang like a bell and the knight stepped back a little. Dai and Robin thrust again with their spears seeking a weak spot in the mail and plate of the Frenchman. He raised his sword again and I realised that the closer we were the less damage he could do, and I stepped forward with the weight of Dai and Robin behind me. I swung the mace at his head, and he tried to block it with his sword. He stopped me hitting his head but not his shoulder. It was a heavy mace with edges to it and I know it hurt him. The knight tried to step back to allow him to swing and I stepped forward smashing my shield into his face as he did so. He took a longer step back and suddenly Robin, Dai and I were behind the red and yellow familia. As the two spears struck, I brought the mace over my head and struck him on the top of the helmet. He tumbled over and Dai rammed his spear between the legs of the knight as he lay helpless on the ground.

The knight, who was doomed, must have been the leader of the group for a man at arms who was in the second rank screamed a French obscenity and rammed his spear at Dai. Dai just had a short mail hauberk and I stepped forward to take the thrust. It found a gap in the plates and entered my side. Robin jabbed his spear into the face of the man at arms. It was now a confused mass of mailed men struggling with tiny battles. The larger one was forgotten. I could not see the French King and I had no idea where our mailed horsemen were. I just knew that the white jupons of Hawkwood were engaged in a deadly duel to the death with the yellow and green jupons of a dead French lord.

I saw that Michael was having the worst of a fight with another of the yellow and green knights. This one had yellow birds on it. I had no compunction about stepping behind him and smashing my mace into the back of his skull. As he fell to the ground, presumably dead or badly wounded, I felt the blood seeping from the spear thrust. I put the wound from my mind and turned to seek my next foe. The open helmet gave me better vision than the French men at arms who all had great helms or visors. I saw my archers able to avoid the predictable swings and thrusts and use their agility to hamstring knights, gut them and ram bodkins through eyeholes in helmets. When the last of the green and white knights and men at arms fell to lie in a very muddy field, I saw that there were no more French close to us.

The Oriflamme still fluttered as did the royal standard but I could see that they were closer to me now and that the French King was surrounded by his best men.

"Hawkwood, to me!"

I tried to run up the slight slope to the ground which was obviously drier. Blood still seeped from my wound and it was a fast walk rather than a run. I hurried, not to the French King for I could see that Prince Edward and Sir John Chandos were hacking their way to him, but to the standard-bearers. A French knight saw my intention and he stepped before me to swing his sword at me. My shield was still in my left hand and holding it before me, took the blow which shattered the shield. I had momentum and as the broken shield fell from my hand, I swung my mace at the side of the knight's head. He stumbled and I battered his helmet again. It sounded like a blacksmith working with iron. He dropped to his knees and I hit him a third and last time. My men at arms and archers were busy disposing of the other knights and I ran to the Oriflamme. I took my dagger from my belt as I ran. The standard-bearer, I later found out he was called Geoffroi de Charny, saw me and swung his sword at me.

His left hand held the red Oriflamme embedded in the mud. I tried to block the blow with my dagger, but I was only partly successful, and it struck my plates and mail. They had been damaged already and I felt the edge slice through my aketon and into my flesh. I knew that I had limited time and I swung my mace with all the force I could muster into the face of the standard-bearer. He wore an open bascinet, and the mace destroyed his features. He fell and with him went the Oriflamme. As soon as it touched the ground we had won the battle.

I stood to look for more enemies but the French who were closest to me saw the standard fall and dropped their swords. I felt the strength go from my legs and I dropped to my knees. Robin and Michael ran to my side,

"Sir John! You are hurt! Robin, tend his wounds, he cannot die on this day!"

I closed my eyes for I felt sleepy and I heard a cheer. Then a voice said, "Sir John, had I not knighted you this morning then I would have done so now for that was a brave act. The French have surrendered, and you have saved many men's lives." I opened my eyes and saw Prince Edward, the Earl of Warwick, all bloodied but whole, looking down at me. I tried to speak but could not manage a single utterance. "Take this hero to the healers and he shall be rewarded when all of the French are taken!"

All went black.

Epilogue

When I woke, I saw that Dai, Robin and Michael remained with me and a healer was sewing up my wounds. Robin grinned and nodded to Michael, "I told you he would not die on this day."

I tried to speak but my throat was so dry that I could not. The healer poured some liquid down my throat. It had a strange taste, "Do not try to speak and rest. I have others to deal with!" He left.

Michael nodded at his back. "He is the Prince's own physician and he tended Sir James Audley before you."

Robin shook his head, "It shows how high you are in the Prince's eyes. You rest, Sir John," he laughed, "I cannot say that enough! It is long overdue! You need not fret, we lost no other but Gareth, Peter Longbow, Ben, Edward, Siôn and Richard of Loidis. Considering the odds that is a small price to pay. and the others are busy collecting the bounty from the field. Your prisoner is safe, and we found the royal wagons. We are rich men."

Michael added, "Our horsemen are pursuing the French who survived. We have won."

Dai asked, "Is it always thus?"

Robin asked, "You mean do we always win when it looks like we should lose?" Dai nodded, "It seems that way. This is the fourth such battle in which I have fought but I never felt that we would lose. We should have but..." I saw him shrug and my eyes began to close. Their voices drifted off and I slept.

When I woke it was daylight and I felt every wound and bruise on my body. I desperately needed to make water. I was outside and I tried to sit up. Dai was at my side in an instant, "Here, my lord, let me help you. The healer put a draught in the drink, and you have slept well." He helped me up and I saw the rest of my men were still sleeping. As Dai helped me to the woods and the area we used to make water he said, "They only returned an hour or so ago. We are rich men, my lord."

"And the knights?"

He laughed, "The people of Poitiers were so afeared of us that they barred their gates to the knights, and we took many men. I hear we have a thousand knights to ransom and that five thousand Frenchmen died!"

I could not believe that for we had barely numbered five thousand at the start of the battle. It was a relief to make water and when I had finished Dai helped me back to the camp.

"I will prepare some food. Martin the Fletcher found not only gold but also food! Today, I think food is more necessary for you cannot eat gold!"

The men awoke, even though they had enjoyed little sleep when they smelled the food. Dai was frying ham and I defy any man to sleep when that smell hits his nose. In addition, they were all keen to speak with me and tell me what we had taken. I say we for we were one company. Whatever we had, including the ransom, would be shared. Robin was right, we were rich men.

We had just finished eating when Prince Edward strode into our camp. He was beaming. "Sir John, you are awake, and my healer says you shall make a full recovery. That is good for we still have work to do. We have the French King, but his son is at large. When you are recovered then you will fetch your company and we will make France our own. Know that I am pleased with you and as well as conferring a knighthood upon you I give to you a pension for life!"

When he had gone, I sat in silence. Robin said, "Did you not hear, Sir John? He said a pension for life. You need not draw sword again if you so choose! We have enough money now to buy a manor if we wished!"

I nodded, "Yet my work, our work, is not done." I smiled at them. "We are small in number and yet on this field, we achieved more than many great knights and lords. Why stop now, Robin? The world is there for the taking."

Dai asked, "You mean France?"

I shook my head, "France is there for the King and his son to take, we have other fields to plough and they will make us richer and garner us even more glory!" I stroked the now bloody white jupon. "And while we will continue to wear the white, I would have a design upon it. While we recover ponder on that and now, Dai, find me some wine for I think we will celebrate, but first, we shall bury our dead, for they helped us to earn this victory."

And so our comrades were buried within sight of the Abbey of Noailles and I like to think that they rested well in that holy ground. We never forgot them and each time we celebrated Gareth, Peter, Ben, Edward, Siôn and Richard were remembered for they were part of my company and now that company had a name; they were Sir John Hawkwood's Company and both the French and English knew it! The Battle of Poitiers ensured that! I was the knight who had taken the Oriflamme!

The End

Glossary

Battle- a military formation rather than an event

Bastard Sword-One requiring two hands to use. The shield hung from the left arm

Bevor- metal chin and mouth protector attached to a helmet

Brase- a strap on s shield for an arm to go through

Brigandine- a leather or padded tunic worn by soldiers; often studded with metal

Centenar- the commander of a hundred

Chepe- Market (as in Cheapside)

Chevauchée – a raid on an enemy, usually by horsemen

Cordwainer- Shoemaker

Gardyvyan- Archer's haversack containing all his war-gear

Glaive- a long pole weapon with a concave blade

God-Damns -derogatory French name for Englishmen

Guige strap– a long leather strap which allowed a shield to hang from a knight's shoulder

Harbingers- the men who found accommodation and campsites for archers

Jupon – a shorter version of the surcoat

Mainward-the main body of an army

Mêlée - confused fight

Oriflamme – The French standard which was normally kept in Saint-Denis

Pavesiers - men who carried man-sized shields to protect crossbowmen

Rearward- the rearguard and baggage of an army

Rooking - overcharging

Shaffron – metal headpiece for a horse

Spanning hook- the hook a crossbowman had on his belt to help draw his weapon

Vanward- the leading element of an army, the scouts

Vintenar- commander of twenty

Wynchchelse- Winchelsea

Historical note

John Hawkwood was a real person but much of his life is still a mystery. At the end of his career, he was one of the most powerful men in Northern Italy where he commanded the White or English Company. He famously won the battle of Castagnaro in 1387. However, his early life is less well documented, and I have used artistic licence to add details. He was born in Essex and his father was called Gilbert. I have made up the reason for his leaving but leave he did, and he became an apprentice tailor. It is rumoured that he fought at Crécy as a longbowman and I have used that to weave a tale. It is also alleged that he was knighted by Prince Edward at Poitiers. The first book in the series and, this, the second will be largely my fictionalised version of his life.

Who knows what would have happened if the Black Death had not reached England in 1348? The plague had struck England regularly but the Black Death, which had its origins in the east was something far more deadly. As I write COVID-19 appears to have much in common with the plague!

For the purposes of my narrative and to give John Hawkwood some action between Neville's Cross and Poitiers I have him honing his skills on the Welsh border. The castle at Cefnllys existed but was largely a Mortimer stronghold. There was a castle at Rhayader but little trace of it remains. That segment is pure fiction!

Most of the incidents I used really happened:

- The sea battle
- The two chevauchée
- The battle of Romorantin
- The catching of the French rearguard
- The clash between Sir Eustace and the German knight
- The mass and the knighthoods
- The battle itself which happened exactly as I wrote it…. According to history!

Sir John will still fight in France for the King and his son but soon he will become that for which he is most famous. He will become the most successful captain of condottiere.

Griff Hosker
December 2020

The books I used for reference were:

- French Armies of the Hundred Years War- David Nicholle
- Castagnaro 1387- Devries and Capponi
- Italian Medieval Armies 1300-1500- Gabriele Esposito
- Armies of the Medieval Italian Wars-1125-1325
- Condottiere 1300-1500 Infamous Medieval Mercenaries – David Murphy
- The Armies of Crécy and Poitiers- Rothero
- The Scottish and Welsh Wars 1250-1400- Rothero
- English Longbowman 1330-1515- Bartlett and Embleton
- The Longbow- Mike Loades
- The Battle of Poitiers 1356- Nicholle and Turner

Other books by Griff Hosker

If you enjoyed reading this book, then why not read another
one by the author?

Ancient History

The Sword of Cartimandua Series
(Germania and Britannia 50 A.D. – 128 A.D.)

Ulpius Felix- Roman Warrior (prequel)
The Sword of Cartimandua
The Horse Warriors
Invasion Caledonia
Roman Retreat
Revolt of the Red Witch
Druid's Gold
Trajan's Hunters
The Last Frontier
Hero of Rome
Roman Hawk
Roman Treachery
Roman Wall
Roman Courage

The Wolf Warrior series

(Britain in the late 6th Century)
Saxon Dawn
Saxon Revenge
Saxon England
Saxon Blood
Saxon Slayer
Saxon Slaughter
Saxon Bane
Saxon Fall: Rise of the Warlord
Saxon Throne
Saxon Sword

Medieval History

The Dragon Heart Series

Viking Slave
Viking Warrior
Viking Jarl
Viking Kingdom
Viking Wolf
Viking War
Viking Sword
Viking Wrath
Viking Raid
Viking Legend
Viking Vengeance
Viking Dragon
Viking Treasure
Viking Enemy
Viking Witch
Viking Blood
Viking Weregeld
Viking Storm
Viking Warband
Viking Shadow
Viking Legacy
Viking Clan
Viking Bravery

The Norman Genesis Series

Hrolf the Viking
Horseman
The Battle for a Home
Revenge of the Franks
The Land of the Northmen
Ragnvald Hrolfsson

249

Man at Arms

Brothers in Blood
Lord of Rouen
Drekar in the Seine
Duke of Normandy
The Duke and the King

New World Series

Blood on the Blade
Across the Seas
The Savage Wilderness
The Bear and the Wolf

The Vengeance Trail

The Reconquista Chronicles

Castilian Knight
El Campeador
The Lord of Valencia

The Aelfraed Series

(Britain and Byzantium 1050 A.D. - 1085 A.D.)
Housecarl
Outlaw
Varangian

The Anarchy Series England

1120-1180
English Knight
Knight of the Empress
Northern Knight
Baron of the North
Earl
King Henry's Champion

Man at Arms

The King is Dead
Warlord of the North
Enemy at the Gate
The Fallen Crown
Warlord's War
Kingmaker
Henry II
Crusader
The Welsh Marches
Irish War
Poisonous Plots
The Princes' Revolt
Earl Marshal

Border Knight

1182-1300
Sword for Hire
Return of the Knight
Baron's War
Magna Carta
Welsh Wars
Henry III
The Bloody Border
Baron's Crusade
Sentinel of the North
War in the West

Sir John Hawkwood Series

France and Italy 1339- 1387

Crécy: The Age of the Archer
Man at Arms

Lord Edward's Archer

Lord Edward's Archer

Man at Arms

King in Waiting
An Archer's Crusade

Struggle for a Crown
1360- 1485

Blood on the Crown
To Murder A King
The Throne
King Henry IV
The Road to Agincourt
St Crispin's Day

Tales from the Sword

Modern History

The Napoleonic Horseman Series

Chasseur à Cheval
Napoleon's Guard
British Light Dragoon
Soldier Spy
1808: The Road to Coruña
Talavera
The Lines of Torres Vedras
Bloody Badajoz
The Road to France

The Lucky Jack American Civil War series

Rebel Raiders
Confederate Rangers
The Road to Gettysburg

The British Ace Series

1914
1915 Fokker Scourge
1916 Angels over the Somme
1917 Eagles Fall
1918 We will remember them
From Arctic Snow to Desert Sand
Wings over Persia

Combined Operations series

1940-1945
Commando
Raider
Behind Enemy Lines
Dieppe
Toehold in Europe
Sword Beach
Breakout
The Battle for Antwerp
King Tiger
Beyond the Rhine
Korea
Korean Winter

Other Books

Great Granny's Ghost (Aimed at 9-14-year-old young people)

For more information on all of the books then please visit the
author's web site at www.griffhosker.com where there is a link
to contact him or visit his Facebook page: GriffHosker at Sword
Books

Printed in Great Britain
by Amazon